# Praise for
# Valerie Wolzien
# and her novels

"Valerie Wolzien is a consummate crime writer. Her heroines sparkle as they sift through clues and stir up evidence in the darker, deadly side of suburbia."
—MARY DAHEIM

"Wit is Wolzien's strong suit. . . . Her portrayal of small-town life will prompt those of us in similar situations to agree that we too have been there and done that."

—*The Mystery Review*

"Domestic mysteries, with their emphasis on everyday people and everyday events, are very popular and the Susan Henshaw stories are some of the best in this subgenre."
—*Romantic Times*

By Valerie Wolzien
*Published by The Random House Publishing Group*

Susan Henshaw mysteries:
MURDER AT THE PTA LUNCHEON
THE FORTIETH BIRTHDAY BODY
WE WISH YOU A MERRY MURDER
AN OLD FAITHFUL MURDER
ALL HALLOWS' EVIL
A STAR-SPANGLED MURDER
A GOOD YEAR FOR A CORPSE
'TIS THE SEASON TO BE MURDERED
REMODELED TO DEATH
ELECTED FOR DEATH
WEDDINGS ARE MURDER
THE STUDENT BODY
DEATH AT A DISCOUNT
AN ANNIVERSARY TO DIE FOR
DEATH IN A BEACH CHAIR

Josie Pigeon mysteries:
SHORE TO DIE
PERMIT FOR MURDER
DECK THE HALLS WITH MURDER
THIS OLD MURDER
MURDER IN THE FORECAST
A FASHIONABLE MURDER

Books published by The Random House Publishing Group
are available at quantity discounts on bulk purchases for
premium, educational, fund-raising, and special sales use.
For details, please call 1-800-733-3000.

# DEATH IN A BEACH CHAIR

## VALERIE WOLZIEN

FAWCETT BOOKS • NEW YORK

A Fawcett Book
Published by The Random House Publishing Group
Copyright © 2004 by Valerie Wolzien

www.ballantinebooks.com

ISBN 0-449-00719-7

Manufactured in the United States of America

First Edition: March 2004

OPM   10   9   8   7   6   5   4   3   2   1

This book is dedicated
to everyone who loves to read.

# DEATH IN A
# BEACH CHAIR

# ONE

"WHAT IS IT ABOUT THE CARIBBEAN THAT MAKES EVERY-one feel so sexy?" Jed Henshaw asked, moving a bit closer to his wife and slipping an arm around her shoulders. "The warm, soft air? The sound of the sea? The scent of exotic flowers? The sugary drinks full of rum? Susan? Honey? Susan, are you sleeping?"

It had been a long day. Susan and Jed Henshaw had gotten up before five A.M. to catch their nine-thirty flight from Kennedy Airport to Orlando, Florida. They may as well have slept in. The flight had been delayed for three hours. Missing their original connection to a small island in the Bahamas, they had been lucky enough to find seats on the last island-hopper. It departed long after dinner. Their luggage had missed their flight, which Susan thought was lucky since the taxi that had picked them up at the airport had the distinctive smell of rotting fish emanating from its trunk.

They had arrived at their resort, expecting to find Kathleen and Jerry Gordon, their best friends, checked in and ready to greet them. But what they found was a message left at the front desk: Kathleen and Jerry were having dinner in town. They'd be back late. They'd all meet for breakfast tomorrow morning at nine. Susan and Jed had gone to their little cottage on the beach, washed up, and headed straight back to the bar.

They were now sitting there on brightly colored chairs, staring out at the inky Caribbean.

"Susan?"

"I'm not asleep. I was just lying here wondering. Jed, don't you think it's weird that Kathleen and Jerry aren't here?"

"Not really. Remember, we should have arrived hours ago. They were probably assuming that we would go to town with them, and when we didn't show up on time, they just went ahead with their plans."

"Yes, but Kathleen said one of the things that appealed to her the most about this resort was its restaurant; it's known all over the island for its food. Kathleen and I liked the fact that everything we wanted was here, that we wouldn't have to leave unless we wanted to. So why would they go off to town to eat their first day on the island?"

"Perhaps they thought you and I would want to stay here all week and decided to take advantage of our absence to explore on their own."

"Well, maybe, but . . ." Susan sat up and looked over at her husband. "Jed, has Jerry said anything to you?"

"Jerry's said a lot to me—at work, at the Field Club, at the boring dinner party the Goldsmiths threw last week. But I gather you're interested in something specific?"

"I was wondering if he'd said anything about Kathleen . . . you know, about their marriage."

"No. What do you know that I don't know?"

"I don't think they're getting along," Susan answered quietly.

Although she and Jed had been married for more than thirty years, her words shocked him more than anything else she had ever told him. "Not getting along? You're saying they have marriage problems? Kathleen and Jerry?"

"I don't actually know anything. That is, Kathleen hasn't said anything specific, but recently I've been getting the impression that she's unhappy about something . . . something to do with Jerry."

Now Jed sat up straighter and turned away from the view. "Hon, I thought this was going to be a romantic, relaxing vacation."

"Oh, it is, Jed. It is. Don't you see? That's why it's so perfect that we're all here together." It was too dark for Susan to see the expression on her husband's face, but she was fairly sure he didn't look happy. She sighed. This vacation was sure not starting out the way she had planned it last month.

The idea had come to her one miserable sleety day in January when she and Kathleen were talking on the phone. Kathleen was stuck in her kitchen, baking cupcakes for an upcoming bake sale at her children's elementary school. Susan was in her kitchen, stuffing her face with leftover Christmas cookies, thinking that her nest was bleak and empty.

"I can't wait until winter break. Jerry's mother and father have offered to take the kids so that Jerry and I can get away for a bit. It's been years since we went anyplace without the kids," Kathleen said.

Susan could hear the KitchenAid whirring in the background on the other end of the line. She looked out the window into her icy backyard and wondered if the dozen red-stemmed dogwoods they had planted in the fall would survive the storm. "It would be nice to go someplace warm," she said. "In fact, Jed and I have been thinking of heading down to the Caribbean. I've been planning to get on the Internet and see what sort of reservations are available. You know, I was thinking—"

"Susan, I have to dash. This dough is beginning to look a little runny. Let me know if you come upon anything interesting the last week of February. That's when the kids are on vacation," Kathleen said before hanging up to tend to her baking.

Susan had headed straight for the computer. A few hours and a couple of cups of coffee later, she was ready to present her idea to her husband and their best friends.

"Compass Bay." She handed Jed a sheaf of computer print-outs along with a goblet of deep amber liquid. A maraschino cherry bobbed in his drink.

"What is Compass Bay? And what is this?" he asked, taking the time to kiss his wife before hanging his Burberry in the hall closet and heading back to his study, where Susan had a fire burning to accompany their usual predinner glass of wine.

"That is rum punch, and Compass Bay is a small, funky resort on an island near Nassau."

Jed sat down on the couch and sipped his drink. "And?"

"And the good news is that Compass Bay has room for us all the last week of February."

Jed took another sip. "This is excellent. A little sweet, but excellent."

"And wouldn't a week spent in the sun, swimming, kayaking, and eating good food and drinking rum punch be excellent, too?"

"Susan, I've been slogging through freezing slush for the past five days. The heat on the train was on the blink tonight and my toes may never thaw out. I had lunch with one of the agency's most important clients today. He ate and drank and I talked and talked and talked, so I'm starving and this rum is going straight to my head. If you're suggesting that we go someplace warm for a few days, the answer is yes, fine, great. Let's go ASAP."

"The Hancock schools' winter break is the last week of February."

Jed placed his drink on the coffee table before him and looked up at his wife. "Susan, we haven't had anyone in the Hancock schools for over three years."

"I know that, Jed! But Alex and Emily are still in elementary school."

"Jerry's kids? What do they have to do with it? Good lord, you're not telling me that you're planning on bringing them on a trip with us. They're cute kids, but they're not the perfect travel companions."

"Of course not, Jed. But I was thinking how much fun it would be if the four of us—Jerry and Kathleen and you and I—went to this place, Compass Bay, together. And they can't get away until their kids are on vacation. Jerry's parents have offered to baby-sit them."

"So you're serious about the last week of February." Jed was reaching into his shirt pocket for his Palm Pilot.

"Yes." She waited a moment while he pressed an amazing number of buttons. "Is it a good time for you to be away from work?"

"It is. Tell me more about this Compass place."

"It's not Compass Place, it's Compass Bay. It's small. Just sixteen cottages and they're all on the beach. I think they all have balconies or porches or decks or something that overlook the water. There's a restaurant, a bar, a pool, a dock, and kayaks, and snorkeling, and . . . and whatever you want, I guess."

"I wouldn't mind another drink like this," Jed said, thumbing through the printout, pausing to admire a young blond in a very skimpy swimsuit before continuing. "You say this place has room for us the last week of February?"

"Yes. In fact, I already made reservations. Two deluxe cottages for two people. They have queen-size beds—"

"In-room safes, refrigerators, CD players, air-conditioning, ceiling fan, handmade batik fabrics, and original art by local artists."

"Huh?"

"Just reading the publicity. The rooms sure seem attractive.

Wood walls, high ceilings, lots of bright colors." He glanced up at his wife and smiled. "I'm really looking forward to this."

"I just hope Kathleen and Jerry are as enthusiastic as you are."

Kathleen and Jerry had been even more enthusiastic than Jed. Kathleen and Susan went shopping in the resort departments of Bloomingdale's and Saks and came home with armfuls of brightly colored shorts and tops. Kathleen bought a gorgeous turquoise bikini. Susan stuck to her black one-piece suit, hoping the brilliant pareo the saleswoman had shown her how to tie around her hips would add an element of dash while covering her cellulite. They both had new straw beach bags, and Susan had bought an amazing Kaminski raffia hat with a wide, droopy brim.

The weather had worsened, and Susan's preswimsuit diet was undermined by the baking she had done to keep depression from the door during the repetitious winter storms. Jed and Jerry were overwhelmed by a project at the advertising agency where they both worked. Kathleen was busy straightening her home for the arrival of her in-laws, but she and Susan spoke on the phone daily, both women claiming to be anxious for the days to pass until they left. A last-minute problem at the office caused Jed to delay his departure by twenty-four hours. He suggested that Susan go on ahead with Jerry and Kathleen, but she decided that beginning their romantic vacation alone wasn't an option. That's how they had ended up arriving this evening, a day after the Gordons.

Susan continued her questions. "So you haven't gotten any hints that Jerry and Kathleen aren't getting along?"

Jed drained his drink, and before he could answer, a good-looking black woman appeared and suggested a refill. "Yes, thank you." He accepted her offer. "And is there any chance that the kitchen is still open? Our plane was late and we haven't eaten much more than pretzels all day long."

With a promise to find them some nourishment, the waitress hurried off, and Jed was left to answer his wife's question. He sighed deeply before doing so. "You know I don't notice the things you do, hon. But, yes, I have noticed that something is bothering Jerry. But I don't know that it has anything to do with his marriage. At least, he hasn't said anything to me that would lead me to think that. But he's been distracted at work and sort of standoffish, I suppose you could say."

Susan had no intention of letting that stand unexplored. "What do you mean? Exactly how has he been acting?"

"It's hard to explain. It's not like there's anything specific. If you hadn't brought it up, I wouldn't have said anything at all. We've been working very hard; maybe he's just tired. We're none of us as young as we used to be."

"You said standoffish. What did you mean when you said standoffish?" she continued to probe.

"Look, I probably shouldn't have used that word. We've been working together almost constantly for the last month and a half. Maybe Jerry's tired at the end of the day. Maybe he just isn't interested in sitting in the bar car and chatting after a long day at the office."

"Like you and he have been doing for decades," Susan pointed out.

"People change," was his brief reply. "Look, Susan, you're not going to ruin our vacation worrying about someone else's marriage, are you?"

"No, of course I'm not! But maybe we can help them out," she suggested.

"How?" Jed sounded hesitant.

"By showing them just how happy we are after all these years," she suggested, reaching out and squeezing his knee.

She could see his smile in the moonlight. "Sounds good to me." He leaned over and kissed the tip of her nose.

A large tray of grilled shrimp, tiny crab cakes with a fruit coulis, and gorgeous tropical fruit kabobs with a dipping sauce was placed on a small table pulled up by Susan's side. Two fresh drinks appeared as well.

"This looks delicious," Jed said. "Thank you. Can you just add it to our bill?"

"Of course. What is your room number?"

"It's . . . to be honest, I don't know. Susan?"

"I don't know, either. We're in the red cottage with the wooden rooster over the door," Susan added.

"No problem. You must be the Henshaws. Welcome to Compass Bay."

"Thank you. Perhaps you've met our friends? The Gordons? Are they in the cottage next to ours?"

"The Gordons? The man with the young wife?"

"I . . . I suppose you could describe them like that." Susan had never thought of her friends in those terms. Jerry had lost his first wife and their two children in an automobile accident a few years before Kathleen had come to Hancock. She was over a decade younger than he, but the difference in their ages somehow rarely came up.

"They are in the cottage on the way to you—the first one in line—the blue one next to the gift shop. They went into town for dinner, I believe. I guess Mrs. Gordon is feeling better."

"What do you mean? Was she ill?"

"I ran into her early in the evening. She was sitting alone in the gazebo." The woman nodded out to sea, and Susan realized she was referring to the straw-roofed platform over the water at the end of the long dock. "I thought she had been crying, but she said she had a headache. I tell her of the island remedy we all use. I guess it worked."

"Crying?" Susan repeated the word.

"What's the island remedy?" Jed asked, ignoring his wife.

"Rum. My grandmother says rum can cure everything. I guess it worked for your friend."

"I guess it did," Jed said.

"I'll leave you now . . . unless you think you'll need something else."

"No, we're just fine, thank you."

Susan waited until they were alone together before speaking. "Jed, she said Kathleen was crying."

"Susan, she said she *thought* Kathleen had been crying. That's all. Now, try this delicious shrimp and have some more punch. Whatever is going on with Jerry and Kath can wait until morning."

# TWO

Susan dug her toes into the sand and leaned back against the stone retaining wall that prevented Compass Bay from washing into the sea. Without waking Jed, she had gotten dressed and slipped out of their cottage. Now she wished she had paused long enough to grab her watch. The sun was rising to her right, and she could feel its heat on her cheek. The water was washing back and forth on the sand, but she slowly became aware of other sounds—cooking sounds. She got up as the lure of coffee became more compelling than the sea.

The dining area had been closed when they arrived last night, but now it was bustling with activity. Waiters in black slacks and white shirts were setting tables with bright-colored linens and heavy pottery. Two young men in swimsuits were raising gaudy umbrellas above tables on the patio overlooking the ocean. The scent of coffee brewing wafted from the kitchen, mixing with the salty air. Susan wandered toward its place of origin.

One of the young men dropped his umbrella and hurried to her side. "May I help you?"

"Is it too early to get a cup of coffee?"

"Of course not. You sit down and I'll bring it."

"That would be nice." Susan chose a small pink table overlooking the water and sat down to resume her contemplation of the sunrise. She had slept well and awakened convinced that worrying about Kathleen and Jerry was pointless. Every marriage had rough spots. And this dreadful winter had probably made small problems appear to be big ones. But things would be different now that they were together in this wonderful place. Not just different, better.

A tray bearing a pot of coffee, cream, sugar, and a small vase of flowers showed up by her side. Susan thanked the young man who brought it and was busy stirring cream and sugar (it was her vacation, after all!) into the steaming brew when she noticed an attractive blond woman strolling down the long pier toward the charming gazebo that stood on stilts a good ten feet above the water. A long peach kimono fluttered behind her in the morning breeze. Susan had seen that robe just a few weeks ago in Bergdorf Goodman. In fact, Kathleen had considered buying it—before checking out its price. Now Susan realized that her friend must have been unable to resist, after all. She sipped her coffee and smiled. If Kathleen had worn the nightgown that went with that kimono last night, there was little reason to worry about the state of the Gordons' marriage.

"What are you smiling about?" Kathleen Gordon slid into the chair across from Susan.

"I—" Susan looked out on the pier. "I thought I was watching you. Out there. I thought that woman walking on the pier was you."

"I'm flattered," Kathleen said. "She's gorgeous. Jerry could hardly take his eyes off her yesterday. Of course, she was wearing the tiniest swimsuit I've ever seen then, not a robe," she continued while Susan's mouth dropped open.

"I . . . you know how men are," was Susan's inadequate comment. Both women had been married for many years. They did know how men were, but that didn't necessarily mean they excused them.

Kathleen didn't respond.

"Would you like some coffee?" Susan asked. "The waiter is around somewhere."

"Someone will be over in a minute. The staff here is very attentive."

"Have you and Jerry been having fun? What have you been doing? How was dinner in town last night?"

"Awful. I think we picked out the worst restaurant on the island. It was dirty, noisy, and the food was dreadful."

"Why did you go there? Did someone recommend it?"

"No, we were just walking by. The menu was posted. It looked okay. You know how it is."

"Sure, but . . . I don't understand why you went into town. The food here is supposed to be wonderful. Don't tell me it isn't."

"Oh, no! We arrived in time for lunch. The food here is fabulous! I had a piece of grilled fish—I think it was grouper—and it was delicious. Really light and the spices were so unusual. And Jerry had a shrimp salad that was sensational."

"Then why did you go into town?"

"Damned if I know." Kathleen frowned. "It was Jerry's idea."

Susan, who was happy to sympathize if a female friend wanted to criticize her own husband, but knew enough not to be the one to start it, changed the subject. "Was your flight on time?"

"Yes. Thank heavens. Alex was up almost the entire night before we left. He claimed to have had a series of nightmares, but I think he was worried about us being gone. I got on the plane and fell asleep almost immediately. I didn't wake up until the pilot announced that we were about to land. So I arrived feeling wonderful. I only wish the same were true of Jerry. He says he didn't even nap, and he's completely exhausted from that mess at the agency. I'm really worried about him. I can't remember the last time I saw him relax."

"You mean that new account Jed and Jerry took over in December?"

"That and everything else," Kathleen answered vaguely. "Oh, there's that nice young man who keeps track of the kayaks. I watched a young couple paddling around in the water yesterday afternoon and it looked like they were having so much fun. I want to reserve two for Jerry and me. Do you and Jed want to try, too?"

"I . . . I think I'd rather watch first. To tell the truth, my plans for today include a short swim in the pool and lots of time spent with a paperback in one hand and a cool drink in the other. Maybe tomorrow I'll feel more energetic."

"Then I'll just ask him to reserve two. Oh, there's Jed! I'll tell him we're over here."

"Great."

Susan picked up her coffee and resumed her contemplation of the ocean.

"Hi, hon." Jed leaned down for his morning kiss. "Sleep well?"

"Sure did."

"I'm surprised you're up so early."

"I'm planning a leisurely day of dozing in the sun. Thought I'd get an early start."

"Just be careful that you don't get a burn," Jed warned.

"I won't. I packed three different sunscreens. Besides, there are umbrellas set up all over the place." She looked around. "It's really nice here, isn't it?"

"It certainly is bright." Jed looked over his shoulder. "Where have Kathleen and Jerry gone?"

"Kath is trying to reserve kayaks for them to use today, and I haven't seen Jerry yet. Maybe he's sleeping late. Kath says he's been exhausted." She thought for a moment before asking a question. "Have things been going on at the agency that you haven't told me about?"

"Probably. I don't tell you everything, after all. But I gather you're referring to something specific?"

"I don't know. Kathleen mentioned problems, and you hadn't told me anything unusual. Oh, here they come. Let's order. I'm starving." If she had been a bit less hungry, she might have noticed the change of expression on her husband's face when she mentioned problems, but Jed had reassumed his relaxed facade by the time Jerry and Kathleen arrived at the table. They were followed closely by a perky waitress who offered menus and coffee.

They spent the next few minutes deciding on their orders. Jed and Jerry stuck to eggs and bacon, but both Kathleen and Susan threw caution—and their diets—into the Caribbean winds and decided on coconut French toast and fresh tropical fruit cup.

The food arrived promptly and it was wonderful. More and more hotel guests began to appear, many of them barefoot, dressed only in swimsuits and flowing cover-ups. Susan noticed that the casual atmosphere hadn't forced some of the diners to leave their jewels at home. One deeply tanned woman wore gold chains around her neck, both arms, and one ankle. A thin gold chain draped around her hips just below her navel completed the ensemble. The man she was with had adopted a yachting theme—boat shoes, navy slacks, a navy and white striped knit shirt—and a hat proclaiming him to be the captain shielded his eyes from the already warm sunshine. Susan leaned toward Kathleen. "Look at the woman over there. She's . . ."

But Kathleen wasn't listening. She was staring at her husband with her mouth hanging open and a distressed expression on her face. "But I thought you wanted to kayak. Yesterday when we were watching that young couple, you said it looked like lots of fun."

"No, you said it looked like lots of fun. I just didn't disagree with you. Kath, I am not going to go out on the ocean in a little slip of plastic that could flip over at any minute. Period."

"But—but I don't want to go out alone."

Susan realized the Gordons' vacation wasn't starting off on the right foot, and she hurried in to help. "I'll kayak with you, Kath. I was just telling Jed that it sounded like fun."

Jed looked up from his plate. "But I thought—"

"I was planning to lie around all day," Susan admitted. "But now that I've consumed about a million calories, I think some exercise is an excellent idea. Maybe we could get another kayak if you want to join us. Right, Kath?"

"Sure. There are five or six available. Do you want me to check with James?"

"Who's James?"

"He's the young man who keeps track of the sports equipment and the towels and stuff like that. There's a little cabana/kiosk building right in front of our cottage; he might be there." Kathleen sat up a bit straighter and looked around. "There he is. He's arranging the seats by the pool. I wonder if we could reserve the four chaises in front of your cottage. Maybe put books on them or something?"

Jerry glanced over at the seats his wife was talking about. A line of about a dozen wooden lounges stood on the patio between the cottages and the seawall that lined the beach. As they watched, a young man wiped the night's dew from them and laid out heavy canvas pads and towels. "Aren't those seats a bit exposed?"

"Exposed?" Kathleen said.

"To the sun," Jerry explained. "I don't want to get a burn. I was thinking of lying by the pool—under an umbrella—or maybe napping inside."

"Inside? Jerry, we're on an island in the Caribbean. No one stays inside unless it's raining!"

"You're the one who keeps telling me that I look sleepy."

"You do look sleepy," Kathleen agreed, looking guilty. "But we're on vacation . . . and I thought . . . oh, I don't know what I thought."

Susan and Jed, simultaneously recognizing a marital argument in its formative stages, chimed in.

"I know just how Jerry feels. A long nap is on my schedule today, as well," Jed spoke up.

"We need to remember to cover ourselves with sunscreen before we go out on the water, too," Susan reminded Kathleen, hoping to change the subject and return to the relaxed conversation of a few minutes ago. "And are there life vests? In Maine we always wear life vests."

"You know, I think that I did see someone wearing a life vest yesterday. We'll ask James. We don't have to go out very far, you know. The reef is only a hundred feet or so beyond the gazebo."

"Reef?"

"Yes, there's a gorgeous coral reef right out there. James told me all about it yesterday afternoon. That's why I want to go out this morning. He said that the tide will be higher later in the day and it will be harder to see the fish and all."

"Oh, Kath! A coral reef! I had no idea! I thought we were just going kayaking for the exercise. How wonderful! When is the best time to go? Now? Or should we wait for a bit?"

"I think an hour after eating is usually suggested," Jerry reminded them. "That gorgeous blue expanse is the ocean, you know."

"An hour. What can we do for an hour?" Susan wailed.

"There's a really nice gift shop right next to our cabin," Kathleen pointed out.

Susan smiled. "Perfect! Lead the way." The women got up and set out for one of their favorite activities. But Susan, turning back to remind Jed where she had stashed the sunscreen when she was unpacking last night, was stunned to see the expression on Jerry's face.

He had turned around so his back was to his friend and colleague and was staring out to sea looking completely miserable.

# THREE

$S$USAN USED A TOURING KAYAK TO CRUISE AROUND THE IS-
lands in Maine in the summer and she was accustomed to its
smooth glide through the water, but the lightweight plastic
kayak Compass Bay provided was another story. It bounced
over the surf like seaweed bobbing on the waves. She found
she could lean out and look into the water without fear of tipping over. There were colorful fish all around, but the biggest thrill was floating over the fabulous coral reef, which
was clearly visible through the water. "This is incredible,"
she said.

Kathleen was paddling by her side. "It is, isn't it? James
takes out groups of scuba divers every few days. They swim
around and through the reefs. I wasn't planning to sign up,
but now that I see this . . ."

"I'll go. And I know Jed won't want to miss this."

"I wish I could say the same for Jerry. Do you know, I think
he really was planning on going back to our room to rest
when we were on our way out here? I couldn't believe it! I'm
beginning to think there might be something seriously wrong
with him."

"You mean his health?" Susan asked, instantly concerned.
Too many men of Jed and Jerry's age were having heart at-
tacks. As a wife, she wasn't taking any chances. She might
eat Häagen-Dazs ice cream herself, but she hid it on the bot-

tom shelf of the basement freezer and offered low-fat frozen yogurt to her husband.

"No, his health is okay. I insisted that he get a complete physical the first week of January and everything's fine." She paused for a moment, slowly moving her paddle in and out of the surf. "I've been wondering if he's depressed. You know, if he should see a psychiatrist."

"Have you suggested it?"

"Not directly. Jerry's too smart to believe that having problems with your mental health is anything to be ashamed of, but I don't want him to think that I think there's something wrong with him. I've wondered out loud if antidepressants would make life easier, when we're watching TV and those ads come on, though."

"How does he respond?"

"He just nods and sort of grunts like he isn't listening too carefully. You know how men are sometimes."

"I sure do. But, if you really think he needs to see someone . . ."

"I don't know what he needs," Kathleen said. The happy expression on her face when she'd been watching the fish had vanished, Susan noticed. "I know he's unhappy, miserable even. But I don't know why and I don't know what to do about it. I just keep thinking . . ."

"What?" Susan urged her friend to continue talking. "What do you keep thinking?"

"I keep thinking that Jerry's regretting getting married to me and . . . and having a second family."

"Kathleen, that's not possible. Jerry loves you and the kids! How could you even consider that?"

"I—there are lots of little things. He really is unhappy, Susan. He says it's just problems at work and that they will clear up. But it's been getting worse for over a month. And last week—" She stopped speaking.

"What happened last week?"

Kathleen was obviously having a difficult time discussing this. She took a deep breath and began. "I was looking for summer clothing to bring on this trip, so I went into the back of Jerry's closet where he stores his golf shoes and things like that and I found a cardboard box full of photos of June and the girls. It was open as though Jerry had been going through it recently. I don't resent it or anything, but when I found that—and then connected it to the fact that he's been so depressed and not like himself at all—well, I just wonder what he's thinking. His personality has really changed in the past few months. He's even been shouting at the kids, and you know that's not like him. Usually Alex and Emily get away with murder when he's around."

"The two things might not be connected," Susan suggested. She heard the pain in her friend's voice and wanted desperately to offer her some solace. "Or the box of photos might have been stored there and just fallen out. You know he must think about them sometimes."

"Of course I do. We talk about them. And he talks to the kids about them, too. After all, Alex has had two of the teachers that Jerry and June's oldest daughter had, and Emily has the same kindergarten teacher that their youngest girl had. Every once in a while someone who doesn't know about the accident will assume that those girls are still alive and that Alex or Emily is a younger sibling. The kids have always had to deal with that, so of course they know about the accident. It doesn't seem to worry Emily at all, although Alex is old enough to begin asking questions about his daddy being sad because of the deaths."

"He's a really levelheaded kid," Susan said.

"I know. And I'm thankful for that, but when he has nightmares like he did the night before we left, I wonder if the tragedy that ended Jerry's first marriage hasn't affected him somehow."

"And now you're wondering if maybe it's bothering Jerry, too?" Susan asked.

"I saw a television show on post-traumatic stress. It can appear years and years after the event. This show was about Vietnam vets, but losing your entire family the way that Jerry did certainly could be as stressful as a war."

Susan didn't respond immediately. She stared down into the water and remembered the night that Jerry had called to tell her that his wife and two daughters had died in a flaming pile of metal on the highway near Hancock. She had been nearly paralyzed with shock and grief, but Jerry had coped with his loss. He had organized the funeral, dealt with June's family, and entertained the many friends and neighbors who had attended the funeral and then come to visit in the following weeks.

A few months later, Jerry had accepted Susan's offer of help, clearing the house of June's and the children's possessions before he put it on the market and moved into a small condo downtown near the train station. At the time, Susan had wondered at Jerry's lack of outward emotion, but Jed, who had known Jerry since college, had claimed that this was Jerry's way of handling things, and in all honesty, Susan had been relieved. She and June had been good friends; her children and Susan's children had been nearly the same ages. They'd gone to school, parties, swimming lessons, and dancing lessons together. They had been inseparable at the Hancock Field Club. They had gone to Disney World on family vacations, trick-or-treated together, joined Brownies and Cub Scouts. Susan and her children were in mourning, as well.

But time passed. An attractive professional and widower in his thirties, Jerry had been invited to numerous parties as the extra man and introduced to many potential mates, but no one had caught his eye until Susan and Jed introduced him to Kathleen, a young state police officer who had come to town to help solve a murder. Less than a year later they were married. Kathleen quit her job and they started a family. Two children later, Kathleen and Jerry seemed to be among the happiest couples Susan and Jed knew. And, more importantly, Susan claimed Kathleen among her best friends. She was having a difficult time accepting the thought that there were serious marital problems in Kathleen's life and that she hadn't known about them.

"Has Jerry talked more about June or the girls recently?" Susan asked.

"You mean since he's seemed depressed?"

"Exactly."

"No. Not that I've noticed. But you know what's beginning to worry me?"

"No, what?"

"I'm beginning to act differently . . . and think differently about him."

"What do you mean?"

"You know those annoying little habits that husbands have?"

"Like leaving socks on the bathroom floor even though there's a hamper less than a foot away? Or putting dirty glasses into the sink instead of bothering to open the door of the dishwasher and plopping them inside?"

"For me it's the toothpaste tube problem."

"What toothpaste tube problem?"

"Jerry leaves the top off. Always. And when I pick it up and put it back on, there's a little drip of toothpaste on the sink that I have to wipe up. It's silly but it drives me nuts."

"Have you tried those tubes that stand up?"

"Sure did. And they are an improvement. He doesn't put the top on, but the toothpaste doesn't drip out. Of course, we have a little travel tube with us here. I'll bet anything that when I go into that bathroom, there will be a top on one side of the basin and the tube on the other. When we were first married, I thought it was sort of endearing—so help me."

"Well, let's face it, during those first few months of infatuation, everything seems endearing. My own theory is that too much sex destroys your judgment, and feeling kindly toward someone who can't remember to put the top back on the toothpaste proves it."

"I had gotten used to it, but recently it's begun to drive me nuts again. I know it's irrational, but . . ."

"But when you're annoyed with one thing, everything else is exaggerated, as well," Susan said.

"I guess. We probably should head back to shore," Kathleen suggested. "James is down by the water with another couple. They may have reserved these boats for the next hour."

"Sure." Susan started to paddle a bit more enthusiastically. "Kathleen, if there's anything I can do . . ."

"Susan, I don't want to ruin your vacation. I don't want to ruin my vacation. I'm glad you're my friend and I know I can always come to you for help. But let's just try to have fun while we're here. Remember, in a week's time we'll probably be up to our knees in snow again."

"Don't remind me!" She put a bit more oomph into her stroke, and the little kayak zoomed across the water.

The movement of the waves pushed them into shore, and in moments they were stepping off their kayaks. That is, Kathleen stepped off. Susan, shifting her weight in the wrong direction, slipped right into the surf. James was in the water immediately, making sure she was okay, helping her get back on her feet.

"I'm fine," Susan assured him, laughing. "I'm just getting to my morning swim a little earlier than I had planned."

"Well, at least you waited an hour after eating," Jed said, appearing on the beach with two large fluffy towels. "Here," he continued, offering both to his wife. "I was planning on offering one to each of you, but your need appears to be greater than Kathleen's."

"There are extra towels piled on the chair out on the gazebo," James informed them.

"We're okay," Kathleen assured him before turning to Jed. "Where's Jerry?" she asked.

"To tell the truth, I have no idea. He went back to his room after breakfast, but when I knocked on the door a few minutes ago, he wasn't there. There was a young woman cleaning, and she said that he had come in for a few minutes and then left almost immediately. But don't worry. It won't take any time at all to find him. This is a pretty small resort and there aren't a whole lot of places to hide."

"I could use something cool to drink," Susan said.

"Why don't you two go find a place to sit and I'll get some juice," Jed suggested. "Orange, tomato, cranberry, or pineapple?"

"Anything as long as it's cold," his wife replied.

"Cranberry mixed half and half with some Perrier if they have it," Kathleen answered. "I'm going to find Jerry, so save me a seat. I'll be back in just a few minutes."

But Susan and Jed had emptied their glasses of juice by the time Kathleen returned, a worried expression on her face.

"I brought cranberry juice and Perrier, but I think it's warm by now," Jed said, standing up. "Why don't I go get some more ice?"

"Don't bother. I'm not really thirsty. I'm worried. I can't find Jerry anywhere."

# FOUR

"HE PROBABLY WENT FOR A WALK." THAT STATEMENT WAS repeated a few times as the Henshaws and Kathleen asked members of the Compass Bay staff if they had seen Jerry. But where? He could have gone for a walk on the beach that stretched out beyond the stone jetty that bounded the resort to the west. He could have strolled down the road in either direction, ending up at the tiny grocery store in the nearby community in one direction or into an enormous stand of palm trees in the other. They couldn't find anyone who had seen him, so they had no way of knowing. Kathleen wanted to organize a search, but Jed and Susan talked her out of it.

"It isn't like Kath to overreact like this," Jed said to Susan as they headed back to their room for more sunscreen. "What's going on?"

"She's worried about Jerry. She says he's been looking at photos of June and the kids."

"Oh, but that might be because—" A loud knock on the door prevented Jed from finishing. He opened the door to discover that the wanderer had returned.

"Jerry was walking on the beach!" Kathleen announced, appearing at her husband's side.

"I didn't mean to make anyone worry—especially this anyone. I thought I would be back before the kayakers returned,"

Jerry said, putting his arm around his wife's shoulder and pulling her closer.

"How is the beach?" Jed asked, grabbing a paperback from the pile by the bed.

"Gorgeous. We should all head up there after lunch, but right now I'm going for a quick dip in the pool and then taking a nap. I'm exhausted."

"Must be this fresh air," Susan said, following her husband's example and choosing some reading material before following him out of the cottage. "I'm planning on reading for a while, swimming for a while, and then, perhaps, I'll feel as though I deserve to nap," she explained.

"James reserved the four lounges right outside our cabin for us," Kathleen said, heading in that direction.

"That's awfully sunny. Why don't we sit down by the pool? Those umbrellas will keep us from getting baked," Jerry suggested.

"I think there are only three lounges available down there," Susan said, counting.

"I'll take a chair and you three can lie down," Jerry offered, starting off to the pool. "Last one in the water buys the rum punch!" he called back over his shoulder.

Jed hurried after his friend, but Susan waited a moment. Kathleen didn't seem in a hurry to join them. "Kath? Are you coming?" she prompted when her friend didn't move.

"I . . ." Kathleen looked up toward the bright blue cabin she and Jerry shared. "I think I'll call home first. I just want to make sure Jerry's mom knows where I keep the—the boxed fruit juice."

"Are you all right?" Susan asked.

"Yes. Definitely. I just want to make sure everything at home is okay. You know how it is."

Susan smiled. She did know. It was sensational to be away

from your children for a while, but that didn't mean that they weren't missed. "We'll see you down by the pool then."

The freshwater swimming pool had been built on a large deck overlooking the ocean. Lined with bright blue tiles, the pool had a mosaic of a coconut palm tree decorating its bottom. Jed was busy arranging the beach towels to his satisfaction. Jerry was already in the water, lying on a bright orange float with his eyes closed. Susan chose a coral-colored lounge near her husband and looked around for a side table to place between them. An attractive, young black man, who apparently could read minds, appeared with two side tables and put one on either side of the Henshaws. "Did you have a good kayak trip?" he asked politely.

"Yes, excellent." Susan smiled up at him and placed her book, sunglasses, and two tubes of sunscreen on the closest table. "Don't you think we should be tipping all these helpful people?" she asked her husband, when they were alone again.

"Why don't we tip them all on the day we leave? Otherwise we'll be passing out money every time we turn around."

Susan leaned back in her seat, adjusted her sunglasses, picked up the latest Katherine Hall Page mystery, sighed twice, closed her eyes, and fell asleep.

When she woke up a bit later, she was vaguely aware of being in a strange place. The skin across her shoulders was hot from the sun, but the air was soft and balmy. She picked out familiar voices from the hum around her. Jed and Jerry might be on vacation, but they seemed to be discussing a colleague from the office. She opened her mouth to protest and then shut it again. Everyone had his or her own way to relax. If they wanted to chat about the problems they had left behind, fine. She had her own ideas. A notice on the dresser in their cottage had explained how to make reservations for a massage. Her arms, stiff from the few hours she'd spent paddling around in the kayak, could use some special attention. She stood up, plopped her straw hat on her head, adjusted her pareo around her waist, and, deciding that she didn't need shoes, headed back to their cottage.

It was close to noon and even those guests who ranked sleeping late high on their list of vacation priorities were up and about. Each chair or lounge seemed to be filled or about to be filled, with colorful beach towels, open paperbacks, and half-finished drinks waiting for their occupant's return. Susan walked slowly. Everything was painted in brilliant colors. But the blue paint couldn't compare with the hue of the sky. The azure sea sparkled in the sunlight. The palm trees rustled slightly in the sea breeze. An enterprising photographer could have pointed his camera in any direction and labeled the resulting photograph paradise. Susan realized she was completely content. She glanced back over her shoulder. Jed and Jerry were still talking. Kathleen had moved her chair under an umbrella and was apparently absorbed in her book.

The maid had cleaned up their cottage, and Susan quickly found the notice of spa services available. Massages—Swedish and deep muscle—could be had day and evening. Reservations were required and could be made in the gift shop.

The gift shop was small, but carried just about all the necessities, from sunscreen to après-sun crème to Solarcaine, as well as lots of luxury items. A tall, elegant black woman was stationed by the old-fashioned cash register.

"May I help you?"

"I understand this is the place I make reservations for a massage?"

"Yes." She pulled a large leather-bound book from underneath the counter. "Do you prefer a male or a female?"

"A woman, if that's possible. Is there someone available this afternoon?"

"Let me see . . . yes, Lourdes could take you at three. Her

specialty is Swedish massage, but if you prefer something different . . ."

"No, that would be lovely. Where does she give them?"

"Right in your room. She has portable massage tables. If that's okay with you, I could make the appointment."

"Three o'clock is perfect!"

"Then you can expect Lourdes at three—or perhaps just after the hour. Sometimes one of her clients keeps her talking and she runs just a bit late. I always say Lourdes knows more about what goes on here at Compass Bay than anyone on staff."

Susan smiled. "Then I know whom to ask if I have any questions."

The woman laughed. "I said she knows, not she talks. Many famous people come to Compass Bay—musicians, politicians, actors, and such. No one keeps his job if he talks about them to the press or other guests." The cordial expression on her face vanished, making Susan feel as though she had been caught doing something wrong.

"I can understand that," she quickly assured the other woman. "I wouldn't want anyone talking about what I'm doing. Not that I'm doing anything wrong," she added quickly. "Or even interesting, for that matter . . ." She realized she was babbling, and the gigantic orange sun hat hanging above the cash register provided a change of topic. "How much is that hat?" she asked quickly.

Five minutes later she left the store, one hat in hand, another on her head. Having no intention of looking like a hat salesman for a minute longer than necessary, she hurried back to her cottage. Noticing that the door to the cottage Jerry and Kathleen shared was open, she glanced inside. A tall woman wearing immaculately pressed white slacks was leaning over the bed. Susan smiled. The room she shared with Jed had been made up hours ago, but in a resort where the guests stayed for multiple days, housekeeping probably had to be very flexible. She had noticed a couple of maids replacing damp beach towels hung over deck railings with clean, dry ones late last night. This was just what every woman needed, she realized, twenty-four/seven maid service. Her own cottage was sparkling and neat, and she tossed the horrible orange hat on the batik bedspread. She would figure out what to do with it later. Perhaps she could donate it to one of the charity sales that organizations in Hancock were so fond of holding. If, that is, she even managed to get it back to Hancock. It certainly wouldn't fit under her airplane seat or in the overhead compartment. She could, she supposed, always wear it.

Back at the pool, Jed and Kathleen were now swimming slow crawls up and down the length of the pool. Jerry was lying on the lounge his wife had occupied, facing the sea. From this angle, Susan couldn't tell if he was napping or just watching the water. But it was obvious that no one needed her. Small boys, so thin that their cutoff jeans were in danger of slipping from their hips, were out on the gazebo dropping nets in the water and pulling them up, full of shimmering silver fish. Curious, Susan turned around and headed in that direction.

Two middle-aged couples were sitting on chairs placed along the deck leading to the gazebo. They shared two small tables. One was covered with half-filled glasses; on the other, one of the women was playing a lackadaisical game of solitaire. "I thought we were going to play bridge," she was saying as Susan passed by.

"After lunch," one of the men said.

"After my nap," the other man added.

The two women exchanged glances. "Perhaps," the one who had just ended her lonely card game said to the other.

"Perhaps we should go see what there is to buy in the gift shop."

"I thought you bought the place out yesterday," growled one of the men, reaching out for his glass.

"Yeah, well . . ."

Susan hurried on, unwilling to allow other couples' squabbles to mar her vacation. For a resort that advertised itself as one of the most romantic spots in the world, there sure seemed to be a lot of bickering going on.

The boys who were fishing turned out to be island natives, not related to the resort's guests. They were thrilled to have an audience and explained that their relatives—older brothers, Susan gathered—would be using what was caught for bait to catch "the big fishes off the boats." Their fishing was energetic, messy, and highly productive. In minutes, they had filled three plastic buckets with fish. They then took a moment to show Susan and another woman who appeared in the gazebo shortly after her the long, thin fish that swirled through the water beneath the dock, causing the smaller baitfish to flee out to sea. "Barracuda!" one of the boys yelled. "You see, you swim with barracuda!" Laughing loudly, the boys ran back toward the shore, the water in their buckets splashing out and wetting the legs of the card-playing women as they passed by.

Susan stared down into the water and realized that, in fact, she may have been swimming with those ugly things. She worked to remember the little she knew about these fish. Certainly they cleared the area of smaller fish, but would they go after people swimming in the same water? She'd try to remember to ask James when she saw him again. She leaned her arms on the railing and stared down into the water.

"Don't worry. They're not sharks. They don't attack people."

Susan had been joined by the tall blond she had seen out here early this morning. Now the woman was wearing white linen slacks and a bikini top that barely covered her ample tanned breasts. She was carrying a long batik scarf.

"I'm glad to hear that," Susan admitted. "I'd hate to stop going in the water on our second day here."

"Don't. I find the water in the Caribbean to be like satin—warm, smooth, delicious to swim in."

"Yes. I guess. I've only been in for a few minutes," Susan admitted, remembering her tumble off the kayak only a few hours ago.

"Well, don't let those fish keep you out. I like going in late, after dark."

"Isn't that dangerous?" Susan asked. "I mean, what about ocean currents, and black sea urchins, and jellyfish?"

"They're all there, but the risk just adds to the pleasure sometimes, don't you think?"

"I—no, not really," Susan said.

"Well, people are different, aren't they? I love it." She turned and looked back toward the beach. "I must be leaving now. I'm meeting someone."

"I—I'll see you around, I guess," Susan said to her.

"Yes, you will. Of course you will." The words floated over her shoulder, and her exit left Susan squinting into the sun. She felt as though she was watching someone play a part. And the actor's face was definitely familiar. Where had she seen this woman before?

# FIVE

IT BEGAN AS THE WORST MASSAGE EVER. LOURDES HAD strong hands and knew what she was doing, and although Susan's shoulder felt better almost immediately, she found it difficult to relax while someone else was talking. And Lourdes had a lot to talk about—starting with her previous client.

Lourdes was waiting for Susan on the deck of the Henshaws' cottage—early, she explained, because her last client had failed to show up for her appointment. It was happening more and more, she continued while setting up her massage table. Susan had retreated to the bathroom to undress. When she reappeared in the bedroom wrapped in one of the heavy terry cloth, one-size-fits-all robes the resort provided, Lourdes was still complaining about being stood up.

"I don't make the appointments. I am told where to go to, what time to show up, and I do what I'm told. Always I do what I'm told. I was brought up poor, but I was taught to be reliable. Some of these rich people who come here could use a little training in reliability." She stopped smoothing out the towel she had laid on the table, looked at Susan, and apparently realized who she was complaining to. "Most of our guests are wonderful people, you understand. I don't complain about them."

Susan smiled. "I understand."

"And since you are on time, you benefit from the guests who are not so responsible. You lie down on table now, please."

Susan did as requested, squirming about until she was comfortable and placing her head on the pillow Lourdes offered. She had barely closed her eyes when Lourdes started talking again. "Of course, there be guests who other guests not like. It not just me. Everyone here is complaining about them. They noisy and they bother the other guests. They demanding. They get up early. They stay up late. They hog the best seats."

"What are the best seats?" Susan asked.

"Many of our guests prefer to sit on the patio between the pool and the bar. It is small. Only a half a dozen lounges and few tables will fit there comfortably. This group has claimed them since last Sunday—the day they arrive. They sit there and play cards in morning. They sit and play cards in afternoon. At night, when the dark come, they sit in bar at big corner table that everyone like and they play more cards. Cards. Cards. Cards. They do not even bet on who win. Can you believe that?"

"I guess," Susan muttered.

"Cards not problem. No one care if they play. But they take best places. They make many guests unhappy. And unhappy guests need care, need to be made happy. Everyone must work twice as hard. Guests must be happy. Unlike staff. No one cares about unhappy staff."

"Yes, I'm sure that's true." Susan yawned. "The sun always makes me so sleepy."

Lourdes didn't take the hint. "We work and we work. And when we do a good job, we have a job. But if anything go wrong. No . . . if nothing go wrong and someone—some guest—complain, then we don't work. There are not many places to work on island, not on this island."

Susan decided that a change of subject was in order. "Have you always lived here?"

"Yes. Always. I leave island to study, then I come back to work."

"Where did you go to school?" Susan asked, realizing she had to say something now that she had started the conversation going in this direction.

"On St. Thomas. They have very good massage school there."

"Oh." Susan had been thinking high school, maybe college. "How long were you there?"

"Two weeks. Our training was thorough, quite thorough." As if to prove her point, Lourdes increased her energetic kneading of Susan's left thigh.

"My legs may be a bit sunburned," Susan said.

"Yes. You must be careful in our sun. The gift shop sells many brands of sunscreen if you forgot to bring."

"I brought and I bought," Susan muttered. Lourdes had moved on to her calves, and she was beginning to enjoy the entire experience. And drift off to sleep . . .

"That woman is a troublemaker. I watch her and I see what she do!"

Susan returned from the edge of sleep with a jerk. "You mean taking the best seats?" she asked, completely confused.

"The best seats? No, I think not. She like to be seen and she like not to be seen. She move from seat to seat. But always the men watch her."

Susan realized Lourdes was no longer complaining about the cardplayers. "I don't know who you're talking about," she admitted. It was obvious that the more she talked, the more Lourdes would respond, but perhaps it was better to give up any idea of sleeping. And listen to the gossip. Susan loved gossip.

"Ms. Allison. That is how she signs up for my services. She

tell people call her Ally. Not staff, other guests," Lourdes explained. "She was supposed to be my massage before you."

"You're talking about the woman who had the appointment
before this. The one who didn't show up."

"Yes. She here on vacation. So she do little. She move from
seat to seat. She swim. Eat. Drink. But she too busy to show
up for massage that she sign up for."

"Ouch!" Lourdes had expressed her frustration with this
unknown woman by digging her thumbs into the arch of Susan's left foot.

"You tell me if I hurt and I stop," Lourdes muttered, moving to the other foot.

"I . . . that feels fine now." It really felt more than fine.
"Tell me about the other guests here," Susan asked, guessing
that she was going to hear the answer to her question whether
or not she asked it.

But to her surprise, when asked, Lourdes refused to answer. "We are told not to talk about our clients," she stated
flatly.

"Oh, yes, of course. I—I just—oh, that feels good." After a
moment of silence, Susan drifted off to sleep as Lourdes
worked on her left leg.

She woke up and realized that she was alone. The door was
closed, but all the windows of the cottage had been thrown
open. Heavy plantation shutters provided privacy but allowed
warm breezes to drift through the room. She could hear
voices—other guests walking by or lounging right outside
the room. There were giggles and she realized that the two
maids were working on the cottage next door. She rolled over
onto her side, being careful not to fall off the narrow table,
and pulled the fluffy towels around her. Sliding to the floor,
she noticed a note and a pale orchid blossom lying on the
middle of the bed. Her feet covered with massage oil, she
slipped across the room and picked it up. It was from Lour-

des, thanking Susan for her patronage and assuring her that the fee for her services would be added to her bill. Susan realized that she would have to tip Lourdes the next time she saw her. Or perhaps, she thought, she could get another massage tomorrow and tip for both services at the same time. The chatter had been irritating, but her shoulders and neck had never felt better. Smiling, she headed off to the shower.

Fifteen minutes later, clad only in a full-length sundress, she set out to search for her husband and friends. And found Jed and Kathleen still in their swimsuits, still sitting beside the pool. Their glasses of Perrier had been replaced by goblets of ruby liquid. Jed was chasing a chunk of fresh pineapple around his glass. He looked up as his wife appeared.

"You look wonderful. How was the massage?"

"Noisy, but good. How do I go about getting one of those?"

"Just go up to the bar and ask for the house special. It's rum and amaretto and . . . I'm not sure what . . . something pink. Anyway, it's delicious. Why don't I order one for you? I was just thinking about taking a shower before I change for dinner. I'll stop at the bar on the way and have someone bring you a drink." He drank the last of his drink and got up.

Susan sat down as he left, turning to Kathleen with what she thought was an innocuous question. "Where's Jerry?"

"Who knows? Last time I saw him, he was heading for the beach. I assume the pool was too tame for him and he was going for a swim in the ocean. Maybe he'll run into one of those jellyfish that sting swimmers."

"Kathleen!"

Kathleen flipped her long blond hair off her shoulders and sat up straight. "Well, wouldn't you think that he would tell me what he was going to do? He didn't have to invite me to go along. But he didn't say anything. He just got up and walked off as though I wasn't even around. I feel as though I might as well have stayed at home with the kids!"

"Oh, Kathleen, don't say that! He may have thought you didn't want to be bothered."

"Susan, you and Jed have been married for over thirty years. Has Jed ever treated you like Jerry's treating me?"

Susan thought for a moment before answering. She didn't want to say the wrong thing or give the wrong impression. "Jed has not always acted as though my presence was the most important thing in his life. After all, I haven't always acted as though he's the most important thing in my life and that doesn't mean that he isn't. It just means that . . . well, after a while you sort of get used to the person you're married to, that's all."

"Susan, I don't expect Jerry to spend all his free time drooling over me, but common courtesy—"

"But you said yourself that he has a lot on his mind."

"Which he won't share with me! Which may have something to do with his first wife. Which—which is the real reason I'm so upset about all this, of course." She picked up her glass and drained it. "I should have asked Jed to order another one of these for me. They really are good."

"I think he read your mind," Susan said as a waiter appeared and set a tray with two drinks, a small plate of spicy nuts, and fresh napkins between them.

"I'll bring the crab cakes out as soon as they're done. Your husband ordered them."

"See, Jed is still taking care of you," Kathleen said.

"Right now he is, but I can't count the times I've asked him to get me something and he assures me he will and then forgets the minute he leaves the room. Heavens, he's always forgetting to tell me people have called. The man can't take a phone message to save his life."

"But he doesn't think about his first wife all the time," Kathleen said sadly.

Susan wasn't sure how to respond. "I think about June and

the kids sometimes, but that doesn't mean I don't consider you my best friend. And you know how I love Alex and Emily."

"I know you're right, but something's changed. I don't know what it is, but Jerry's feelings for me have changed. Sometimes I get the feeling that he regrets marrying me!"

Susan picked an almond from the nut cup and examined it carefully before popping it in her mouth. Kathleen was a savvy woman with a lot of self-confidence and her feet on the ground. She was not the type to imagine problems where none existed. Susan suddenly found herself wondering if what her friend was saying might be true. Men did lose interest in the women they married. What if that was what was happening in the Gordons' marriage? What if Jerry did regret marrying Kathleen? How would Susan know? Who really knew what went on in someone else's marriage? She chewed and carefully considered what Kathleen was saying. Jerry claimed to be concerned about a problem at work, but Jed said things at the agency were just a little more hectic than normal. Jerry was distracted and looking at photos of his past life. Kathleen claimed he acted as though he no longer loved her. For the first time, Susan considered the possibility that this was true. By the time Jed returned, she was seriously depressed.

Dinner didn't improve her mood. Their table was placed at the south end of the patio, and they had watched a glorious sunset while eating. As soon as the sun sank into the inky sea, the staff had scurried around lighting small votives on the tables and large pillar candles set in heavy hurricane lamps upon the shell-studded cement wall that prevented guests and the resort itself from falling into the sea. It was quite romantic.

"Storms tomorrow," their waitress said, placing their orders before them.

"Can you tell that from just looking at the sky?" Susan

asked, as a sautéed grouper fillet surrounded by tiny vegetables was placed before her.

"No, I can tell that just by listening to the radio."

Everyone but Jerry laughed.

"Can I get you anything else?"

Jerry didn't even bother to look up.

As the evening wore on, Susan was ready to believe the worst about Jerry. He had arrived late, apologizing perfunctorily without explaining the reason for his rudeness. Refusing to join the others in their preferences for island drinks, he had ordered a double Scotch, gulped it down, and then ordered another. Susan and Jed and Kathleen chatted throughout the meal, but by the time they had finished their main course, Susan, at least, was tired of making an effort.

Everyone refused dessert, although Jerry ordered a large brandy to take back to their cottage. The couples parted quickly, barely bothering to say good night. Jed had flung himself down on their bed, claiming exhaustion and a surfeit of rum. He was asleep before Susan had washed her face and brushed her teeth.

But whether the result of her long nap earlier in the day or because she was worried about Kathleen and Jerry, Susan realized she wasn't ready to sleep. Quietly, so as not to bother Jed, she let herself out of the cottage.

There were diners still on the patio and in the dining rooms. The bar was full of carousing vacationers. Susan turned and walked away from the commotion, toward the pier leading over the water to the gazebo. She would sit for a while. Perhaps the cool breezes would make her sleepy.

# SIX

THEY GOT THE NEWS AT BREAKFAST. THE STORM HAD AR-
rived overnight, and the resort staff had rolled down heavy
clear plastic tarps to protect the diners from the wind and
rain. The view through the plastic was blurred, and the sound
of the pounding rain could not be ignored. The resulting am-
biance was gloomy. As Susan looked around at the almost
empty room, she realized that many vacationers had decided
this was the perfect occasion for room service. The Henshaws
were having coffee as they waited for Jerry and Kathleen to
arrive.

Susan had wondered if this was the perfect opportunity to
question Jed about Jerry's strange conduct and then discarded
the idea. They were on vacation; there must be something
else to talk about than their friends' marriage.

"Too bad it's raining," Jed said, looking out at the sea. "I
was thinking we might take a walk up the beach. Jerry found
some sensational sea urchin shells yesterday."

"Where? There were some shell fragments under the pier,
but I didn't see any intact shells."

"Back that way." Jed pointed west past all the cottages and
the pier. "You can either wait until low tide and walk around
the seawall or you climb over it. Apparently there are miles of
pristine beach in that direction. James told me about it while
you and Kathleen were kayaking."

"And Jerry walked up there while we were out?"

"I don't know when he was there, but he told me about it while we were all sitting around the pool yesterday afternoon. That's when I thought we might go this morning. I know how you love to collect shells."

"Yes, but I don't want to collect them in the rain," Susan said, as their waitress appeared with a platter of fresh fruit. "How long do you think the storm will last?" she asked her.

"Oh, our weather comes and goes. This will not ruin your vacation. It will have blown out to sea by the afternoon. You'll see. Oh, here is your friend. I'll bring her coffee."

"Bring two coffees," Jed suggested as Kathleen ducked under the tarp. "Her husband will be close behind."

Susan wished she could be so sure about that. "Where's Jerry?" she asked as Kathleen sat down in the chair between them.

"There's some sort of commotion at the end of the pier. He went out to see what was going on." She smiled at Susan. "I think he's beginning to relax. He's almost his old self this morning."

"Oh, Kath, that's great news! Now the weather doesn't matter so much. Jed was just telling me about the beaches up beyond the last cottage. Jerry told him there were sensational shells up there. We don't have to let the rain stop us. We can walk up in the rain. Heaven knows, it's warm enough and we're not going to melt."

"All four of us?"

"Sure, why not? We need to get as much exercise as possible. We're certainly eating enough. Those macadamia nut pancakes on the menu look interesting."

"I was thinking about the coconut muffins with mango butter," Kathleen said, picking up the large sheet of paper on which the morning's offerings were printed. "Or maybe the tarragon omelet with English bangers."

"I wonder where our waitress has gone," Jed spoke up. "We ordered coffee for you and Jer, and she said it would be out in just a moment."

Susan looked around. "She seems to have disappeared."

Jed, who was in a position to look out toward the sea, frowned. "Is that our waitress running toward the dock?"

Susan turned and looked over her shoulder. "Wow! It looks like the entire staff is heading in that direction. What do you think is going on?"

"We were just passing by on our way here, and your friend was walking back from there." One of the women from the card-playing group leaned over from a nearby table to explain. "He said that some young boys—they must fish out there no matter what the weather—had found a body."

"Someone drowned?" Kathleen said, starting to stand up.

"No, now I don't know about that, but I couldn't be sure in all this blowing. The sand does make an incredible racket, doesn't it?"

"But where did you see my husband?" Kathleen asked.

"He was coming in this direction. I can't imagine where he's gotten to. It was only a few minutes ago. Oh, look, here he is."

Jerry Gordon was walking toward them. Raindrops had stained his shirt, and a towel hung around his neck. "I went back to the room to change," he said, not bothering to greet anyone.

"Jerry . . . this woman says that you told her that a body has been found."

Jerry looked at the woman his wife had pointed out before answering. "Yes. That's what I was told. They found her in the gazebo."

"So that's where everyone is going," Jed said.

"Actually, it looks as though everyone is coming back here now," Susan said, watching.

"It's Lila's fault. She's ordering the staff back to work," the woman they'd been chatting with announced. "She runs a tight ship, I can tell you."

"Who's Lila?" Jed asked.

"She manages this place," Jerry answered. "She introduced herself to us the day we arrived, didn't she?" he continued to his wife.

"If she did, I don't remember it," Kathleen said. "But it does look as though the staff is returning. Thank goodness. Maybe someone will bring us more coffee."

"And some news about the body," Susan added quietly. "I hate to think of someone drowning right where we were kayaking yesterday."

"I told my husband the day we arrived that this place was unsafe. No lifeguards. You'd have to look for quite a while to find a beach without a lifeguard in New Jersey. That's where I live."

"Oh, where? We have friends who have a summer house in Avalon," Susan, ever gregarious, said.

"Avalon is lovely. We have a place in Loveladies, but—"

One of her companions, a heavyset man with what looked like a painful sunburn on his bald head, interrupted her. "We can order now, Ro. Our waitress has returned."

"We'll talk later, dear. Such a dreadful thing. A death right at the beginning of your nice vacation."

Susan turned back to her own party. Jerry and Kathleen were studying their menus intently, but Jed was still looking toward the now thinning crowd on the beach, his coffee cooling before him. "I think I'll go see what's happening," he said. "Order the pancakes with bacon for me, Sue."

"Don't you want to try the coconut pancakes with burnt sugar syrup?"

"No, just the regular kind with regular syrup," her husband answered, getting up and pushing his chair away from the rain that was blowing through a slit in the heavy plastic. "I'll be right back," he assured her. Then he pulled the tarp aside and disappeared into the rain.

Susan looked over at Kathleen. "I wonder what that was about."

"I wonder where our waitress is. I could really use some coffee." Almost before the words were out of Kathleen's mouth, their waitress was at their side, coffee in hand.

"Can you take our orders now?" Susan asked.

"I . . ." She rummaged in her apron pocket. "Oh, I forgot my pad. I'll be right back." And before anyone could protest, she was gone.

"Well, at least she left the coffeepot," Kathleen said, picking it up and filling all their cups.

"You can't expect the service to be normal when a murdered woman was just discovered close by," Jerry said, pouring cream into his coffee.

"Who said anything about murder?" Susan asked.

Jerry seemed startled by this question. "I thought everyone knew. She's dead. There was a fishing line pulled tight around her neck. It couldn't have been an accident."

"But—"

Kathleen interrupted before Susan could ask another question. "I don't understand why you say that. She could have drowned accidentally. She might have become entangled in the fishing line after her death."

"But she wasn't found in the water. She was found sprawled on one of the deck chairs. She was wet, but it was from the rain. She was murdered." And suddenly, without any warning, tears were running down Jerry's cheeks. "I—I think I'd better go back to our cottage," he muttered, getting up.

Kathleen didn't waste a second before following him.

Their waitress reappeared, notebook in hand, to discover Susan sitting alone at the table. "Why don't you just put the coffees on our bill and we'll get back to breakfast in a bit," Susan suggested, standing up. "I think I should find out what's going on."

"They've taken her away," their waitress said. Then she moved closer and lowered her voice. "She was a guest, you see. They don't want to upset other guests. They don't want everyone to think they might get murdered in their sleep. Not good for business." She stood up and spoke more loudly. "Of course, maybe you weren't going to join your husband."

"Actually, I was."

"Your husband may've gotten the last look before they covered her up. You can't see her anymore. I told you. They've taken her away."

But Susan had gotten up and was heading for the pier, despite the rain, despite the woman's protests. Jed was among the least impulsive of men. If he had felt the need to check out the dead woman, there was a reason for his behavior. And she was going to find out what it was.

# SEVEN

SUSAN FOUND JED SITTING ON THE PIER IN ALMOST EXACTLY the spot she had stood the night before. He looked miserable and she slid down beside him on the bench and took one of his hands in hers.

"I can't believe this," he said, staring out into the rain. "It doesn't make any sense."

Susan squeezed his hand in what she hoped was a comforting manner. "No one expects a murder to happen while they're on vacation, but we should try to not let it bother us too much, Jed. After all, it's not as though we know the woman who died."

"That's just it, Sue. We do."

"We do what?" she asked slowly, hoping she didn't know the answer.

"We do know her. That is we did. I was just sitting here trying to remember the last time we saw her—before yesterday, that is. I mean, I saw her. We both must have seen her. But we didn't recognize her then, and now . . ."

"Jed, I have no idea what you're talking about."

"Allison. I didn't recognize her yesterday. She's changed a lot—and for the better, too—but something seemed familiar, and just now, even though she looked awful—pale and grayish with that horrible thing around her neck, and her tongue—"

Susan interrupted quickly. "I get the idea, Jed."

"What I'm saying is I knew who she was. This time."

Susan was becoming more confused as every second passed. "You said her name was Allison?" she asked, mentally reviewing the women with that name in her circle.

"Allison. You know, June's sister."

Now Susan had two unknown women to deal with. "June and Allison," she repeated slowly. "Jed, the only June I've ever known was Jerry's wife."

"Exactly! June Gordon! Jerry's first wife! You must remember her sister, Allison. She came to visit for holidays. Heavens, she must have had Thanksgiving dinner at our house half a dozen times."

"Or course I remember. She was the only person I've ever known who was allergic to cranberries. Although I did wonder—June's sister is here? Was here? Was murdered here?" She asked the questions breathlessly, suddenly realizing the import of what Jed had told her.

"Exactly."

"But . . ."

"Listen, Sue, I didn't recognize her at once, either, but we have to talk some things over right now. While we're alone."

"But . . ."

"We have to decide what—how much—to tell the police and whoever else ends up in charge here!"

"Jed, I don't understand. You're not making any sense."

"I'm trying to tell you. June's sister was here. She was killed here. Jerry could end up on the list of suspects. He—"

"Why would Jerry be suspected of killing anyone?" Susan paused and examined the expression on her husband's face. "Jed, you know something about this that I don't know, don't you? Something about Jerry and Allison?"

"I think someone's coming," Jed said, not answering her question. "Why don't we talk about this later—when we're alone."

Susan, completely mystified, could only agree. She got up and followed her husband back down the dock, toward the shore. The rain had almost let up, and on the horizon, a thin line of sunlight promised better weather to come. "Did Jerry recognize her—"

"Sue, not now!"

"Okay, but let's go back to our cottage and you can explain exactly what's going on."

"No. We'll go back to the restaurant and continue eating our breakfast. And we won't say anything to anyone that might indicate that we knew Allison."

"But . . ."

"Let's not say anything in public that might be misunderstood, okay?"

"I guess."

The restaurant had filled up, and Susan realized immediately that they would be conspicuous if they didn't talk about the murder. Everyone, staff and guests alike, was discussing nothing else.

"The rain has stopped. Why don't we see if they'll serve us out on the patio," Jed suggested.

"The seats are awfully wet. But I guess that doesn't matter. I have my swimsuit on underneath this dress." She glanced around. "I don't see Kath or Jerry."

"They're probably in their cottage."

"Then we—"

"We are going to go sit down and eat breakfast—in public. Maybe once Kathleen and Jerry see where we're sitting they'll come join us," Jed said, taking her elbow and guiding her over to a table beside the pool.

"Why here?" Susan asked. Then suddenly, and without benefit of a second cup of coffee, she realized what was going on. "We're sitting here because Kath and Jerry can see us by looking out the window of their cottage, right?"

"Yes, and we're as far as possible from the police as we can get," Jed added.

Susan looked over her shoulder and spied the group of uniformed men sitting around a large table next to the bar.

"They're policemen? They're certainly not acting like policemen. They all seem to be drinking rum punch. Don't you think that's a little unprofessional so early in the morning?"

"I think we don't know anything about the police force on this island. They could be highly qualified and professional or just the opposite. I don't know which possibility is the worst." Jed stood up abruptly. "I'm going to go see if I can find someone to serve us." He walked off, leaving Susan to worry about what all this meant. She and Jed had been married for years, and as far as she knew, he had never known more about the private lives of their friends and neighbors than she did. But in this case, at least, she had apparently been wrong. She turned around in her seat and studied the other guests. Who was missing? Who had she failed to recognize as the sister of Jerry's first wife yesterday?

Jed returned, accompanied by a waitress she hadn't seen previously.

"This is Trina. She's helping out in the kitchen today. I told her we'd understand if she took a little more time than her experienced colleagues."

The young woman giggled until her hair, wrapped in dozens of braids bound with little silver beads, flew out in all directions. "My cousin . . . he work here always, but today with the death, they expect big crowd and he call me to help out."

"Big crowd? You mean people will come here from other parts of the island? Other resorts?"

"Maybe. My cousin say Lila might hire me if I do well in emergency. I don't want to work other places. I want to work here."

"Oh, what—"

"I'm starving. Tell Trina what you want for breakfast, Sue," Jed interrupted, sitting down across from her.

Susan was beginning to wonder if she knew her husband at all. "I'll have the pecan pancakes with coconut syrup and bacon . . . and coffee . . . and some fresh fruit, please," she answered, glaring at him.

"I'll have the same," he agreed. "And you'll remember to tell our friends that we're out here if you see them?"

"Of course. I see them. I tell them. And I bring your breakfast back here faster than you can believe."

"We can only hope," Jed said when they were alone together again.

Susan was still examining the guests. "Except for Kath and Jer, I don't know who else is missing—That gorgeous blond. The one who was carrying that beautiful scarf! I thought she looked familiar. She is—she was—that was Allison?"

"Yes."

Susan tried to accept what she was hearing. It had been at least ten years since she had last seen Allison McAllister. She remembered that day well. She sat back in her seat, stared out at the clouds making way for the returning blue sky and the sparkling sun, and remembered.

June Gordon and her two children had been killed when the car she was driving had spun out of control and careened off a raised bypass on the highway right outside of Hancock. She had been an excellent driver, and no one had ever known what caused the accident, although Susan often wondered if June had taken her eyes off the road to check on one of her children—something every mother did but usually without fatal results.

Jed had been on a business trip, and Susan had accompanied a stunned Jerry to the trauma center morgue to identify the bodies of his wife and children. She had had nightmares about that event for years afterwards. Seeing June had been bad, but the children . . . Susan shook her head and sat up straighter. It was Allison's death she should be concerned with now, not something that happened over a decade ago.

She had last seen Allison about six months after June's death. Jerry had readily accepted Susan's offer to help. He had asked her to clean out his children's rooms, and she had done that, sending boxes of clothes to the local women's shelter and their toys and books to the state Head Start collection agency to be distributed where needed. She had also gone through June's closets, removing clothing and personal items and donating them to charity after checking with family members and friends to see what, if anything, they wanted.

June's parents were both dead and she had only one sister: Allison was an artist who made a living by freelancing. Most of her work, Susan remembered, was done for various advertising agencies. Allison didn't want many of her sister's possessions. She lived in a loft on the Lower East Side. Susan remembered her describing it as high rather than wide. Allison had spent a few days helping sort through her sister's possessions and then, claiming the call of work, returned to the city, leaving behind a small shoe box filled with June's possessions. Less than a year later Jerry put the house on the market and Allison arrived to claim that box. Susan, hearing from Jerry of the proposed visit, had made a point of being at his home while Allison was in town.

Jerry had thought Susan was being unselfish, but actually the opposite was true. She wanted to speak with Allison about the bracelets. June and Susan both had small children they adored—and desperately wanted to escape for a few hours once or twice a week, so they had started going to craft fairs held in local church halls and featuring items like stenciled pot holders and Christmas tree ornaments molded from bread dough. Then they had moved up to juried craft fairs featuring

artists who worked in gold and diamonds. At one of these
fairs, June found and fell in love with a pair of rose gold and
diamond cuffs. Susan had dutifully reported this love affair to
Jerry, who tracked down the artisan and gave the cuffs to June
the Christmas before her death. They had been the one thing
Allison wanted from her sister's estate. They had not been
found. Not that Susan hadn't looked. After searching through
June's personal possessions, she rummaged through kitchen
cupboards and drawers, thinking June might have removed
the bracelets while cooking. When she found nothing there,
she had searched around the washer and dryer in the laundry
room, on the shelves near June's gardening equipment in the
garage, and, finally, in the tote bag where her tennis togs lay.
Nothing. Susan finally concluded that June had been wearing
them when she died and that they had been stolen between
the time her body was cut from the car and she arrived at the
morgue.

But she had always suspected that Allison didn't believe
her theory. She had even gotten the impression that Allison
didn't trust her. And that was what she wanted to discuss with
her on that last day in Hancock. But Allison had swept through
town, picking up her box of reminders of her sister's life, and
left, only waving to Susan as she got into the taxi to take her
to the train and back to New York City.

And now she was dead. Susan shook her head. It all
seemed unbelievable.

"It seems unbelievable, doesn't it?" her husband said,
echoing her thoughts.

"Yes . . . but . . . oh, here's our breakfast." She smiled, but
wondered if she still had an appetite.

Jed hadn't lost his, picking up his fork and digging in as
soon as Trina put his plate on the table.

"You like island food," she commented approvingly.

"Yes, too much." Jed patted his almost flat stomach.

"Your friends like it, too," Trina commented.

"Our friends? You mean Kathleen and Jerry?" Susan asked.

"Yes, your friends in cottage by gift shop. They sitting with police now. They order island specialties, also."

Susan decided she didn't have to worry about gaining weight today. She had definitely lost her appetite.

# EIGHT

JED AND SUSAN COULD ONLY WAIT FOR JERRY AND KATH-
leen to join them. Somehow their food disappeared. Jed, in
fact, claimed to be thinking about what he'd order for lunch
when Jerry and Kathleen finally appeared.

"You won't believe what those guys are planning to do,"
Jerry said. He sat down beside Susan and reached out for the
last slice of cinnamon toast in the bread basket.

"What guys?" Susan asked, glancing over at Kathleen as
she did so.

"The island police apparently have different ways of doing
things than we do at home," Kathleen said.

"Yeah, you wouldn't believe it. Apparently they think that
they can just watch and wait and the murderer will somehow
identify himself. Most goddamn stupid thing I've ever heard."

"Jerry, I don't think we should underestimate them. A lot
of what they were saying made sense to me. They seem really
relaxed and casual, but . . . well . . ."

"You're saying that the police on the island are incompetent?" Jed asked for clarification.

"I'm saying that it would be easy to get that impression,
but I really don't think it's true," Kathleen answered. "They
may not have a whole lot of fancy equipment to check out the
crime scene, but they were asking some very good questions."

"Whatever," Jerry said. "I know that I'm just glad I'm not depending on them to find out who killed Allison."

"You recognized her!" Susan cried out.

"Well, of course, I—"

"Jerry! Shut up! Listen," Kathleen continued in the shocked silence that followed her order. "There's been a murder. There will be an investigation. Someone may be arrested. We have to make sure it isn't the wrong person—and I do mean you, Jerry Gordon!"

"Kath—"

"Wait! Our waitress is on the way over. We don't want to be overheard."

"But—"

"Wait!"

Susan and Jed exchanged one of those embarrassed looks that couples share when the other couple they're with begin to fight in their presence. They'd been through this before, but not with Kathleen and Jerry. Susan, studying Jed's expression, realized she wasn't the only person who was worried.

"Can I get anyone anything else?"

"I could use some more coffee." Jerry answered Trina's question.

"Maybe we could have it up in our cottage." Kathleen reached over and placed a hand on her husband's arm.

"In the cottage? But the sun is coming out; the day is going to be gorgeous. Who wants to spend a beautiful day like this indoors—"

"Jerry's right," Susan spoke up. "Why don't we all go kayaking?"

"I think the storm stirred up the surf," Jerry protested immediately.

"Then how about a long walk on the beach?" Susan knew they needed to talk someplace where they wouldn't be overheard.

Jerry was as quick to agree as he had been to protest. "Sounds good to me. What do you think, Kath?"

"I guess . . ." She looked around the tiny resort. "Apparently everyone is settling in for the day as if nothing unusual has happened."

Susan glanced around. The other guests did seem to be stretched out in lounge chairs around the pool or on the beach. Well, they were all on vacation, and the death really didn't relate to their lives—as far as Susan knew. Had Allison come here alone or was someone—a friend, relative, or significant other—hidden away in a cottage, mourning her death in private? "Do we know if Allison was here alone?" she asked quietly.

"Yesterday she was eating lunch with one of those men who always seem to be playing bridge," Jed answered. "Maybe she's here with that group."

"That doesn't sound like Allison," Jerry said. "At least, not the Allison I know."

"The Allison I knew didn't even look like the Allison that was here," Susan said. "She may have changed more than her appearance since I last saw her."

"So we'll head up the beach for a nice, long walk and burn all these calories, right?" Kathleen interrupted as Trina arrived, steaming coffeepot in hand.

"Oh, you're going for a walk?" Trina asked, filling Jerry's cup.

"We thought we would," Susan said quickly. "Any suggestion which direction we should go?"

"The beach is beautiful both ways. West is quieter, of course. No homes or hotels in that direction. Just watch out for the sea urchins. You don't want to walk on one. Their sting can make you pretty sick."

"We'll be careful." Kathleen stood up and turned toward Jerry. "Why don't you bring your coffee back to our room, and you can drink it while I change? I want to put a two-piece swimsuit on and get another hat."

"I'll wait out here," Jerry said, picking up his cup and taking a sip.

"I'll come with you, Kath." Susan jumped up quickly. "Jed can keep Jerry company."

The two women walked away together, and Susan, displaying what she thought was an amazing amount of self-discipline, waited until the door of the Gordons' cottage had closed behind them and they were alone before asking the first of many questions. "What is going on with Jerry?"

Kathleen responded with a question of her own. "Why didn't you tell me that gorgeous woman was June's sister?"

"I didn't know."

"I don't know," Kathleen's answer almost echoed Susan's.

"Look, we only have a few minutes before either Jerry or Jed comes to see what we're doing, so you tell me about the police and Jerry and—and whatever you know and I'll tell you what I know about Allison while we're walking on the beach."

"But—"

"Kathleen, we can talk about Allison with Jerry and Jed. We might even learn something we don't know, but if you think Jerry might be arrested for murder, don't you think we'd better talk about that while we're alone?"

Kathleen was silent for a moment, picking at the terry cloth robe she had retrieved from the large queen-size bed she and Jerry had shared last night. "Okay. You're right.

"The problem . . . I think the problem," she began, "is that Jerry thinks the police here are stupid."

"And that would mean what?" Susan prodded when Kathleen didn't continue.

"I don't know. I mean, I know he didn't kill anyone, but he does have a connection to the victim. Jerry seems to think the police will ignore that, but . . . well, only the most incompetent investigator wouldn't look into their relationship."

"Don't you think maybe you're making too much of that? I mean, they just happened to be here at the same time, right?"

"That's not necessarily true."

"Of course it is! And I can prove it to the police. I was the person who made reservations for all of us, and I certainly didn't know that Allison was going to be here when I did. I didn't even recognize her when I first saw her. There was no connection between our vacation time and hers! Unless—" Susan suddenly realized what she was missing.

"Unless Jerry told her when we were planning to be here," Kathleen filled in the blank.

"Do you think that's possible?"

"I have no idea. Of course, Jerry's mentioned Allison to me, but the truth is, it's sometimes difficult hearing Jerry talk about his life before we met so I don't necessarily listen as closely as I might. And recently—" Kathleen stopped talking, and Susan began to fear for the hem on the robe she was picking at.

"You know, we can just ask Jerry if he's seen Allison recently and if he mentioned our trip to her," Susan said.

"No, we can't! Susan, we can't!"

"Kathleen, you just said that Jerry is putting himself in jeopardy by ignoring the police, but now you're also trying to pretend that there isn't a serious problem here."

"No, no, I'm not. You weren't sitting nearby when the police were interviewing us. You didn't see the expressions on their faces. You didn't hear Jerry blabbing on and on about how long he had known Allison, how she used to spend every Thanksgiving with him and his dead wife. How she used to bring such interesting gifts to his dead children."

"It sounds a little weird."

"That's what I'm telling you! It was more than a little

weird! It was bizarre and strange and odd and peculiar and—
and damn near self-incriminating. Jerry made Allison sound
like a long-lost . . ."

"A long-lost what?"

"A lover."

Susan was shocked. "Kathleen, you know that's not true. It
doesn't even make any sense! Jerry was married to Allison's
sister. There was never, ever a hint of anything between them.
Believe me, I would have known if there was. June would
have told me!"

"That's not necessarily true."

"Of course it is! Kath, you don't understand. I knew June
as well as I know you. She would have told me—" Susan
suddenly realized exactly what she was saying. "You're not
telling me something."

"I told you how Jerry was distracted about work. I didn't
tell you that there was something else."

"Another woman?" Part of Susan couldn't believe she was
even asking this question.

"It's possible."

"Anything is possible," Susan said, completely miserable
at the direction their conversation was taking. "What do you
know?"

Kathleen dropped the robe back onto the bed before answering. "That's the trouble, of course. I don't know anything. Not really."

"But?" Susan asked.

"Jerry being involved with another woman would explain
a lot of things."

"He said it was problems at work," Susan interrupted to remind her friend.

"Well, he would, wouldn't he? And remember that Jed told
you nothing unusual was going on at the office."

Susan couldn't argue with that.

"Although I don't think he was stupid enough to give the police the impression that his relationship with Allison was anything other than the loving relationship between in-laws . . ."

"Which is in itself a bit strange."

"Why?"

"I always got the impression that he and Allison didn't get along all that well. In fact, I thought that was why they always ended up with us at Thanksgiving."

"What do you mean? We always eat Thanksgiving dinner with you."

"Oh, but that's because . . . well, it's because you hated cooking so much when you and Jerry first got married."

Kathleen smiled for the first time since hearing about Allison's murder. "I still hate cooking and last year we celebrated at my house. What you mean is that I didn't know how to cook when Jerry and I got married and no one in their right mind would have trusted me to prepare a meal as elaborate as Thanksgiving dinner."

Susan smiled back. "True."

"I'm thinking that you're thinking that June was a wonderful cook, so that's not the reason why she and Jerry and their kids celebrated Thanksgiving at your house when Allison came to visit."

"That's one thing I'm thinking."

"What's the other?"

"I'm thinking that we're going to have to get over being uncomfortable talking about June and the girls if we're going to help Jerry."

Kathleen took a deep breath, stood up a little straighter, and became the woman Susan had been friends with for the past decade. "Damn right. So let's go on that walk."

# NINE

THE POLICE CAME BETWEEN THE HENSHAWS AND GORDONS and their walk.

"I'm so sorry, but we've been told to insist that everyone remain within Compass Bay for the time being." A tall woman with an impeccable auburn French twist and skin so pale that Susan could only wonder at how much sunscreen it took to accomplish this in the Caribbean stopped them as they began to walk around the jetty.

"By whom?" Jed asked.

"By the island's police chief," the woman said, while Susan tried to adjust to her husband's impeccable grammar.

"Is everyone being asked to remain on the premises or just some of the guests?" Kathleen asked.

"The staff has been interviewed and allowed to get on with their work. Those who work different shifts have been allowed to go home and rest before returning to work to pick up their regular schedule later in the day. This is a very small island and everyone knows everyone else. Anyone doing anything unusual will be quickly reported."

"The police seem very sure of your staff," Kathleen said.

"They have reason to be. They know that we are very careful whom we hire and who remains in our employ."

"Yes, but there do seem to be fewer people around," Susan

said. "Perhaps many of the guests have decided to remain in their cottages."

"Well, there were two parties of guests who were scheduled to fly back to the mainland later this morning and who have been allowed to do so." For the first time since she had barred their way, the woman faltered slightly. "The police apparently determined that those who were allowed to leave had nothing to do with Ms. McAllister's death."

"And how did they know that?" Susan asked.

"I can't tell you how their minds work, but I can suggest that you not underestimate them. Now, if you will excuse me, I have many extra things to deal with immediately due to this unfortunate event."

"I gather that was Lila. The woman who manages this place?" Jed asked.

Jerry and Kathleen nodded.

"This is weird," Susan said when the two couples were alone together. She didn't expect anyone to disagree.

"Maybe it's not. Maybe there's something more sinister going on here," Kathleen suggested.

"What do you mean?" Jed asked, wandering over to an upturned kayak and sitting down.

"Kath thinks the police are going to arrest me for Ally's murder."

"Do you know who killed her, Jerry?" Kathleen asked angrily. "Do you even know anyone else here who knew her? Are you willing to put your future in the hands of a police department you know nothing about in a foreign country? Are you?"

"Do you know if Allison was here with someone else?" Susan asked.

"Did you speak with her?" Kathleen asked.

"I think we should find out who else knew Allison," Susan said, pressing her point when Jerry didn't answer.

"I believe our guidebook to the island mentioned something about a local U.S. embassy office. Perhaps we should call there before any more time passes," Jed said quietly.

"Did you speak with her?" Kathleen asked Jerry again.

"I think Jed has made an excellent suggestion. We should find that guidebook—or a phone book—and insist on speaking to a representative of our government," Jerry said, ignoring his wife.

"Fine. You and Jed go call the embassy. Susan and I will just sit here and twiddle our thumbs." Kathleen, despite her words, folded her arms across her chest and turned to look out at the sea.

"We'll be here when you're done," Susan said, speaking more calmly than her friend.

"We won't be long," Jed said, getting up and following Jerry back toward the cottages.

"Don't you think it's a little odd that the police are allowing some guests to fly home and others aren't even permitted to leave the resort?" Susan asked after a moment of silence.

"I think it's more than odd. I think it's sinister. They've focused their investigation on one or a few suspects, and they don't care about anyone else."

"If that person is Jerry, then Jed's suggestion that we call the embassy office is probably a good idea," Susan said.

Kathleen didn't answer right away, and when she did she changed the subject. "Who keeps moving around those chairs on the pier?"

Susan frowned. "I think everyone does. James seems to straighten out the chairs around the pool and on the patio in front of the cottages, but everyone moves them wherever they want to sit. The day we got here someone had dragged two chairs down the stairs to the beach, and there were a few chairs out on the gazebo during the day yesterday and then late last night they were gone, and the chair Allison was found on was moved out."

"You were out there last night? I thought you and Jed went to bed when we did."

"We did, but I wasn't tired and couldn't sleep so I wandered outside. I actually sat for a while on the edge of the pier. The stars were amazing!"

"Did you see Allison?"

"I didn't see anyone. I did think that maybe there was someone in the gazebo. In fact, I might have stayed there a lot longer, but I heard strange noises and I was afraid that I had interrupted a couple who were enjoying the fresh air and each other at the same time."

"Or perhaps someone was killing Allison as you sat there."

"I—my God, do you think that's possible?" Despite the sultry heat, Susan experienced a sudden chill. Had Allison been killed while help was only a few feet away? So much had happened in the past few hours, but she could still remember the feeling that she wasn't alone in the dark. She turned back to her friend. "Kath, do you think—"

But Kathleen, without a word of explanation, had turned around and was jogging back toward the cottages. It took Susan only a moment to realize that Jed—and only Jed—was loping toward her, a very nonvacationing expression on his face. "Jerry's been taken away," he explained when they met.

"By—By the police? They've arrested him?"

"I don't know. I just know he's on his way into town with a police escort."

"Then we've got to get hold of the U.S. embassy right away."

"There are embassy representatives here already. One of them was looking for Kath. They're probably together now."

"So what do we do?"

Jed shook his head, obviously perplexed. "Wait and see, I guess."

"Wait and see? Are you nuts?"

"What do you propose? I'm willing to consider any other suggestion."

"I—I can't think of anything," she admitted.

Jed surprised her by reaching out and putting his arm around her shoulders. "Why don't you snuggle over here next to me?"

"Jed, I know we're on vacation, but—"

"Let's try to look as though you're upset and I'm comforting you." He interrupted her protest and pulled her closer. "We need to talk and this is not exactly a private place," he added in a whisper.

Susan got the idea at once. "What?" she asked, turning and snuggling her face into his chest where she was sure no one would overhear or overlook their conversation. "Is Jerry actually under arrest?"

"I didn't hear anyone put it quite like that. He was asked to come to the police station in town to answer some questions about Allison. I thought it was pretty obvious that they knew about his relationship with her. Anyway, the woman from the embassy suggested that it would be a good idea to do as requested, and she went along with them without anyone questioning her right to do so, as far as I could tell."

"And Kathleen is with someone else from the embassy? Where are they?" Susan asked, leaning back and gulping a deep breath of fresh air.

"I'm not sure."

"What do these women do at the embassy? Who called for them?"

"I don't know what their positions are, but they got here in a timely fashion and they seem to be respected by the islanders who are in control of the situation."

"I suppose that's good. But do you think we can trust them?"

"Trust them?"

"To help us. To make sure Jerry isn't accused of Allison's murder."

"I don't think that's their job, Sue. I'm wondering if I shouldn't go over to the office and make some calls. I thought cottages without phones were such a good idea when I read about them in the brochure, but it's turning out to be a real inconvenience."

"Who would you call?"

"Friends at home. Lawyers. Anyone who might know the law down here and what we're becoming involved in—"

"Yoo-hoo! Henshaws! Up here!"

Susan and Jed turned and looked up. Standing on the top of the breakwater was a heavyset woman Susan recognized as one of the card-playing group. She smiled weakly.

"I need to speak to you and it's a lot easier for young people like you to come up the steps than for an oldster like me to waddle down."

Susan and Jed exchanged glances.

"Now I might be interrupting a romantic moment or I may not, but I really think we should have a little chat. It has to do with the murder."

The Henshaws acted as one, moving up the stairs as quickly as their "young" legs could carry them.

"What do you know?" Susan asked.

"What's happened?" was Jed's question.

"I know that you're going to need my help here. Why don't we find someplace to sit down and talk—preferably in the shade. In all the excitement, I'm not sure I applied sunscreen evenly before I left my cottage this morning."

"There are some umbrellas leaning up against the wall over there," Jed said. "I could find James and ask him to set some up for us."

"Oh, my. You could try, but I imagine James is somewhere

with the rest of the staff, gossiping about this horrible thing. He's one of the best of the staff, but under the circumstances, I think we will have to fend for ourselves." She looked Jed up and down and then turned to Susan. "Perhaps you could ask your husband to bring us an umbrella or two."

"Of course. Jed . . ."

"I'd be happy to set up an umbrella for you both, but then, perhaps, I should go make those phone calls we were discussing." He looked at his wife, and Susan realized that he had decided she was better off dealing with this woman alone.

"That's a good idea," she agreed. "In fact, why don't you go do that and . . . and we can go over to the restaurant, sit in the shade, and we can talk there."

"Better yet, we'll go back to my cottage, order room service, and sit on the porch. Number 16 with a seagull by the door, down by the breakwater. Your husband can find us there if he needs to."

Susan couldn't think of any reason to refuse. "You'll let me know if Kathleen needs me, or there's anything else I can do, won't you?" she asked her husband pointedly.

"Sure," he agreed, hurrying off.

Susan suspected he had missed the point. She was stuck talking with this woman whether she liked it or not.

# TEN

"Now, I suppose I should introduce myself. I'm Rowan Parker. Most people call me Ro and you should, too."

"I'm Susan Henshaw, but you seem to know that already." Despite Ro's previous statements, she was no frailer than Susan, and moved quickly over the cobblestone walkway toward her cottage.

"I make it my business to learn the names of all guests the very day they arrive. My husband says I'm nosy, but I'm just interested in the people around me. And, over the years, you wouldn't believe the fascinating people I've met here."

"So you've been here before," Susan said, following Ro up the steps to her place. The cottages at this end of the resort were comprised of two floors. Ro headed for the stairs on the far side.

"There's an intercom upstairs we can use to call for food. Damn inconvenient—we have to climb up and down a dozen times a day—but what can you do?" she said, starting up the stairs. "And, yes, to answer your question, this is our fourteenth year here. My husband likes continuity. I'm always suggesting we try something new, but he says when you like something you stick to it. He has a point, of course. Best not to be disappointed when you're on vacation.

"Sit down and I'll order us something to drink," she

continued as they reached the second floor. "It's foolish to risk dehydration in the tropics."

"Thanks," Susan murmured, looking around. "This is fantastic," she said honestly.

"Yes, the large cottages are quite roomy, and, of course, the view from the balcony is incomparable." Ro nodded toward the open plantation shutters, which revealed a second-story porch facing the sea. "Go on out and have a seat. I've gotta use the little girl's room, and I'll be right with you."

Susan wandered onto the porch and sank down in one of the pair of batik-covered wicker lounges. A substantial glass-topped trunk of woven straw was the only other furniture. A couple of back issues of *The New Yorker* and *Bon Appétit* had been flung down beside a worn paperback thriller. On the other lounge a pigskin binocular case lay open, containing what Susan suspected were very high-powered spyglasses. She was still staring at them when Ro returned.

"Bird-watching," Ro stated flatly, seeing Susan's interest. "My husband says it relaxes him. Can't imagine why watching a bunch of flittery little birds would relax anybody, but you never really know with people, do you? Even if you're married to them, you never really do know."

Susan agreed that this was true and then tried to change the topic. "You seemed . . . at least, I thought you knew something about Allison's murder."

Ro moved the binoculars and sat down across from Susan. "I know quite a bit about Allison. And some of it just might have to do with someone killing her."

"Oh, you should tell me. I . . ." Susan hesitated. She didn't want to sound foolish, but decided she had no real alternative but to go on. "I have helped the police solve a few murders in the past."

"That's what I understand. That's one of the reasons I came to you when I heard about the murder."

"How did you know about—about what I've done?" Susan asked.

"Why, Allison herself told me about it just the other day when we were sitting around the pool."

"Allison told you?"

"Yes, she said that you had come up with the identity of a murderer when the police had been quite unable to do so, and done it more than once. I must say, that from what she was saying, Hancock, Connecticut, must be a terribly dangerous place to live—so many murders! Is it very near New York City, dear?"

"Not really." Susan didn't waste any time defending her hometown. She knew exactly how close her upper-class affluent suburb was to New York City; it was nearly in another world. The *New York Times* didn't report on the things that happened within Hancock's confines unless a famous or infamous person was involved. And Susan didn't know any celebrities—either dead or alive. If Allison had known what had been going on in Hancock, Connecticut, in the years since her sister had died, she had made an effort to do so.

"Well, Allison made living there sound very exciting."

"But Allison—" Susan didn't finish her sentence. She didn't know this woman at all. She should be more careful about what she said. "What did she say about Hancock?"

"Oh, that's not important right now, is it, dear? What's important now is keeping your friend out of jail. I must admit that while we have done extensive sightseeing on the island, we've never visited the jail, but this is a poor island. They don't educate their children beyond age ten. I cannot imagine that their expenditures on prison facilities are anything like adequate."

"Jerry would never kill anyone," Susan insisted.

"I'm sure you're right, dear. That's why I felt it so important that we talk immediately. You see, I think we should get our stories straight."

"Our stories straight? I'm sorry, I have no idea what you're talking about."

"Of course, you don't. How could you? Let me begin at the beginning. You see, I have insomnia."

"So . . ."

"So I don't want to bother my husband. Burton gets so cranky when he doesn't get his eight hours a night. At home, I just go downstairs to our den and turn on the TV. Some of those shows advertise very interesting products, I find."

"But you can't do that here," Susan guessed.

"That's absolutely true." Ro beamed as though Susan had made a deduction that would have made Sherlock Holmes proud. "I can't do that here, so while we're on vacation, I get up and sit out here. I have a battery-powered light so I can read my books or magazines—I always bring along all the reading material that I get at home and have no time to read—and I look around, as well."

Susan glanced down at the water. She was pretty sure she knew what was coming. "You were here the night Allison was killed," she guessed.

"Yes. I was."

"Did you see her?" Susan asked, leaning forward.

"I saw a few people . . ." Ro didn't finish her sentence.

"I went out on the pier for a while," Susan said. "Did you see me?"

"I'm glad you brought that up," Ro said approvingly. "Yes, in fact, I did."

"Who else?" Susan decided to ignore the possibility that this woman thought she was the murderer.

"Well, the place was pretty busy that night. Let me think. James and one of the kitchen workers were walking on the beach when I came out. A girlfriend, not one of his many relatives who work here, I think, from the way they were holding hands. They're not supposed to use the facilities for their own purposes, of course, but at night, Lila isn't around to keep her staff up to snuff.

"After a minute I saw your friend Jerry. He was walking with someone back and forth in front of his cottage. Then, when James and his girlfriend came up from the beach, Jerry and his companion hurried out to the gazebo. They were there for quite a while. Then one of them—I couldn't see which one—came back alone. The other stayed out there."

"In the gazebo."

"I assume so. To be honest, I was feeling a bit peckish and went back inside to see if I could find something to eat. We keep a stash of fruit and pastries downstairs for when the kitchen is closed. You must help yourself if you're hungry in the middle of the night."

"How long were you inside?" Susan asked, ignoring the suggestion. Just what she didn't need—more food.

"Certainly not more than five minutes. Very little could have happened in that time."

Susan didn't agree with that; she could even imagine an improbable situation where everyone in every cottage exchanged places in those five minutes. But she didn't share her thought. "So when you came back," she prompted.

"That's when I saw you leave your cottage and walk out on the pier."

"And did you see me return, as well?"

"Yes. I could see you, you understand, but I couldn't hear you or any conversation you might have had with anyone out there."

"I didn't talk with anyone," Susan said honestly. "I wasn't even sure who, if anyone, was out there at the same time I was."

"Really?"

"Really," Susan assured her. "I thought—well, I assumed, I really didn't think about it—that I was alone, but I did notice some noises. To be honest, I thought I might be interrupting a couple who was out there . . . ah, making out."

"Oh, yes, that little gazebo is a favorite spot for romantic trysts." Ro glanced over at the binoculars lying beside her, and Susan wondered if birdlife was the only thing Ro's husband spied on. "I gather you were too polite to look over and see who was there?"

"I didn't want to interrupt."

"And naturally you had no idea Allison would be found there less than eight hours later."

"Exactly." Susan frowned. "I can't remember the last time I saw her alive, to be honest. Not that I knew who she was."

"My goodness. She said she had changed a lot, but I didn't really believe her. You know how it is. You dye your hair a shade lighter and think everyone you know will notice, but, in fact, the only person who knows—or cares—is you."

"She had done a whole lot more than dye her hair," Susan said. "She had lost about forty pounds. Her hair was a completely different color, and long and straight rather than short and curly. She dressed differently. She had contact lenses. She might have even had cosmetic surgery. She looked familiar, but I never realized who she was."

"Was she much more attractive than when you knew her?" Ro asked.

"There was no comparison. She used to be . . . well, not hideous or anything, but rather plain—homely if you want the truth. And yesterday . . . well, she was smashing!"

"She had a very interesting theory, and from what you say, she was living proof of it."

"What theory?"

"She said you lived the first forty years of your life in the body your genetic makeup decreed, but once you turned forty, your appearance depended on how hard you worked at it."

Susan was silent for a moment. "I never thought about it like that, but it's probably true. The funny thing is, I never would have thought that Allison cared about her appearance. She always looked so dowdy and dull."

"Those are two words I certainly wouldn't have applied to the Allison I knew." Ro leaned closer and lowered her voice as though about to convey a dirty secret. "I'm positive she saw the plastic surgeon more than once."

"Do you know if she was here alone?" Susan asked, wondering if Allison had a man in her life these days.

"Yes. She told me she was alone the evening we met. I was a little concerned. A gorgeous single woman can cause a lot of mayhem in a place like this. I've seen it happen with my own eyes."

"What do you mean? What happened?"

"Well, naturally not everyone comes here with a husband or what everyone these days calls a significant other. But this isn't the type of resort that appeals to swinging singles looking for a vacation pickup. There are lots of those places available. But every once in a while someone comes here looking for a holiday fling. The second year we were here—or was it the third?—no, I'm pretty sure it was the second—there was a woman who damn near caused a divorce when she set her cap for a married man."

"That really doesn't sound like Allison," Susan said.

"Perhaps not, but there aren't many men who didn't look up when she walked by in one of those tiny bikinis she wore."

"No, I guess not." Susan thought for a moment. "Not counting last night, when did you last see Allison?"

Ro frowned. "You should remember that I didn't identify Allison as one of the people I saw last night. In fact, if anyone asks, I wouldn't be able to tell them if your friend's companion last night was male or female."

"That's interesting," Susan said, noting that this could be the most important thing she had heard so far. "But what I'm wondering is when you last saw her here—just walking around or whatever."

"That's easy. We had lunch together yesterday. And she was sitting at the bar having a rum punch last night when Burt and I went in before dinner."

"Was she alone?"

"Yes, but I must tell you that I got the impression that she was waiting for someone."

"What did she do that gave you that impression?"

"She was looking over her shoulder at everyone who came in. She seemed rather nervous."

"Do you know who she was meeting?" Susan asked.

"No, we left before anyone joined her, I'm afraid. But I think we can rule out your friend. After all, they had just spent the afternoon together," Ro added before Susan could ask another question.

# ELEVEN

THERE WERE QUESTIONS SUSAN WANTED TO ASK IMMEDI-
ately, but she had to wait until the drinks Ro had ordered were
served. An obsequious young man, apparently familiar with
the Parkers' requirements, placed a tray on the trunk and
poured deep amber liquid into ice-filled glasses, dropped in
lemon slices, and passed one to each woman. Susan, realizing
she was thirsty, took a large gulp immediately. And gasped:
There may have been a touch of the tea she was expecting, but
most of the glass was filled with sweetened dark rum. "Oh,
wow!" she muttered.

"Don't worry, dear. They always use artificial sweetener,"
Ro assured her.

"And what else?" Susan asked, realizing that her eyes were
watering.

"Mount Gay rum and spring water," the waiter answered,
picking up the empty tray and preparing to depart. "Anything
else?"

"We're fine now," Ro said, raising her own glass and sipping. "Excellent, as usual. Thank you," she dismissed him.
"Now where were we?" she asked Susan when they were
alone again.

"You had just told me that Allison and Jerry spent yesterday afternoon together."

"Oh, he didn't admit that to you?"

"It wasn't a question of admitting anything to anyone," Susan answered, annoyed. "I never asked him what he was doing yesterday. I haven't even spoken to Jerry about Allison . . . or about her murder."

"The police did take him off rather abruptly, didn't they?"

"I'm sure they'll discover that they've made a mistake and he'll be back here soon," Susan stated flatly.

Ro didn't seem convinced. "Perhaps you're right. But I certainly would feel much better if I could tell the police that someone else was out on the beach last night, someone else who had a reason to kill Allison."

Susan stood up so quickly that she spilled her drink. "Jerry Gordon had absolutely no reason to kill Allison. She was his sister-in-law. They were family. The police have made a terrible mistake."

"She was his sister-in-law? She didn't tell me that!"

Susan realized that she was giving away as much information as she was getting. "What exactly did she tell you about herself?"

"Well, let me think. She mentioned her career, that she was an illustrator who did mainly freelance work. But when I asked about it—and it sounded very interesting—she said she was on vacation and didn't want to think about work."

"Did you think that was odd?"

"Not at all. She wouldn't be the first person to try to forget problems back at the office while on vacation. Why, there was a famous senator here a few years ago and he absolutely refused to talk politics."

Susan didn't think that was exactly the same thing, but she didn't mention it. "So what did Allison talk about?"

"Oh, the places she had visited on other vacations, things she had done, books she had read. She didn't speak a whole lot about what you could call her personal life. Which must be why I didn't know she was anyone's sister-in-law."

"But she must have mentioned some people. After all, she told you that I had investigated murders, right? She wouldn't have talked about me and no one else."

Ro took another sip of her drink before answering. "But you were different than other people. Your name came up because we were talking about murder."

"Not exactly a topic you expect to come up on vacation, is it?" Susan heard the coldness in her own voice. She was beginning to suspect that Ro was lying.

"Not unless you're a big reader of mystery novels. In fact, it was the books we were reading that drew Allison and me together. She was just finishing up a book by Carolyn Hart, and I was just starting the latest by Kate Grilley. We agreed to switch when we were done. The gift shop's collection of mysteries leaves a lot to be desired."

"So you started talking about real murders after discussing favorite authors?" Susan asked, thinking it an unlikely segue.

"Yes. You see, some of the authors I like best write series mysteries and their characters are always stumbling on dead bodies—sometimes two or three times a year! I mentioned the fact that you had to suspend your disbelief to read them, and that's when she mentioned knowing a real person who had had this very experience!"

"Oh. Did she mention me by name?"

"Well, not when we were first talking, but then you and your party checked in and she said something about you being the woman she had described earlier in the week."

Susan realized this might be more than a little important. "Did she seem surprised to see me? Surprised that I was here?"

"Oh, dear, I know what you're getting at. If your presence wasn't a surprise, it would seem that she and Mr. Gordon had communicated sometime before their arrival, wouldn't it?"

"I don't know about that. There might be other explanations."

Ro beamed. "That's why you're such an excellent detective. I must admit I can't think of a single other explanation for why Allison wouldn't have been surprised to see you."

"Perhaps Allison was in the office and just happened to see our name on some sort of list of future bookings," Susan improvised.

"Yes! That would explain it, wouldn't it? We should remember that in case anyone asks, don't you think?"

"I suppose, but frankly, I can't imagine why anyone would ask us anything."

"Not only is the man arrested your friend, but you knew the deeeased—and this is a very small resort. Word gets around." Ro drained her glass so quickly that Susan would have worried about her sobriety if she didn't have other things on her mind.

"You're not the only person who knows about Allison's connections to us, are you?"

Ro smiled. "I'm not here alone, you know. And I may have mentioned the things Allison told me to my husband or one or two of my friends. And, of course, Allison may have spoken about these things to other guests or staff."

There was nothing Susan could do about that now. "You said you saw Jerry with Allison during the day yesterday. What were they doing?"

"I can't tell you that. I saw them come back to the resort together. A taxi pulled up outside the restaurant and they got out. Most of the taxis drive right into Compass Bay's courtyard. Theirs didn't. I suspect they were trying to hide."

Susan didn't like anything she was hearing. "Isn't it possible that the driver didn't realize that he could drive into the courtyard?"

"Oh, my dear, you don't know this island. A job driving a taxi is coveted. Absolutely coveted. The men here have very few employment opportunities that could be said to be macho. Taxi driver is one of them."

"And the others?" Susan asked, momentarily distracted.

"Oh, crewing on some of the ships that take tourists out for deep-sea fishing, bartending . . . I can't think of any more at the moment. But I can assure you that tearing around the island roads in those old Cadillacs that are used for taxis are jobs passed down from father to son. All the drivers know where to pick up their clients."

"What time did you see them?" Susan asked.

"Around four. Right before my friends and I met for predinner drinks and a game, I guess."

"You said you had lunch with her yesterday."

"Yes, that's right, I did."

"And did she tell you that she was going to spend the afternoon with Jerry?"

"No, no." Ro appeared to think for a moment. "I don't believe either of us discussed plans for the day. That's one of the nicest parts of being on vacation. You can just do things without planning. Free as a bird! At least that's what I think."

Susan didn't bother to agree or disagree. "And did you happen to notice when they left?"

"No."

"What about later in the evening?"

"I only wish I had! I saw Mr. Gordon eating dinner with your party, but I didn't see them together again until last night on the beach."

"And you said they were walking together on the pier at that time."

"Yes. I did. I thought it was a little odd."

"Why?"

"It seemed to me that Mr. Gordon was spending rather a lot of his vacation with a woman other than his wife. You know, I'm not the only person who noticed. That young couple—I can never remember their names—the ones on their honeymoon—were talking about it when I passed them by at dinner last night. The bride seemed to be concerned that her groom might treat her like that sometime in the future."

Susan had noticed this particular couple cavorting in the pool, bronzed and bikini clad, as well as lying in the late afternoon sun, hands clasped. The bride wore a skimpy white lace bikini that had attracted Jed's attention, as well. "I didn't see them at dinner last night," she said.

"Everyone who has been here for a while noticed. They arrived five days ago and have ordered from room service for most meals since check-in. My husband insists that they don't want to get dressed for any reason other than to lie in the sun, not that they wear very much for that particular activity."

Susan agreed. "But they aren't the only ones wearing scanty swimwear. In fact, the first time I saw Allison she was wearing an amazingly tiny bikini." That might have been exactly why she hadn't recognized Allison, Susan realized. During summer visits, Allison had spent time at the Hancock Field Club and, as far as Susan remembered, had been seen only in a navy blue maillot—with a skirt.

"Yes, Allison was very proud of her figure, wasn't she?"

"It certainly looked that way," Susan said. She was interested in other things right now. "Was it odd that Allison spent so much time with Jerry? I mean, she was here alone. Did she . . . well, sort of team up with anyone else while she was here?"

"Let me think." For the first time since Ro had introduced herself, Susan got the impression that her hostess was worried about how she answered the question.

"You said that you and she spent a lot of time together talking," Susan prompted.

"I don't believe I said a lot of time. We just chatted a few times. I like to get to know the other guests here. I told you that."

"Yes, of course. It's natural to talk to the person in the chair next to yours while you're lying about the pool or whatever," Susan assured her. Ro was getting nervous. Susan didn't want their conversation to end just as she was about to learn something. "And I can't tell you how thankful I am that you're trying to help Jerry."

"Well, he seems like a very nice man. And Allison seemed to think highly of him."

There was a moment of silence as Ro seemed to realize that she had said more than she meant to—and Susan tried to figure out how to keep the revelations flowing. "Allison mentioned him and didn't tell you that she had been his sister-in-law?" She finally settled on asking the question that most interested her.

"Allison never mentioned having a sister who was divorced."

"Did she mention having had a sister who died?"

Ro was obviously shocked. "Her sister was dead? I never thought—no, no, she never mentioned that. My memory may not be what it once was, but I would have remembered that! So Mr. Gordon is a widower."

"Was. He's been married to Kathleen for almost ten years."

"Oh."

"Oh?" Susan repeated the word.

"I thought I heard someone."

"Who—"

A short, balding man, incredibly knobby knees shown off by his bright green plaid shorts worn beneath a purple polo shirt, had joined them.

"Ro, dear, we've all been wondering where you were. Did you forget our game?"

Ro, as if on cue, looked at her watch and gasped. "I had no idea it was this late!" she cried, standing up. "Everyone will think I've been terribly rude." She turned to Susan. "You will understand if I dash off. My friends are waiting for me. The game cannot start without me."

Susan stood up, too. "Of course I understand. My husband is probably wondering where I've vanished to, as well. I . . ." She didn't know what else to say. "Thank you for—for showing me all this and talking to me and—and the drink," she added quickly, moving into the Parkers' bedroom and heading toward the stairs. "I guess we'll see each other around." Susan, feeling awkward, waved at the couple and started down the stairs.

She hurried across the first floor and back out onto the beach. She had gotten the distinct impression that Burt Parker was unhappy to discover his wife talking to her. Her impression was confirmed when these words floated down from the balcony:

"Meddling in the lives of others has gotten you in trouble before, Ro. I would have thought you had more sense than to get involved in a murder."

# TWELVE

Susan had hoped to speak with Kathleen, to assure her friend that she wasn't alone, to start the investigation that would free Jerry from whatever hellhole the local police had locked him in. But she returned to her cottage to discover a note from Jed explaining—complaining—that he had not been able to find her, and as Kathleen had been given permission to see Jerry and hadn't wanted to go alone, he had been forced to leave without talking with his wife. Susan, reading his message, realized he had been upset when he wrote it. Well, there was nothing she could do about that now, she decided, folding and putting it in the pocket of her shorts. She turned to leave the cottage and wondered what, if anything, she could—or should—do now.

She heard a knock on the door behind her and turned, hoping whoever was there would provide a solution to her problem. The worried expression on her face morphed into a smile when she recognized James.

"Mrs. Henshaw, your party signed up for kayaks today. I didn't want to change your reservations or offer my boats to anyone else until I was sure you wouldn't be wanting them. I—" He stopped and looked embarrassed. "I can't say I know what to do in this situation."

"Never had anyone die here before?" Susan asked, trying to sound casual.

"Oh, no, ma'am. We've had people die here. But not killed . . . except by love. Once."

"What do you mean?"

"Well, a few months ago this old guy came here. He must have been over fifty and he'd just gotten married to this young girl. Well, they scuba dived, kayaked, swam, ate and drank, and . . . and did what couples do on their honeymoon. And he was dead in less than twenty-four hours after check-in. Heart failure. He was too old to keep up with her. She should have married a young buck. At least, that's what Lila said at the time. And he was not the only one," James hurried on, possibly afraid he had offended her.

"Who else died?" Susan asked.

"Just a few months ago a woman stepped on something on the beach. No one ever really knew what, although her husband said it was some sort of jellyfish. Anyway, she had some sort of horrible allergic reaction, went into some sort of shock."

"Anaphylactic shock," Susan suggested.

"Maybe. All I know is she was dead before anyone could call a doctor. Scared the hell out of me. It was in all the papers. Perhaps you saw it up north? I know Lila was worried about bad publicity hurting us."

"I didn't see anything. Anyway, an allergic reaction is individual. Most people aren't allergic to the same things. But is there anything else deadly around here? On the beach?"

"Well, many people step on black urchins. Happens more than you'd think. Their feet swell up something awful and they have a whole lot of pain for a day or two."

"And then they die?" Susan asked.

"Nah, they get better. It's no biggie. We can warn people, but we can't get them to listen. We had a guy here from Maine last winter. He said he knew all about urchins—used to go out in the cove in front of his house, pick them up, smash them, and serve them over homemade pasta. Sounded disgusting to me, not that anyone asked. Anyway, we took out the kayaks, paddled over to a beach just south of here, and got out for a walk. Don't say I didn't warn him."

"He stepped on one?" Susan guessed.

"Nope, two. But one at a time. Stepped on one with one foot and jumped up and stepped right onto another with the other foot. Who woulda thought it could happen like that? Both feet swelled up like pillows by the time we got back here. Last I saw of him, he was getting into a taxi, saying he'd be real glad to get back to the frozen north."

"But no one else has been murdered here?" Susan asked.

"Not that I know of, but, I tell you, I only been here for three years. Things could have happened before I got here." James shifted his weight from one foot to the other, and Susan realized he was anxious to be on his way.

"You know, I'd enjoy going out in one of the kayaks again. Everyone else seems to be gone for a while."

"Yeah, your husband and your friend went in to town to see that man who was arrested—at least, that's what I heard," James added quickly. "So you could paddle around for a bit on your own. Don't go out too far. You be perfectly safe."

"I don't think I want to go out in the ocean alone," Susan answered slowly. "But if you have the time, maybe we could go out together—just for a bit?"

James frowned and then glanced back over his shoulder. "I guess I could—just for a bit—but I gotta make sure I'm not needed here and—and all."

"That would be fantastic. I'll grab some sunscreen and be right with you. I don't want to be gone long either, but it would be great to get away—just for a bit." Susan repeated the phrase they seemed to have agreed on. She wasn't actually interested in getting away alone. But Ro had said James was on the beach last night. He might have seen something that related to Allison's murder. Susan grabbed a tube of sunscreen and dabbed a bit on her nose as she left the cottage.

James was standing just outside the open doorway of the gift shop, apparently talking to someone inside. Susan called out his name, and he turned and waved, a big smile on his face. "You go on down, ma'am. I come down presently."

Susan waved, turned, and discovered herself face-to-face with a woman whose resemblance to a tubby Buddha was emphasized by the white flowing beach dress she wore.

"My dear, my husband and I have been looking for you. What a dreadful thing to happen. I was just telling Martin, this will just ruin your vacation."

"It certainly isn't improving it," Susan admitted.

"This seems to be the morning for husbands and wives to get separated. Your husband was looking all over the place for you, too. Just a few minutes ago. And your friend, too. How sad it is that her husband was arrested. She looked distraught the last time I saw her, and I can't say I blame her one bit. It's bad enough when your husband falls for someone else on vacation, but to kill someone . . ."

"Jerry did not fall for Allison. They've . . ." She paused and decided not to say anything more than necessary. "They've known each other for years and years. And he certainly didn't kill her. They—they've always gotten along well." She paused for a minute, knowing that wasn't true. Hadn't June once told her that it was so much easier to celebrate the holidays at the Henshaws' because everyone was much more polite when there were no family members present? At the time, Susan had assumed she was talking about the children. Certainly she was more confident that Chad and Chrissy would mind their manners at someone else's home. But was it possible that June had meant the adults? Had Allison and Jerry gotten along? She noticed that the other woman was staring at her curiously.

"I'm sure this is all going to turn out to be a huge mistake and everything will be fine," Susan insisted. "In fact, I'm so sure everything is going to be fine that I am going to go kayaking until everyone returns." She hoped the smile on her face didn't look as forced as it felt.

"Why, you brave thing! Why don't my husband and I go along with you? We can keep you from becoming depressed. Let me just go find Martin. That man can vanish more quickly than anyone I know. My name's Joann. I'll just see if I can find my husband . . . but you call on me if you need anything. Anything at all." Joann turned and moved away remarkably quickly for someone her size.

Susan took a deep breath and hurried down the steps to the beach where the kayaks waited. James was nowhere to be seen. She paced back and forth, watching out for anything with spines or gelatinous substances. Who would have suspected these gorgeous beaches could be dangerous—or even lethal? On the other hand, who would have imagined going on vacation and becoming a suspect in a murder investigation? She sat down on an upturned kayak and looked around. The stone wall behind her blocked her view of the resort's buildings, so she turned and looked out to sea—and realized she had a sensational view of the spot where Allison had been found.

A Compass Bay beach towel was still draped across the lounge. Instead of the yellow police-line do-not-cross tape that would have been wound around the area in the States, here a bright red rope strung across the middle of the pier prevented the curious from getting too close to the crime scene. On the other hand . . .

As she watched, a head popped up out of the surf, looked around, and apparently spying her, ducked back down.

Susan jumped up and ran across the few feet to the water and waded in, trying to keep an eye on the underwater swimmer, but he—she was pretty sure it was a he—was impossible to spy beneath the lambent sunlight on the water.

"See something interesting, Mrs. Henshaw?"

Susan looked up and over her shoulder and discovered James striding down the stairs to the beach.

"Someone—there's someone swimming out there—underwater."

"Snorkeling?"

"Excuse me?"

"One of the guests snorkeling?" He paused in his descent and, shading his eyes with one hand, peered out to sea.

"Yes. I guess that's who it was. I was surprised by how long whoever it was remained underwater."

"Probably someone snorkeling and you didn't see the tip of the snorkel above the water," James said, putting down his hand and turning to Susan. "Good news. The Robbinses are going to kayak with us. The more people we have, the more fun we have," he added without much enthusiasm.

"Can she—I mean—" Susan was too much of a lady to ask the question.

"Many of our larger guests do just fine on the sea kayaks," James said, answering the question she hadn't asked.

"I know the kayaks aren't as unsteady as they appear. But I still have trouble getting on and off," Susan said, chatting as though nothing untoward had happened. She was still staring out at the sea. "How long can someone stay underwater when they're snorkeling?"

"All day if they're good. You don't want to get water in the snorkel. Or in your eye mask, of course. You never tried to do it?"

"No."

"You try. You might like it. Many of our guests like it. Oh, here are our companions all ready to go out to sea."

"Yes. We're ready!" Joann agreed, making her way slowly down the steep steps.

"Some of us are readier than others of us," her husband said, trailing behind.

Joann threw him an angry look over her shoulder. "We're here to have fun. We're here to experience new things. There's no reason we shouldn't go kayaking."

Martin Robbins flushed. "I don't think I said anything to imply that I wasn't going along." His pale blue eyes glanced up at Susan for a moment before looking down at the boats.

Susan suddenly realized that Martin must have been exceptionally good-looking when he was young. He still seemed to be in excellent shape—tall and athletic. The contrast with his wife made her look even dumpier. Susan wondered what had brought them together when they were younger. Had she been thinner, less demanding, less annoying? Had he been the dominant partner in their relationship in the early years? She sighed. There was no time to speculate about such things now.

"Mrs. Henshaw, do you want to use the same kayak you used yesterday?" James asked, pushing the red plastic crescent toward her.

"I guess."

"And I'd like that yellow one over there," Joann spoke up. "Martin, you take the blue one."

Susan couldn't help hoping Joann would get soaked while trying to board her kayak, but, in yet another example of the lack of justice in the world, Joann slid onto her kayak without even mussing her hair. Martin, benefiting no doubt from the long list of instructions his wife offered, followed suit. The dunking that Susan got almost made her forget why she had suggested this activity in the first place.

James waited patiently for her to right herself, regain her

balance, and begin paddling. Then he jumped into the last kayak and began to paddle. "Where do we go?" he asked.

"I don't know," Susan answered honestly.

# THIRTEEN

SUSAN'S EXPERIENCE IN TOURING KAYAKS WAS ONCE AGAIN not helping her to get the hang of the little sea kayak on which she was perched. She was having so much trouble, in fact, that she was forced to accept James's offer to travel by her side.

Joann smirked and Martin looked concerned, but Susan had gotten what she wanted—the opportunity to talk with James in relative privacy.

"I heard you were walking on the beach last night." She jumped right in, not knowing how long Joann would be content to bounce around on the waves, displaying a surprising skill in this sport.

"Ah, you know about that, do you? I am courting a lovely young lady who works in the kitchen. Her parents are very old-fashioned. They think I'm unsuitable for some reason." James offered his most charming smile, and Susan could understand why a young woman's parents would worry if their daughter was interested in him. "So we spend time together here when we can," he continued. "The staff isn't really supposed to be using the beach," he added, lowering his voice. "I'd appreciate it if you didn't mention seeing me to Lila."

"I'd never do that," she assured him. "I mean, you have a

right to your privacy. I'd imagine the beach was pretty deserted yesterday evening, wasn't it?"

"No, ma'am! Cottages are all full this week. At least, they were until three emptied out this morning. But, still, there are few places where a man and his girl can be alone."

"Did someone interrupt you yesterday?" Susan asked.

"We are always interrupted. You all okay?" he called out as the Robbinses steered their kayaks to the east.

"We want to see that large coral reef we've heard so much about," Joann called back. "Just follow us."

James looked over at Susan and shrugged. "That one, she likes to have her own way."

"She seems to get it, too," Susan muttered, guiding her kayak toward the east. She looked down into the water at a row of sand dollars lying in a line on the floor of the sea. "It's amazing how close everything looks," she said, momentarily distracted.

James chuckled. "It is close. Tide is low. Water not more than one, one and a half meters deep here."

"You're kidding!"

"No. Course, tide coming in. Soon it will be much deeper."

Susan paddled along, considering whether or not this might have any bearing on the murder. "Can a person walk—wade—to the gazebo when the tide is low?"

"A tall person, yes. The water is maybe five meters at low tide this time of year. Later, in the summer, it is less. There is a blackboard in the bar. There, low tide and high tide are listed. The person who tends bar makes daily change."

"That's good to know." Susan thought about this for a moment.

"You are wondering if someone walked out to pier and kill that woman," James said.

"I was thinking of that, yes. Do you think it's possible?"

"Not last night. Last night tide was high. Killer either walk on pier or swim."

"Or kayak," Susan suggested.

"Not kayak. Not in one of my kayaks. They are locked up when sun go down."

"Why? Are you afraid someone will steal them?"

"No. Kayaks used to spend the night up by gift shop. They were leaned against walls. No one thought anything about it. Then one night some guests got drunk, took two kayaks, and drifted out to sea. They were rescued by U.S. Coast Guard the next day. Suffered sunburn and nothing else. Damn lucky they didn't drown. One man was a lawyer. He threatened to sue. Said kayaks should be locked up. So now we lock them up. Can't let stupid people do stupid things."

"Where?"

"In lockers. Behind gift shop. There's lots of things locked up behind the gift shop."

Susan frowned. They didn't seem to be getting anywhere. "How well did you know Allison—the woman who was killed?"

"I do not fraternize with guests. It is a rule."

"I'm not accusing you of anything like that," Susan assured him. "I just was wondering if she talked to you about anything—anything that might help my friend."

"Yes, of course you must help your friend," James agreed. "Many people here—we worry about your friend."

"Then you'll help me?" Susan asked, relieved.

"How can I help you? I don't know what you want."

Susan could hear the hesitation in his voice. "I need two things. I need to know who you saw on the beach yesterday. They may have had nothing to do with the murder, but anyone who was there might have seen something. And I need to know if anyone on the staff saw something—or was told something—that might give me a clue to what really happened."

James didn't respond for a few minutes.

"I've investigated murders before," Susan explained.

"Yes. But the staff here has not been involved in anything like this until this. And this is good place to work. People who work here want to keep working here. These people, they are my friends, my family."

"Of course. I understand. That's a nice way to feel. Do you think—maybe I should talk to Lila and she could assure everyone that their jobs aren't in jeopardy?"

"No. Lila already told staff what to do. We are to help police and keep the guests from being upset. And we are not to talk to press."

"But I wouldn't involve Lila in my investigation. I wouldn't want to bother anyone here or cause anyone to lose their job. Really. And I think I could investigate, just ask a few people a few questions, without doing anyone any harm." She stopped talking and concentrated on her paddling. She realized she was going to need James's help in gaining the cooperation of the rest of the staff. And she had no idea how to convince him that she wouldn't hurt anyone. "I—"

Before she could say anything more, Joann coasted over to her side. "Have you gotten the hang of this yet?"

"I'm doing fine now," Susan said, immediately offended. "I'm just not accustomed to this type of kayak. In Maine—"

"Really? I find this very easy. Almost relaxing."

Something about Joann's voice implied that Susan was a complete klutz. "I'm just not used to this type of kayak," she started her explanation again. "See, in Maine—"

"I've been thinking about the murder," Joann interrupted. "I think it's possible that Allison knew someone was going to kill her."

Susan was astonished. "Why?"

Joann scowled at Susan and then managed to give James a look that was both imperious and demanding. "I believe my husband could use your assistance."

"Of course. If Mrs. Henshaw doesn't need me . . ."

"You go ahead. I'll be fine," Susan assured him. "I'll call if I think I'm going to fall in."

"What's he going to do? Pull you out and dry you off?" Joann asked as James spun his kayak around and pointed it toward her husband.

"I've got the hang of this now. Why did you say what you said?"

"Not in front of the servants," Joann said, putting one pudgy finger to her lips.

Susan waited until she deemed James out of hearing range to ask the question again. "You said that you thought Allison knew someone was trying to kill her?" She liked this woman less and less, but was curious to know where this would lead.

"Yes. I said that. And I can tell you why."

"Why?"

"I must tell you that Allison and I had a very interesting talk two days before she was killed."

Susan made an effort to keep her impatience to herself. "Really? You talked about murder?"

"In a way. We talked about death."

"What about it?"

"Perhaps I should start at the beginning."

"Please do."

"Well, I was lying by the pool—in the shade, of course. I cannot understand what these people are thinking when they sprawl out in the scorching sun for hours and hours. Haven't they heard of melanomas?"

"Was Allison lying in the shade, as well?"

"No. And now that I think about it, that was unusual. She

was talking about the value of life when, in fact, she was practically squandering it."

"She was talking about the value of life? Is that what makes you think someone was trying to kill her?"

"No, that's what led to the comment that makes me think she knew someone was going to try to kill her. I do think I should tell this story in my own way."

Susan doubted if Joann was capable of telling anything any other way. "That's fine."

"So there I was, lying in the shade, relaxing, enjoying being on my own—and then Allison sat down a few chaises away from me and almost immediately began to talk about herself. To tell you the honest truth, I was irritated. Yes, I was irritated and I can honestly admit now that she is gone that I'm ashamed of feeling that way."

"But how could you know she was going to die?"

"Exactly! How could I have known she was going to die?" Joann shook her head so hard that her kayak rocked back and forth.

Susan hoped Joann wasn't going to fall into the water now that they were finally getting to the topic she found interesting. "Go on," she urged. "What did she say about herself?"

"She started out by saying that she was relaxed for the first time in years. Well, I disregarded that. We're all here to relax. It would be almost immoral to say anything else. I don't remember how I responded. I probably said something like, 'I know how you feel.' In fact, now that I think about it, I'm pretty sure that's exactly what I said. I know I didn't encourage her to keep talking about herself. But she did anyway. You know how some people are."

"Yes. What did she tell you?"

"She said she was here alone and that she was using the time to examine her own life. Well, I don't know about you, but I consider all this self-examination stuff a load of cow doo-doo. I never waste any time examining my own life. I do what I do and that is that. I've always been that way."

Susan suspected that Joann was too busy talking about herself to examine anything, but that isn't what she said. "Apparently Allison didn't feel the same way."

"No, and her conversation was a fine example of where all this life-examining garbage can lead. No sooner did she start talking about life, the value of life, what she had done with her life, all that crap, than she started talking about death. Her own death!"

"In what way? I mean, she didn't just say, 'I've been thinking about my own death.' "

"She did! Well, she almost did. At least that's what she began rambling on and on about. Very boring. I almost didn't bother to listen. But then she said something that will interest you." Joann stopped dramatically, brushed a stray curl of hair off her forehead, and almost toppled her kayak.

Susan willed her lips not to curve upward. "Are you all right?" she asked, when Joann had stopped wobbling.

"Of course. But I will admit that what I'm about to tell you is very upsetting. It upsets me to think of it and it upsets me to talk about it. But I believe in doing what is right so . . . Allison said she didn't think her own death would be peaceful."

"What did you say?"

"I actually don't remember. It's possible . . ." Susan heard a hint of insecurity in the other woman's voice for the first time. "It's possible that she said she expected to die a violent death. Well, you can imagine how I felt."

"Of course, I'd be horribly upset if someone said anything like that to me. I mean, you must have been shocked and horrified and—"

"I was appalled. What a thing to say to me on vacation. I'm here to relax. I have a very complex life to return to in a few weeks. I certainly don't expect to be burdened with a stranger's silly worries."

"Oh. Did you ask her what she meant?" Susan asked. "I mean, what sort of violence?"

"Of course not! I just told you that I was quite upset by what she said. Why would you ever imagine I'd encourage her to continue talking about it?"

"But—you said she predicted her own murder?" Susan protested.

"I believe what I said was that it was possible she knew she was going to be murdered. She talked to me about a violent end to her life. What is more violent than murder?"

Susan wouldn't have argued with that even if she had thought there was half a chance that Joann would listen to anything she said. She just paddled back toward land with the rest of her group, wondering if she had learned anything this morning.

Later, reviewing what little she had been told, she realized the high point of the morning had been Joann's kayak flipping over and dumping its passenger in the water as she passed the gazebo. Even Martin had smiled at that one.

# FOURTEEN

KATHLEEN WAS SITTING ON THE DECK OF HER COTTAGE, apparently writing postcards, as relaxed and content as any tourist.

Susan, recognizing a facade when she saw one, rushed to her friend's side. "How's Jerry? Did you see him?"

The smile that appeared on Kathleen's face was real. "He's okay, at least for now. There's an American embassy office here. Not a big one, but the woman who runs it has been wonderful. I don't know how she did it, but she managed to convince the higher-ups in the local police department that everyone concerned would be better off if Jerry was incarcerated on U.S.-held property. Fortunately, the embassy offices were built on the ruins of an old English fort. Jerry's locked up in a guarded room on the ground floor. It's a bit musty and damp, but he has a sensational view out over the sea. For the time being at least, he's safe."

"What did he say? Did he tell you anything about Allison, or—" Susan stopped, realizing that Kathleen probably didn't know that Jerry and Allison had been together the day of her death. "—or anything," she concluded.

"A police officer stayed in the room with us, so we were both careful about what we said," Kathleen answered. "But we talked for a bit. In fact, I've been writing notes here. I'm

trying to figure out whether or not he was trying to tell me
something that no one else would understand."

"What do you mean? Some sort of code? What did he actually say?" Susan repositioned the card closest to her so
that she could read the words written in Kathleen's perfect
Palmer-method script.

"Not a code. I thought he might be saying things that only
he and I would understand. If that's what he was trying to do,
he failed. At least, I didn't get it."

"What did he say?" Susan asked again.

"He started out by telling me that he was fine, being treated
well, not to worry. All that type of thing. He's worried about
the kids. What will happen to them if this hits the news back
home and they hear about it."

"Is there any reason to worry about that? Has there been
any sort of news coverage about this?" Susan asked, momentarily distracted.

"Not that I know of. And Ms. Adams—she's the woman in
charge of the embassy office—says that as far as she knows,
nothing has been reported back to the States about it. But she
also said that all it would take for the story to hit the news at
home is for one bored American journalist here on vacation
to hear about it."

"Let's just hope Jerry's out of there before anything like
that happens."

"Yes. I can't imagine trying to explain this to the kids."
Kathleen was silent for a moment, playing with the rest of the
postcards she'd written.

Susan sat quietly, waiting for her friend to continue.

"We didn't have much time to talk," Kathleen began again.
"Jerry asked about the kids and then he asked about you. He
wanted to know what you were doing—where you were."

Susan nodded. "He was probably wondering if I was
investigating."

"I thought that at first, but then he said something interesting. He said that you were the only person who could help him."

"He's saying that he wants me to investigate Allison's murder."

"No, he emphasized *only*. The word *only*. I'm pretty sure of that. I got the impression that he was making this point for a reason. He may have been trying to say that he doesn't want me involved in any investigation." Kathleen picked up a card showing a gaudy sunset behind palm trees and examined the words she had written on it. "I'm pretty sure he said you were the only person who could help him. But it may have been *should* help him. I wish I could remember."

Susan was still thinking about Kathleen's first thought. "What does he expect you to do? Lie around the pool working on your tan?"

Kathleen dropped the card she had been studying. "You don't think he was trying to tell me to go home, do you?"

"I don't know," Susan answered slowly. "Maybe he thinks you should be with Alex and Emily. If that's what he means . . . are you thinking of leaving?"

"Absolutely not! I'm going to call Jerry's parents and tell them what has happened. If it does hit the news, they should be prepared to deal with the kids—or maybe just get them away from town for a while or something—but I'm not leaving Jerry here alone and I am going to investigate this with you!"

"Of course you are! And I can't imagine Jerry thinking you would do anything else. So what could he have been talking about?"

"I have no idea. But he wasn't upset. I mean, he knew perfectly well what he was saying. And he probably knew we were only going to have a short time together. It must have meant something." Kathleen picked up her cards and placed them in a neat stack. "Maybe Jed will be able to tell us more."

"Where is Jed?" Susan looked around as though expecting to discover her husband nearby.

"He's still at the embassy offices. They're trying to find a lawyer to represent Jerry. The lawyers he called in Hancock all suggested he find someone familiar with the laws—and customs—on the island."

"Have they actually charged Jerry with the murder?"

"Not officially. The term they're using is *assisting with the investigation of the untimely death of Allison McAllister*. But apparently there aren't a lot of laws on the books here to protect the rights of suspects. They can hold Jerry pretty much as long as they want. Ms. Adams agreed that a lawyer familiar with the island's laws and court system, such as it is, should be hired. She suggested two names—expatriates who are practicing here—and they should be talking with Jerry right now. Jed offered to help us out. He's contacting our bank at home to have money transferred here so we can give the lawyer a retainer. He said to tell you that he'll be back as soon as possible." Kathleen picked up her pile of cards and tucked them in the pocket of her linen slacks. "So what have you learned this morning?"

"I've been talking to people," Susan said, realizing again that she was going to be uncomfortable discussing Allison and Jerry with Kathleen. "To tell the truth, they've been talking to me. Allison's been here for a few weeks and she spent time chatting with other guests. They've been seeking me out and—and telling me about her. In fact," she continued, suddenly inspired, "why don't we go get some lunch and see who else wants to talk to us?"

"I'm not hungry."

"You should eat something. But even if you just have some

iced tea, we'll learn more in the restaurant than we will sitting here alone."

"I suppose. But these people don't know us. They might think Jerry actually did kill Allison."

"They might, but that's not important now. What's important is that we know Jerry didn't do it. And it's more than likely that a guest—or someone on the staff here—did."

"You know, I hadn't considered the possibility that someone on the staff killed her."

"I think it's unlikely. I spoke with James and he said it's against the rules for staff to fraternize with guests and that everyone here wants to keep their jobs. If there's no connection to Allison, why would one of them kill her?"

"Perhaps someone who works here is a psychotic killer and Allison just happened to be the next victim."

"I suppose that's possible." Susan spoke slowly. "Allison was here alone."

"But she and Jerry had a connection. So Jerry's the only suspect."

"Unless we can find someone else she had a connection to. She might even have been here to see someone else."

"That's true," Kathleen agreed. "But isn't it possible that the killer thought he or she was killing someone else, that Allison's death was a case of mistaken identity? Doesn't one woman lying on a lounge in the dark look pretty much like another?"

To Susan, this sounded less like a serious possibility than wishful thinking on Kathleen's part, but she had two tasks here: to find out who had killed Allison McAllister and to keep Kathleen's spirits up. "It's possible. Let's go get that lunch and check out the other women here, see who might resemble Allison under those circumstances."

"That's a great idea!" Kathleen stood up, and Susan had to hurry to keep up so they arrived at the restaurant together.

"We'd like a table for lunch," Kathleen told the hostess who was seating guests.

"Of course, Mrs. Gordon. Would you like your usual spot overlooking the water, or would you prefer something a little more . . . ah, a little more private?"

"A table overlooking the water," Kathleen stated firmly.

Susan smiled. For the moment, at least, Kathleen was all right. "My husband might be joining us. So perhaps we could have a table for three?" she asked.

"Naturally."

If Madonna or Hugh Grant had arrived for lunch, they would have been seated at the table Susan and Kathleen were led to. Set right next to the seawall, it offered a stunning view of the horizon, while allowing other diners an unobstructed view of its occupants. Susan glanced across the table at Kathleen, now studying the menu the hostess had offered her. "We seem to be attracting a lot of attention," she said quietly.

"Not surprising," Kathleen responded without looking up. "Do you see anyone who resembles Allison?"

Susan scanned the room. "I suppose . . . one or two. The young woman here on her honeymoon is tall and thin and has long hair. From behind, I suppose, someone might confuse the two of them."

"I don't think I know who you're talking about." Kathleen put down her menu and looked around.

"The good-looking couple sitting at that small table by the bar," Susan said.

Kathleen glanced in the direction Susan indicated and raised her eyebrows. "Allison was good-looking, but not that good-looking."

"Of course not. That girl—young woman," Susan corrected herself. "She's about twenty years younger than Allison. But they both have long blond hair and they're both tall and thin. From behind . . . in the dark . . . it's possible they might be mistaken for each other."

"You could say that about the groom, too," Kathleen pointed out. "He's also tall with long hair."

"He is, isn't he? On the other hand, if we're looking for a lone woman—or man—lying on a chaise lounge, we can probably eliminate them both. I don't remember seeing one without the other, do you?"

"True." Kathleen looked out at the room again. "You know what's interesting about being stared at? When you stare back, everyone looks away."

"So who else is tall with long hair?" Susan asked, getting back to their search. "There are three women at the table to our right—I think they're here together—and all three of them have long hair. And if they're not tall, at least none is incredibly short."

"But they weren't even around when the murder happened. They just checked in this morning. They were busy at the front desk when I was on my way to see Jerry. And I don't see anyone else who could be mistaken for Allison."

"Except . . ."

"Except who?"

"You. You're tall and you have long hair."

Kathleen offered her friend a rueful smile. "But the only people I know here are you and Jed and Jerry, and I don't believe any of you would kill me."

"So I suppose we can eliminate the mistaken-identity theory," Susan said. "Which means we have to find the connection between Allison and someone other than Jerry."

"Let's order our lunch and eat quickly," Kathleen said. "Sounds like we have a lot of people to meet and a lot of questions to ask."

# FIFTEEN

LUNCH TURNED OUT TO BE MORE SUCCESSFUL THAN SUSAN had anticipated. The bread basket arrived along with a note from someone named Rose Anderson, who wished to speak with Kathleen "concerning a matter of some importance." Susan and Kathleen were still discussing that rather stilted statement when their main courses—seared swordfish Caesar salad for Kathleen; conch chowder with cornmeal croutons for Susan—arrived. The note that accompanied this course suggested that the women meet for drinks at four P.M. with the writer and her husband, who wanted to help in "this unfortunate situation." That note was signed "Peggy and Frank from Connecticut."

"Connecticut," Susan repeated. "This is great! They may have some relationship with Allison! This note may have been written by the killer!"

"Who are these people?" Kathleen asked. "Do you recognize their names?"

"Nope, but they'll be waiting for us in the bar at four. We'll figure it out when we arrive. Now, how about dessert?"

"I don't think—"

"I think we should ignore the calories today. The longer we sit here, the more likely it is people will contact us."

"Then I'll have key lime pie," Kathleen said.

"And I'll have the coconut flan and some iced coffee. I could use the caffeine."

"That's a good idea. I didn't sleep well last night."

"Did you leave your cottage?" Susan asked, leaning closer to her friend.

Kathleen looked down at her plate. "Maybe there are some things we should only talk about in private."

Susan had no trouble with that. "Of course!" She picked up her spoon and sipped the chowder. "We're going to have trouble keeping all these people straight. I mean, we don't know any of them. I don't suppose you brought a notebook to the island with you?"

"No. I never thought about it."

"I have my journal. I suppose I could rip some pages out of the back, but . . ."

"The gift shop probably has paper," Kathleen suggested.

"Good, let's go there right after we're finished here. I hate to wreck a perfectly good journal, especially since this one is almost new." Susan had been keeping journals for decades, nothing organized, writing in them when she had time, ignoring them when life was busy. As a result, she sometimes thought that she had recorded only the low points. On the other hand, at least she had some record of her life. The journal was in the top drawer of the built-in dresser in her cottage. "I wonder what's going to happen to Allison's things."

"Her things? You mean, like has she left a will?"

"No, I mean here. In her cottage."

"Good question. Which cottage was she staying in?"

"I'm not sure. But I'll bet every single member of the staff knows."

"Do you think we could get someone to tell us?"

"We could try. James was pretty forthcoming this morning. And why shouldn't he tell us? Anyway, Allison arrived a while ago; probably a lot of guests could tell us where she was staying." Susan turned and looked out to sea. "Are you thinking what I'm thinking?" she asked.

Kathleen turned and feigned an identical interest in the horizon. "That having a look around her cottage just might tell us something significant about Allison McAllister. Something that might lead us to her murderer."

"You got it! So first we find out which cottage it is and then we figure out a way to get inside."

"Sounds good to me," Kathleen said, turning back to her meal.

Susan did the same, somewhat reluctantly. The food was wonderful, but they had things to do and people to see. Kathleen apparently felt the same way, but, as agreed, they took their time, enjoyed their desserts, and were just about to leave when Lila strode across the room toward them.

"There's a phone call for you," she informed Kathleen. "You can take it in the office if you like."

Kathleen got up immediately. "Of course."

"And I wonder if I could possibly speak to you for a moment, Mrs. Henshaw."

Susan repeated Kathleen's words, albeit a bit less enthusiastically. "Of course. Why don't you sit down?"

"I . . ." Lila looked over her shoulder. Most of the guests who had stopped eating to watch her passage across the restaurant and Kathleen's retreat in the opposite direction, now turned to their plates and their lunch companions. "I think perhaps we should speak someplace more private. You see, it's my job to make sure our guests are satisfied with the time they spend with us."

"Of course. We could go back to my cottage," Susan suggested.

"Good idea. If you're done with your meal?"

Susan grabbed the notes that still lay on the table, stuffed them into the pocket of her slacks, and, followed by Lila, walked back to her cottage. Their progress was slow as Lila stopped at table after table to check on her guests or just to chat. Susan stood by awkwardly. Now that Kathleen was gone, Susan was the focus of many curious looks, and she found herself wondering which of the diners had sent the notes—and why.

Lila finally disengaged and they continued on their way to the Henshaws' cottage. Once inside, Lila wasted no time getting straight to the point.

"The murder—and the arrest of your friend—has become something of an amusement here and I wanted to talk to you about it."

"An amusement?" Susan said. "I don't understand." And I don't know what I can do about it in any case, she added to herself.

"It's just one of those things that happen in a resort," Lila explained. "This is a small place and we're somewhat isolated. So the guests themselves can have quite an impact on everyone's vacation. For instance, we once had four cottages of competitive chess players staying here. By the end of the week they were in residence, more than half of the other guests had learned to play the game, and there was talk of a resort chess tournament. And then the players left, and everyone lost interest and went back to lying in the sun, swimming, and beachcombing—our more usual offerings."

"But murder isn't exactly a game."

"Certainly not. But I believe I'm beginning to see evidence of an emerging group of Miss Marples and Hercule Poirots."

"I don't see how I can help that. If the other guests want to—to pretend to be detectives. I don't see that anything I can do will stop it," Susan protested, feeling a bit guilty about the notes stuffed in her pockets. She was, in fact, planning to encourage the guests who had sent them to become involved in her investigation.

"You misunderstand me. I'm not trying to discourage them. That's the last thing on my mind. Many of the guests I've talked with seem to be quite well informed about your past, and they assume you will be working hard to make sure your friend is freed."

"Of course, but—"

"And apparently many of the guests want to help," Lila continued before Susan could explain that any knowledge of her past had not come from her. "Your waitress told me of the notes sent to your table during lunch. And I believe there are more in your mailbox in the office."

"I don't see what I can do to—to discourage them. And, to be honest," Susan added, "I was hoping to talk to any guests who may have seen something unusual the night of the murder, or who spoke with Allison the week before she died."

"Oh, I'm sorry. You misunderstand me. I want you to include—or at least make the other guests feel as though they're being included in your investigation."

"But I thought—"

"I confess that my original feeling was that the guests should not be involved in all of this. And I was worried about the police being around, although the local police are always exceptionally considerate in their attempts not to annoy the guests."

Why should they? They've already made an arrest, Susan thought.

"But there is so much sympathy for Mrs. Gordon and, of course, for her husband. I believe many of our guests want to help them. I'm asking you to accept their kind offers of help—if you possibly can."

Susan contemplated what Lila was saying. She was sure that Lila didn't think she—or any of the guests—would find the murderer, and she wondered at Lila's apparent willingness to add some sort of murder weekend theme to the resort's list of activities. On the other hand, she was going to talk to some of the other guests as soon as Lila left her alone. She didn't need Lila's permission to talk to anyone about anything. But if she could get Lila's assistance . . . "I'd be happy to include anyone who's interested," she said. "And it would help if I could speak with some of the staff about all this."

Lila looked at Susan, seemingly considering her statement. "I keep the staff busy. They have very little free time, although it does not always appear this way to the average guest. The staff understands that they are to be pleasant to the guests, so they are willing to stop and chat and answer questions anyone might ask, but not at the expense of their work."

Susan realized immediately that while Lila was perfectly content for her guests to be occupied in some rather strange murder game, she didn't want her employees distracted from their work. She was about to ask for permission to look around Allison's cottage when Kathleen walked in. "How is everything?" Susan asked immediately. "Who was on the phone?"

"It was Jed," Kathleen answered, glancing over at Lila. "He says everything's fine. The lawyer was there for a bit and talked with Jerry. He's gone on to the police station. Apparently he has some friends there or something.

"Jed also said our bank at home is going to wire money directly to a branch here on the island—apparently it isn't that difficult to do—and that he's going to hang around with Jerry for a bit." A frown appeared on her face for the first time. "He said they were playing cards."

"Wow! They must be bored! That doesn't sound like them at all."

"I was thinking the same thing. How is everything going here?" Kathleen asked, including Lila in the question.

"Fine. We were just—" Susan began.

"I'm sure you and Mrs. Gordon will be able to handle this.

If I can do anything, please let me know." Lila was walking toward the door of the cottage as she spoke. Had she not been forced to go around Kathleen to get outside, she would have been out of sight before finishing her sentence.

"Thank you." Kathleen's response was polite, but her voice puzzled.

Susan waited until the door had swung shut and they were alone before speaking. "She wants us to include the other guests in our investigation. She came here just to make that point."

"Really? How odd."

"The strange thing is that she hasn't even considered the possibility that it might be dangerous."

"Of course not. Because she thinks Jerry is the killer. You and I know that he would never kill anyone. So we know the one thing she doesn't. We know there's still a killer loose at Compass Bay."

# SIXTEEN

A TIMID KNOCK ON THE LOUVERED DOOR TO THE COTTAGE interrupted their discussion. "Mrs. Henshaw? Mrs. Gordon?"

"We're both here. Come on in," Susan called out as Kathleen opened the door to admit a mousy woman in her mid-fifties.

"Hi. I don't want to bother anyone, but I think I might be able to help you—I mean, your husband. I'm Rose Anderson? I wrote you a note?"

Rose Anderson had a bad haircut, topped by an even worse highlighting job, and styled by someone who thought curlers were still in fashion. Her skin was dry and uncared for. Her blush was too bright and her lipstick too dark. And her clothing was an example of the very worst of some designer's "cruise line." She wore wrinkled periwinkle linen capri pants with a hideous pastel plaid gauzy big shirt, and brown leather sandals adorned with clunky gold rings. Gold earrings, three copper bracelets, a watch, and two silver and turquoise necklaces completed her ensemble. She was a mess. An expensive mess, but still a mess.

"Of course. It's good to see you," Kathleen said.

"I was wondering if we could talk for a few minutes," Rose said. "There's something bothering me. Something that doesn't make sense and in so many mystery novels—especially the

English ones—what doesn't make sense is what turns out to
be important, isn't it?"

Susan realized the smile on her face was beginning to fade.
Jerry was under arrest. Their vacation was supposed to end in
less than a week. Regardless of Lila's wishes, they didn't have
time to listen to the theories of people playing detective. It
might meet with Lila's approval, but for the first time, she
realized just how difficult it was going to be to get credible information from people she didn't even know. But what else
could she do? "We certainly never know what will turn out to
be important," she said. "Why don't you sit down and tell us
about it?" Susan pointed to the batik-covered rocking chair in
the corner and sat down herself on the edge of the bed. Kathleen leaned against the dresser and waited for Rose to begin.

"First, I should tell you that I am the type of woman people
confide in. Complete strangers tell me about their lives. It
happens in the strangest places. Just last month, I was in the
Amsterdam train station waiting for my train to Germany
when a woman came and sat down next to me. It turned out
that she was waiting for a train to take her to Zürich. Her
schizophrenic daughter was in a clinic there and she was going to visit her."

"Heavens, people really do tell you about their lives," Kathleen said.

"Exactly. So I can't say I was at all surprised when Allison
sat down next to me the day after I arrived and started talking
about herself."

"What did she say?"

"I've been going over this in my mind all morning long
trying to remember exactly. I do want to get it right."

"Just take your time," Kathleen urged, in her best police-
officer manner.

"Well, she started out by telling me her name and asking if
I'd been here before. I haven't, so we didn't have a whole lot

to discuss about that. I had been out snorkeling and we discussed that and other activities available here. She said she'd been snorkeling on St. John's a few years ago. We talked about that a bit. I hadn't known that there was a national park there—I'm sorry. You're not interested in that. We chatted a bit about the various vacations we'd taken. She was very well traveled, you know. Every place I mentioned, it seemed she had been there before me—and been able to do all the right things. Which is not what happens when I travel, alas."

"What do you mean?" Susan asked.

"Oh, you know how it is. I get to Florence on Tuesday with plans to leave on Saturday. And it turns out that Sunday and Monday are the only two days an important museum is open."

"I've had that happen to me, too," Susan said.

"I thought it happened to everybody—until I met Allison. She said that when she went somewhere for a limited time, she made sure everything she wanted to see would be open while she was there. Always."

"Sounds like a smart woman," Kathleen said.

"What else did she tell you about herself?" Susan asked.

"Well, she talked about her career. I think advertising and illustration are very exciting fields myself, but she was thinking of doing something else. She said if her book was a success, she might even retire."

"What book?" Kathleen asked.

"Allison wrote a book?" was Susan's question.

"Yes. It's going to be published next fall. She was quite proud of it. And she was using part of her advance to pay for her time here."

"Did she tell you anything about the book?" Susan asked.

"Yes. She talked about it a lot. It's a novel, but she may have based many of the characters in it on her own life and the people she knew."

Susan looked across the room at Kathleen. Kathleen looked back. Each of them knew what the other was thinking.

"What's the title?" Susan asked.

"That's the problem," Rose said. "I don't know. And I don't know how I'm going to find it. She's not using her own name. But I don't know what name she was going to be using."

"But you said she talked about the book a lot," Kathleen pointed out. "Didn't she mention its title?"

"She must have, but I just don't remember. And it didn't worry me until she died. She carried around the big beach bag and there was a notebook inside. She took my name and address and was going to send me some publicity information when she got home. I didn't think it made any difference whether or not I knew the title."

"What exactly did she tell you about the book?" Susan asked, suppressing a sigh.

Rose's eyes lit up. "Well, it was sort of a modern-day Cinderella story. At least, that's what it sounded like to me. There were these two sisters. I guess Cinderella has three sisters, but . . ."

"That doesn't matter," Kathleen assured her. "Go on."

"Well, these two sisters grow up competing with each other. They competed for their parents' attention. Apparently the parents were a busy couple who didn't spend much time with their children. They competed to see who could get the best grades in school, the highest SAT scores, get into the best college, get the best job, *and* to see who could get married first!

"Of course, I didn't think anything at all about this at the time. Frankly, I thought it was probably just fiction. You're always hearing about how writers get ideas and then write about them. I mean, the book doesn't necessarily have anything to do with the writer's real life. But Allison kept dropping hints."

"Hints? What sort of hints?" Susan asked.

"She kept saying that she was writing about something she knew. That she could have put in more details, but had decided not to. And then, this morning, a few of us were sitting around talking and someone said that Allison's sister was your husband's first wife. Well, I was amazed! Completely amazed! I knew I had to talk with you both as soon as I could." Rose fiddled a bit with one of her necklaces before continuing. "I would have been here earlier, but I'm afraid that something I ate last night didn't agree with me. I had a terrible time getting to sleep last night. And what with all the excitement, you know . . ." She glanced at Kathleen, and her expression changed from enthusiasm to embarrassment. "Not that I think your husband's arrest is exciting! Please don't misunderstand me!"

"Please, I do understand what you're saying. Go on," Kathleen urged.

"Well, Allison said that one thing had happened in life and something different in the book. That the sister who won the competition in real life was the loser in the book."

"Do you know which sister won?" Susan asked. "In life or in the book?"

"I got the impression that the narrator—Allison herself probably—wins in the book. So I guess she lost in real life. I can't be sure of that, of course. Allison talked to me about herself and her life, and she talked to me about her book, but she didn't exactly explain who the characters in her book were. Today I realized that the two sisters in the book were probably Allison and her sister."

"That could be significant," Kathleen said.

"Well . . . I was thinking that the logical person to suspect in the murder is Allison's sister! It sounds to me as though she certainly wouldn't want this book published, and—" Rose looked from Susan to Kathleen. "You don't agree with me, do you? You don't think that Allison's sister killed her, but think about it for a bit. Just because her sister isn't a guest here doesn't mean that she isn't on the island. She could be staying someplace else. She could have slipped in under cover of darkness and killed her sister. She could have—"

"No," Kathleen interrupted. "She couldn't have done anything. Allison's sister died in an auto accident years ago."

Rose turned pale beneath her makeup. "I—I had no idea. I thought your husband and she had gotten a divorce. I never thought she might be dead." She rocked back in the chair and closed her eyes for a moment. "I thought I would be helping by telling you all this. And it doesn't matter at all, does it?"

"Of course it matters!" Susan cried, getting up and moving closer to Rose. "We know very little about Allison. Kathleen's never even met her, and I haven't seen her in years and years. Anything you tell us about her might lead us to the killer." That sounded a bit dramatic even to Susan's ears, and she shut up and perched back on the edge of the mattress.

"Oh, well, then you would be interested in knowing that she was in love. Head over heels in love. Those are her words, not mine," Rose added quickly, twirling one of her rings around her finger.

"Do you know who the man is? We understood that she was here alone," Kathleen said.

"She was here alone. She said it was very freeing to be on vacation alone. That she could do what she wanted when she wanted. And she didn't tell me who she was in love with. She said he was wonderful. The most wonderful man she'd ever met. She—frankly—she talked about him as though she was a teenager and this was her first crush. She said he was handsome, and smart, and rich, and kind."

"Did she mention any names?" Susan asked.

"No. I'm sure she didn't."

Kathleen frowned. "Did she say anything that might help identify him? How long she'd known him? What he does for a living?"

Rose thought that over for a while. "I got the impression that he worked with her. She said they had a lot in common and she could talk to him about anything. But I think the only thing she actually mentioned was some help he'd given her on an account. I don't know much about advertising, but . . ."

Susan and Kathleen both nodded. "Both of our husbands are in advertising," Susan explained. "We hear about it all the time. In fact . . ." She paused.

"What?" Kathleen prompted.

"I think it's possible that Jerry and Allison met at work and she introduced him to June . . . Allison's sister," Susan explained to Rose.

"I remember Jerry telling me that," Kathleen spoke up. "But Allison hasn't worked with Jed and Jerry for decades, has she?"

"No. She quit around the time June and Jerry were married, and she moved to an agency in Chicago. She came back to visit on holidays, but she was in the midwest for years and years. I think she returned to New York around the time of June's death." Susan stopped and considered all this for a moment.

"Do you think that could be significant?" Rose asked, leaning forward. "Because in the book, one of the sisters leaves the country, and moves to Paris, and changes her life—becomes beautiful and then returns home and marries the man of her dreams."

"Sounds a bit like the script for *Sabrina*," Kathleen said.

"Such a beautiful movie. It's one of my favorites," Rose responded enthusiastically. "I actually bought the videotape so I can watch it over and over again."

"But it does sound kind of like Allison's life. She really doesn't look at all like she did when June was alive," Susan mused.

"What else did she tell you about her novel?" Kathleen asked.

"She said it had a surprise ending. I could tell that's what she liked about it the most. She kept saying that readers would never know what hit them when they got to the end. She seemed really pleased about that."

"What else did she say about her life?" Susan asked. "Did she tell you how she ended up here? How she even knew about Compass Bay?"

Rose thought for a minute before answering. "No. I told her about my wonderful travel agency and how they got me such a great deal here, but I don't believe she said anything about how she found Compass Bay."

"When you came in here you said that something Allison said didn't make any sense," Kathleen pointed out. "What was that?"

"Oh, heavens. I do get off the point, don't I? She said that she had thought about writing a murder mystery, but that was too close to her real life. But the murder happened after she told me that. And, of course, it happened to Allison herself. So how could her life be close to a murder mystery without a murder in it? And that's not all. We were talking about our lives and she said that she had spent much of her life being a victim, but now all that was changing."

"But it didn't, did it?" Kathleen mused. "She ended up being a victim. A murder victim."

"I know." Rose's jiggling with her jewelry became almost frantic. "That's something else that doesn't make any sense."

# SEVENTEEN

"WHAT DO YOU THINK ABOUT THAT?" KATHLEEN ASKED Susan when Rose, promising to return if she remembered "anything else important," had departed.

"She's not the most reliable reporter, but she wants to help and she may be the type of person people talk to. I was stunned to hear that Allison was going to have a book published."

"Do you think it will turn out to be as autobiographical as it sounds?" Kathleen asked.

Susan looked at her friend. Kathleen was staring into the large mirror hung between the two windows on the wall across from the bed, idly arranging and rearranging her hair. Her shoulders were sagging, and even from behind, she looked tired and discouraged. "You know, I can't imagine Allison writing a book, but then I guess I really didn't know her all that well. I thought about her as an extension of June."

"You know what's bothering me?" Kathleen spoke up, still facing the wall. "What's bothering me is that you won't talk to me about June."

"I—"

"You never wanted to talk to me about June. No one wanted to talk to me about June. Damn it, even Jerry keeps me in the dark about her."

Susan, realizing Kathleen's shoulders were shaking as she began to sob, hurried over and embraced her friend. "You're right. I didn't realize. I've been stupid. Maybe we've all been stupid."

With a loud sniff, Kathleen pulled herself together. "I've been stupid, too. I should have encouraged Jerry to talk about her before we got married, but I didn't. To tell the truth, he talked so much about their children that I thought he was talking about her. It wasn't until we were married and living together that I realized how little I knew about her."

"What do you mean?"

Kathleen sat down in the rocking chair Rose had so recently vacated, bit her lips, and started to explain. "When you introduced me to Jerry he was living in that condo down by the water, remember?"

"Yes." Susan couldn't imagine what was coming.

"Well, he was subletting the place and it was furnished—pretty much. He'd brought his computer, stereo, and some personal things. Then we got married and both agreed that it was a good idea to buy a house. I had some savings and Jerry had the profits from the home he had sold just sitting in the bank getting almost no interest. So we found our house, bought it, and a week later a huge moving van pulled up from the company that had been storing his stuff and began to unload."

Susan nodded. "I remember."

"That's right! You came over to help. I'd forgotten."

"Probably because you were so upset."

Kathleen laughed bitterly. "And I thought I hid it so well."

"Nope. And I didn't blame you. It was insensitive of Jerry—and me—not to realize what you were going through. God, Kath, I feel awful about it now and that was years ago. You may have thought you were hiding things, but when the first piece of furniture out of the van was that pencil bed—"

"Their bed," Kathleen agreed, nodding.

"Yes. Of course. I remember the expression on your face."

"And you offered to go furniture shopping with me. I'd forgotten."

"Do you remember the salesman at Bloomingdale's?"

Kathleen laughed. "I sure do. He was positive that they couldn't deliver the bedroom furniture for at least a week."

"And we convinced him that it could be done in twenty-four hours."

"And it was!"

"I'd forgotten all about that."

"And you probably never even knew that the next thing off the truck, the double dresser, was full of June's clothing."

"I had no idea. I thought all of that had been cleaned out." Susan paused, walking over to the window and looking out at the beach before continuing. "I helped Jerry clean out the house before he sold it. Emptying the children's rooms was heartbreaking. I remember emptying June's closet. And the nightstand on her side of the bed. I guess I just missed the dresser."

"You missed her desk, too."

"Her desk? Oh, that's right. The little cherry desk. It sat in the corner of their kitchen." Susan had a flash of June sitting there, organizing a fund-raiser for the PTA, piles of paper before her. "Was it full of stuff?"

"Yes. Mostly notebooks and sheets of paper. I became obsessed with those papers. I put the desk in the guest room— that's what it was then, now it's Emily's room—and went through those papers over and over. They told me a lot about her. How organized she was, how involved in the lives of her children, what a wonderful cook she must have been. There was even a box of letters that Jerry had written her before they got married."

Susan didn't know what to say. This didn't sound at all like her self-confident friend. Kathleen and Jerry had always seemed so happy. Susan had no idea that Kathleen might be haunted by the memory of his first wife.

"I think my problem was that everyone loved June. I mean, I didn't want Jerry to have been married to an awful person, but June was always talked about as being perfect. She was everything I wasn't. She was petite and cute, she was domestic, and she had perfect children—"

"It wasn't really like that at all," Susan interrupted gently.

"Of course it wasn't. No one's perfect. I know that. Ask any cop and he'll tell you that no one has any idea what goes on in other people's lives. In my head, I knew June couldn't have been perfect, but I was so overwhelmed. Living in the suburbs with a new husband, leaving behind my work in the city—was just too much."

"I'm so sorry. I had no idea. None."

"You might have if it had gone on for long, but after a few months, I pulled myself together. It wasn't all that hard to do. Jerry and I were so happy. I would have been a fool to keep beating myself over the head for not being the perfect suburban housewife."

"But, Kathleen, June wasn't perfect."

"Do you know that's the first time you've ever said anything at all negative about her!"

"I—I don't know what to say. She—we—we had a lot in common. Jed and Jerry were best friends in college and they always spent a lot of time together, so of course June and I did, too. We joined the Field Club the same year, had our children around the same time, and then the kids went to school together. Heavens, we were class mothers and taught Sunday school together. The truth is that we were together a whole lot. But that doesn't mean that we were close."

"You're kidding."

"No. You know how it is. How many women are you quote-unquote friends with that you wouldn't even talk with if your kids and their activities didn't throw you together frequently?"

"I suppose that's true. But I'm surprised that June would fall into that group."

"I—" A knock on the door interrupted Susan.

The door opened and a scarf-covered head peeked in. "I'm sorry. I bring towels. Bath towels," the young black woman explained.

Susan looked around. "But the room's already made up."

"I work here earlier in day, but towels still in laundry."

"Just leave them on the bed and I'll put them away later," Susan said.

"Yes, ma'am."

Susan didn't resume speaking until the door had closed behind the maid and they were alone again. "To tell you the truth, I didn't realize this until about a year after her death. I didn't miss June enough. Other women filled in the spaces in my life, and I began to realize that my relationship with June had been more casual than the amount of time we had spent together would lead anyone—including me, apparently—to believe."

"So tell me about her."

"Well, she was pretty. You've seen pictures, so you know that." Susan sighed. "I don't know. She was a good wife, a good mother, a good member of the community. But, that's about all. She did what was expected of her and she did it well, but there was no spark, no excitement, no creativity. Do you remember when Emily was a baby and Alex got all his Magic Markers together and put all those bright-colored streaks in her hair?"

"How could I forget! I could have killed him before I realized that they weren't permanent. And she looked so silly and happy." Kathleen smiled at the memory.

"And you took all those photos of her and sent them to all your friends the next Halloween."

"Yeah. Not a great lesson for Alex, but I couldn't resist. And he did seem to understand that drawing on his sister is absolutely forbidden. At least, he never did it again."

"June would never, ever have done anything like that. She wouldn't have laughed about it. Babies aren't supposed to have multicolored hair and that would be all there was to it."

"Her kids were probably much better behaved than mine are," Kathleen said.

"No, they weren't. But it's June we're talking about. She couldn't hold a candle to you, Kath."

Kathleen smiled. "Okay. Enough self-indulgence. I feel better, but Jerry is still locked up. We need to help him. And it will be a lot easier for me to ask questions about Allison now that we both feel more comfortable talking about June."

"Of course, if we could just get hold of Allison's book, we might find out a whole lot about both of them."

"You do think it's about them! Were you aware of them competing with each other?"

"Not really. But it sounds like the book is written from Allison's point of view. I do know that June found Allison's visits to be somewhat trying. She wasn't a relaxed hostess. She wanted everything perfect and that's why I had them over to dinner for holiday meals. But, you know, now that I think about it, that competition thing may have been a dominant theme of their relationship. And it may have been the reason June was so nuts when Allison came to visit—she wanted everything to be perfect—so she could show it off."

"Was Allison ever married?"

"Not when she used to visit in Hancock. She made a big deal about her exciting single lifestyle. To listen to her, life was just a series of parties, trips to exotic places, and affairs with gorgeous men—but we never met any of those men. In fact, I remember June making a rather nasty comment about that one Thanksgiving."

"What did she say?"

"Oh, Allison was going on and on about a trip she and some man were planning to his family's villa on Capri. It was a bit boring for everyone listening. No one at the table had been to Capri, and June was just getting over the flu and feeling rotten. Anyway, June asked why all these rich and good-looking men never came to Hancock. I don't remember what Allison answered, but she implied that Hancock was just too, too suburban and she didn't think her lovers would be happy there."

"How did June react to that?"

"I remember looking over at her and realizing that she was absolutely furious. But she didn't say anything."

"Did you think that was odd?"

"Not really. It was Thanksgiving. All our kids were there, as well as Jed's mother and Jerry's parents. No one wanted a family argument erupting in the middle of the meal. It was almost as though Allison knew she could say anything she wanted to say and get away with it."

"Did Jerry's parents like June?" Kathleen asked, changing the subject.

"I guess so. I never thought about it . . . although I do remember Jed saying that there was some sort of argument or conflict or something the night before they were married. To tell you the truth, I don't remember the details—if I knew them."

"You were there?"

"Yes. I was a bridesmaid—hideous green polyester satin dress and a big floppy straw hat with ribbons down the back. All I needed were some sheep. I hated it. You know, I met Allison at that wedding. She was maid of honor and hated her dress as much as, if not more, than I did. The female attendants

wore various shades of green. Mine was jade—ugly, but not
bad. Hers was sort of dark avocado. She thought it looked
like she was wearing a refrigerator—and it did, sort of."

"Ugh."

"Yes. Who—"

The door opened and both women turned around, expecting to see the maid again. But Jed stood there. He looked
exhausted.

# EIGHTEEN

"How's Jerry?" Kathleen asked immediately.

"How are you? You look exhausted!" Susan cried.

"Jerry's just fine. He was just getting ready to take a nap when I left him. I promised I'd be back in an hour or so. The kitchen here is going to pack up a lunch to bring him."

"So you came back just to pick up lunch?" Kathleen asked, sounding dubious.

"That was an excuse. I came back to give you two a message. And I'd be a lot happier if I had some idea what message I'm supposed to be delivering."

"What?" Kathleen and Susan asked simultaneously.

"Look, Kathleen, you've been there, you know how it is with Jerry. There's absolutely no privacy and no way to talk without being overheard. The doors and windows are louvered. Anyone could be standing right outside and listening to anything we say. And a guard remained in the room for the entire time I was there, as well."

"So you couldn't write each other notes or whisper or anything like that," Susan guessed.

"Exactly. We kind of stood around together and commented on the weather and stuff until Jerry suggested playing cards."

"We thought that didn't sound like you two," Kathleen explained.

"It isn't, but once we started, I realized it was a brilliant idea on his part. We played and chatted, trying to sound casual. At first, I didn't realize what was going on."

"What was going on?" Kathleen asked.

"A whole lot—at least, that's what I started thinking on the drive back here. The most important thing is that Jerry kept mentioning you, Kathleen. And in sort of a negative way."

"What?"

"That's not what I was trying to say." Jed ran his hands through his hair and took a deep breath. "I'm sorry. I didn't mean that to sound so awful. Jerry kept mentioning you, Kath, and after a while, I realized he was trying to give me a message."

"What message?" Susan asked.

"What sort of negative things was he saying?" was Kathleen's question.

"He kept saying things like Kathleen shouldn't go out in the kayaks here. That it's too dangerous. And that he didn't want Kathleen to swim in the ocean. That he thought that might be dangerous, too. Frankly, I thought he was getting a bit paranoid. I said something about you going out kayaking," Jed explained to his wife. "And Jerry said that was just fine. That Susan was safe kayaking and being in the ocean and Kathleen wasn't."

"I swim as well as Susan," Kathleen protested.

"But I don't believe Jerry was talking about the ocean. I think he was talking about looking into Allison's murder. I think he thought that Susan should and you shouldn't."

"Why? Does he think I will find out something about him that he doesn't want me to know?" Kathleen asked bitterly.

"I don't think that's what he was saying at all," Susan protested. "I think he was trying to warn Kathleen."

"About what?" Kathleen asked.

"I think he wants you to stay put inside the cottage. I think he thinks you might be in danger."

"Oh, please. I'm not going to fall off a kayak. I'm not going to drown in the ocean. And I sure as shit am not going to sit in my cottage and twiddle my thumbs while Jerry is under arrest on an island in the Caribbean. Period."

Susan nodded approvingly. "Of course not.

"So what else did Jerry tell you?" she asked, turning her attention to her husband.

"I think—but I'm not sure—that he was trying to tell me something about the cardplayers."

"What cardplayers?" Kathleen asked.

"Those two couples who are always playing bridge?" Susan guessed.

"I don't know which couples you mean, but you know how I am about people."

Susan nodded. She did. He was unobservant. Not in a normal husband "have you worn that dress before? when she'd worn it weekly for over three years" sort of way, but in a "who was sitting next to us last night when that happened" sort of way. It was unlikely that her husband would have noticed two bridge-playing couples in their mid-sixties. "So what did Jerry say about them?"

"He didn't say anything about them. He just kept talking about playing cards. At first he said maybe we should find a deck and play a game, that it was amazing how you could play cards and think and talk about something else."

"So?"

"So I called a guard and asked if he could find us a deck of cards. There were two guards right outside Jerry's door playing cards when I arrived, so I knew there wouldn't be any trouble finding us a deck."

"So?"

"Look, even after I had brought the cards and after we

started playing, he kept talking about how interesting it is what people say when they're playing cards. I thought he was trying to make a point—so I would listen to what he was saying. But he kept repeating himself over and over. It finally occurred to me that maybe he was trying to make a point about something back here."

"And you're sure he said the important thing is what people talk about when they play cards?" Susan asked.

"I can't be sure of anything, hon. It's possible that he was just making sure that I was listening carefully to what he was saying. And if that's true, all he's worried about is keeping Kathleen indoors."

"And since I'm not going to do that, I guess we can ignore the entire thing," Kathleen said.

"Do you want to come see him when I take back his lunch?" Jed asked her.

Kathleen hesitated. "I love being with him."

"You know he would love to see you," Susan said.

"And you might understand what he's trying to tell you better than I do," Jed added.

"On the other hand, those people who wrote us notes are expecting to talk to both of us," Kathleen pointed out.

"That's true."

"And it could be important that I talk to them."

"That's true, too."

"Rose certainly wanted to talk to me, as well as you."

Susan nodded. "So you think you should stay here."

"Yes. After all, we're meeting Peggy and Frank for drinks, right?"

"So you want me to tell Jerry that you can't come see him because of your full social schedule?" Jed asked.

"No, don't tell him that. He might worry."

"These are all guests who want to talk to us about the murder," Susan explained. "If Jerry doesn't want Kath to investigate, he won't be happy to hear about any of it."

"Do you mind lying to him?" Kathleen asked.

"Yes. And, as Susan will tell you, I'm not really any good at lying."

"Why don't you tell Jerry that Kathleen will bring him dinner tonight? That she's lying down."

Kathleen obliged by immediately flopping onto the middle of the bed and closing her eyes. "Now it's not a lie."

Jed frowned. "I'll tell Jerry I left Kathleen resting in our cottage. If he asks me what she's going to do this afternoon—"

"Tell him you have no idea, but you're sure I'll be safe."

"And she will be, Jed," his wife added. "I won't leave her side."

Jed looked from one woman to the other. "I'm not sure that makes me feel a whole lot better. You both be careful."

"We will be. Don't worry."

"I'll worry," Jed said. "And I'll be back as soon as possible." He glanced down at his watch. "I'd better pick up Jerry's lunch and get it to him."

"Why don't we walk over with you and ask about having a dinner prepared that Kathleen can deliver to him later," Susan suggested.

"So much for telling Jerry that I left you resting in our cottage," Jed said, opening the door for the two women.

"You can tell him that you left me in the restaurant. He'll believe it. He knows that I eat when I get nervous," Kathleen said.

Jed stopped. "Kathleen, everything's going to be all right."

"It will be if I have anything to do about it," she answered.

He smiled. "I'd place my bet on you two any day of the week. But—"

"—be careful." Susan finished his sentence for him.

Jed placed an arm around his wife's shoulders and gave her a quick hug. "You read my mind."

"Nothing like thirty years of practice," she said, grinning.

"So thirty years is what it takes," Kathleen muttered.

Susan and Jed exchanged looks. "Why don't you go on back to the kitchen alone? You can order Jerry's dinner and check to see if his lunch is ready at the same time," Susan suggested to her friend.

"I spoke with a woman named Sissy when I called, so you might look for her," Jed added.

"Got it. I'll be back in a few."

"How's she holding up?" Jed asked, watching Kathleen walk away.

"I don't know. We had a long conversation about June. Jerry hadn't talked much about her, and Kathleen was curious." They had come to the large coral stone retaining wall, and the Henshaws leaned against it and looked out to sea. "I hadn't thought about June in years," she continued, watching as the honeymooning couple horsed around in a two-man kayak.

"Not surprising. Kathleen is a better friend—and probably a better wife—than June ever was."

Susan's mouth dropped open, and she looked over at her husband, astonished. "Didn't you like her?"

"Not really."

"I can't believe it. Why didn't you ever say anything?"

"What good would that have done? Anyway, she was married to Jerry. It didn't really matter how I felt about her."

Susan was astounded. "I had no idea!"

"Well, you two were such good friends. I thought saying anything would be inappropriate."

"But you like Kath."

"Of course I do. I'm crazy about her. And so is Jerry."

"Were Jerry and June having problems with their marriage when she died?"

"You'd probably know more about that than I would. Jerry and I don't talk about our marriages as a rule."

"June didn't talk to me like that. We weren't particularly close."

It was Jed's turn to be surprised. "Susan . . ."

"I don't think I realized it at the time, Jed . . ."

"Susan . . ."

"And I still miss the kids . . ."

"And maybe you don't want to talk about this right now. We could be overheard. And considering the situation . . ."

Susan looked around. The newlyweds had fallen overboard and were enthusiastically dunking each other. A man was sunning himself on a float in the middle of the swimming pool, and half a dozen other guests were lounging on the patio. The bridge players had resumed their tournament, and as Susan watched, Ro became the dummy and got up and walked around to examine her partner's hand. "Jed, have you ever played cards with Jerry before today?"

"Of course. Sometimes there's a game going on in the locker room at the club. A bunch of us get together for golf and have to kill time until we can tee off. You know how it is."

She didn't, but she nodded anyway.

"Why do you ask?"

"I don't know. I was just wondering about the two couples that play bridge. Why would they come to a gorgeous place like this and just sit around and play cards? Couldn't they do that at home?"

"Sure. But at home it's cold and wet if not actually snowy. Here it's warm, beautiful, and they can get a tan while they play. Why were you thinking about them?"

"I don't know. I keep thinking that it's odd that Jerry would mention card playing to you. Those two couples are the only thing I can think of that he might be talking about."

"Maybe they saw something."

"But that's not what you said. You said that Jerry said to listen to what the cardplayers were saying."

Jed shrugged. "I have no idea what he was talking about. Guess it's up to you and Kathleen to figure that one out."

"Just one of the small mysteries. Maybe if we find an answer to that one, we'll be a bit closer to finding the murderer."

# NINETEEN

WHEN PEOPLE HAILING FROM THE SAME STATE MEET IN A foreign country, they usually spend some time discussing the locations of homes and the possibility of having acquaintances in common. Susan and Kathleen and Peggy and Frank Romeo initially followed this convention.

Peggy and Frank Romeo were from northwestern Connecticut, over sixty miles from Hancock. But the foursome did manage to discover three friends in common, as well as a fondness for the cheese soufflés served at the same country inn. Formalities over, they got down to business.

"We were really sorry to hear about your husband," Frank said to Kathleen, brushing his red hair off his forehead. A tall, thin, and rather tired-looking man, he had done most of the talking. His wife, short, dark, and heavyset, had spent their time together quietly sipping her rum punch and smiling.

"Thank you," Kathleen replied politely.

"We're sure the police will discover that they've made a mistake soon and they'll let him go," Susan added.

"Some people here are saying that you have some experience investigating murder," Frank said.

"Yes, I do," Susan answered.

"So, of course, you are trying to help your friends," he suggested.

"Yes." Susan paused. "Kathleen and I thought that's why

you wanted to talk to us. Not that we don't appreciate your sympathy . . ."

"And the cocktails," Kathleen added, raising her gin and tonic to her lips.

"We did think you needed to relax," Frank began.

"And we wanted to offer our support," Peggy said. "Here you are, far from home, among strangers. This must be so distressing."

Susan nodded. "It is. We need all the help we can get if we're going to help Jerry."

"That's what we were thinking. It's why we sent that note to your table at lunch," Frank explained. "You see, we know something you don't know."

Susan almost giggled at the childish expression. "Something about Allison," she guessed.

"And something about your husband," Peggy added to Kathleen. "We think we know why he was arrested."

"He was arrested because the police have made a terrible mistake," Kathleen said.

"Oh, we don't think he was guilty of murder," Frank explained quickly. "We think he was guilty of love."

"My husband believes—and I must say I have come to agree with him—that your husband was in love with Allison McAllister," Peggy explained, reaching across the table and placing her hand on Kathleen's forearm.

Kathleen shook off the caress and sat up straighter. "And exactly how did you get that impression?" she asked coldly.

"I can assure you that we didn't make it up," Peggy insisted.

"And we in no way want to distress you," Frank added.

"You see, Allison herself told us," Peggy answered.

"How did that happen? Were you sitting together and she saw Jerry and just said, 'I'm in love with that man and he's in love with me'?" Kathleen sounded furious.

"I'm afraid you need to explain more. We have to understand exactly how this all came up," Susan pointed out.

"My husband was not in love with another woman," Kathleen insisted, ignoring Susan.

Peggy reached out for Kathleen again and then, apparently thinking the better of it, put her hand around her glass. "I understand exactly how you are feeling. You see, about a year ago, my best friend came to me and told me that Frank was in love with someone else. I was shocked. I had had no idea. But before we go on, you should look at Frank and me. We're here on our second honeymoon. Our marriage is stronger than ever. This could be the enlightening moment when you see your marriage for what it has become. And only by confronting reality can you change it. You and your husband will be just fine. I promise."

"My husband is not in love with someone else," Kathleen repeated.

"But—"

"Perhaps we should tell these women just why we're saying this," Frank said to his wife.

"That's an excellent idea," Susan agreed.

"I'd like another drink." Kathleen drained her glass.

Frank Romeo was apparently one of those men who could demand instant attention from waiters and waitresses. One wave of his hand, a quick order, and less than five minutes later, everyone at the table was enjoying a fresh drink and Peggy began their story.

"I suppose I must begin by explaining honestly that I did not like Allison McAllister."

"But I did—" Frank started.

"Of course you did. She flirted outrageously with you," Peggy said, glaring at her husband. "Now if you will allow me to continue . . ."

"Please." He narrowed his eyes and glared back. Susan

wondered if this was going to be one of the shortest second honeymoons on record.

"Allison approached us the first morning we were here. We had spent the night in a motel near the airport in Miami, took the first plane out in the morning, and were here in time for brunch."

"That way we get an extra day at the resort without paying for an extra night," Frank explained. "We always do that on vacation."

"I'm sure these women aren't interested in your cheap ways." Peggy picked up her glass and then put it back down without drinking. For one moment, Susan had thought she was going to pour it over her husband's head.

"So Allison approached you," Kathleen prompted.

"We were placed at a table right next to her. And, of course, we said hello right away."

"Frank has a hard time ignoring attractive women. Even when he's on his second honeymoon."

"We don't have all day," Kathleen announced, downing her drink in a few gulps and acting as though she was about to get up.

"And we're going to tell you about meeting Allison," Peggy said. "I'm sorry. Sometimes it's difficult to forgive and forget. As you will learn," she added to Kathleen.

"You sat next to Allison while you enjoyed the first brunch of your second honeymoon," Susan prompted.

"Yes. And, of course, we introduced ourselves, as people do in a place like this. And Allison was very helpful. We couldn't get into our cottage immediately, and she suggested we use her cottage to change in so we could use the pool and start to get some sun."

"How nice of her," Susan said. "Which cottage was she in?"

"Number nine. It's the first two-story cottage you come to walking down the beach. I think she may have been the only single person here staying in a cottage that large. I must admit I was disappointed when I discovered that we had reserved one of the smaller cottages nearer the restaurant."

"We're all staying in one-story cottages," Kathleen said. "So you went to number nine and changed into your swimsuits."

"Yes, and we—the three of us—went out to sit in the gazebo. We were actually sitting together so close to the spot where she died that it makes me shiver. Perhaps even in the same deck chair. Even now when I think about it . . ." Peggy actually shivered.

"My wife is very emotional," Frank said.

She glared at him before continuing. "Frank was tired and he took a rather long and noisy nap, but Allison and I got along so well. We chatted about ourselves—you know the way you do—and I told her about our second honeymoon. And she told me that she was here to meet a man, a man she has been in love with for years. At first she didn't mention your husband by name. But then she started saying Jerry. She did seem to feel slightly uncomfortable admitting that this Jerry—well, your Jerry," she added, glancing at Kathleen. "That he was married. I mean, I'd told her about the woman who wrecked—almost wrecked—our marriage, so it was quite natural that she wouldn't feel comfortable admitting to being the other woman, although in a very different situation, of course."

"Why do you think the situations were so different?" Susan asked.

"Well, Frank's affair was just a physical thing." Peggy looked over at her husband, and Susan thought the expression on her face just dared him to disagree with her. "Allison, on the other hand, had been in love with your husband for years and years. I believe she actually said decades."

"So she claims she was in love with him when he was married to her sister," Kathleen said.

"Yes. I suppose that's why they kept their affair a secret."

"And did she explain why they didn't get together after she died?" Kathleen asked.

Apparently Peggy didn't hear the sarcasm in Kathleen's voice. "She did mention that. She said he was so broken up over her sister's death that he didn't know what he was doing for years afterward."

"He didn't know what he was doing?"

"She said he had a breakdown. Poor man. Anyway, he married you and had children and then, years later, Allison ran into him."

"Where?"

Peggy looked at Susan as though she had asked something odd. "In the town he lives in, of course."

"Oh." Susan looked over at Kathleen. She knew they were both wondering what had brought Allison back to Hancock after all these years.

"Yes, she said she ran into him on the street while she was shopping. I told her that their meeting like that sounded like it was meant to be, and she agreed with me."

"And then what happened?" Susan asked.

"Their affair started up again almost immediately."

"She kept coming to Hancock?" Kathleen asked coldly.

"No, she said they met at her place in New York City. He took her out to dinner, to see the latest plays, and to art exhibits, as well. She said the last few years have been the best of her life."

"Years?" Susan asked. Kathleen merely glared at her empty glass without speaking.

"Yes, years," Peggy affirmed.

"And you're saying that Jerry and Allison went to restaurants, theaters, museums, and art galleries without running into any of our friends?" Kathleen asked.

"Oh, but don't you see? That wasn't a problem for them—

unlike my husband and his trashy paramour who couldn't explain to my best friend why they were together in the lobby of the Plaza in the middle of the afternoon in the middle of the week."

"Why wasn't it a problem?" Susan asked.

"Because she was his ex-sister-in-law. They had a relationship that everyone knew about. They didn't have to worry about being seen together."

"And you don't think that a mutual friend might have told Kathleen if she ran into Jerry and Allison together in the city?" Susan asked.

"Actually, a friend of mine did see them together a little over a month ago. They were having lunch together in the bar of the Four Seasons," Kathleen said slowly.

"But that doesn't mean anything really," Susan insisted. "Jerry works near the Four Seasons. He has to eat lunch. That meeting could have meant nothing."

"And why, if Allison and Jerry really were seeing each other all over the city back in the States, did they meet here?" Kathleen asked.

"Because Jerry wanted to tell you about their relationship without your children around. He wanted to ask you for a divorce so he could marry Allison."

# TWENTY

KATHLEEN CAREFULLY PUT DOWN HER GLASS AND PUSHED
her chair back. She stood up, snatched her straw bag off the
floor, slung it over her shoulder, and stamped out of the bar
without saying a word. Susan followed immediately.

Kathleen headed straight for her cottage, climbed the stairs
to her deck, yanked open her door, and stormed right in.

"You didn't lock your door," Susan said, trailing her friend
into the cool, dark interior.

"Jerry's in jail, a strange woman just informed me that my
marriage is a big lie, and you think I should be worried about
locking the cottage door in case someone wants to steal a few
suitcases full of overpriced resort clothing?" Kathleen's final
words were muffled.

"Kathleen! You're crying!" Susan was shocked. "You don't
believe the garbage that woman was saying, do you?"

"Part of me doesn't. And part of me knows that every
woman whose husband has betrayed her has refused to believe the truth when she first heard it."

"Kathleen, it's not the truth. Jerry wasn't in love with Allison. I'm sure of it."

Kathleen grabbed some tissues from the box by the bed,
blew her nose, and dried her eyes. "Okay. Susan, think about
this as though you don't know the people involved. If we had
been told that story about someone we had never met, you

and I would be sitting here discussing those poor, foolish women that Jerry had cheated on."

"Not Jerry! I know Jerry, and the man Peggy described—a man who had an affair, then was so shaken by the loss of his wife that he married—"

"That he married me. The first woman to come along," Kathleen said bitterly.

"The first woman to come along?" Susan squeaked. "Are you nuts? Jerry was the most eligible widower in Hancock for years. I introduced him to at least a dozen women, and I'll bet half our friends did the same thing. You were not the first woman to come along. You were the first woman he fell in love with! Period! Jerry was miserable after June and the kids died, but he didn't go insane and he had recovered any emotional stability he had lost long before he met you! And he was not in love with Allison."

"Susan, you can't be sure of that."

"I—well, probably not, but she was always kind of an odd person," Susan insisted, realizing her argument was losing steam. "I mean, her own sister had trouble with her coming to stay."

"What if the reason June had such a difficult time being her sister's hostess was because she suspected there was something going on between Jerry and Allison? Now, don't have some sort of knee-jerk reaction and tell me I'm wrong. Think about it! It could be true, couldn't it?"

Susan considered that possibility for a moment. "I suppose it could be true, but it probably isn't. And I can't believe Jerry would cheat on two wives with the same woman. Why didn't he just marry Allison after June died?"

"I don't know. But I know you don't know, either."

"Look, what if what Peggy told you was the truth? What if they were in love? Do you think Jerry could have killed her?"

"No. I can't believe that. I won't believe that."

"And you still want to find the killer and get Jerry released?"

"Of course I do! But what if Peggy is telling everyone the story Allison told her? What if everyone believes Jerry came here to tell me about Allison?"

"You know that is the oddest part of her whole story! Why would Jerry come on vacation with the three of us to meet Allison and tell you that he wants a divorce?"

"Maybe he did want to protect the kids. If he told me at home, I might become hysterical. They would see me hysterical. It wouldn't be good for them. If he told me here, I would be over the first shock before seeing Alex and Emily again. And you and Jed are here to help me through this." Kathleen shook her head. "That does not sound like something Jerry would do. It doesn't sound like something anyone would do."

"What have I been telling you?"

"Okay. You're right. It makes no sense. But—"

"But it's the story Allison told Peggy and Frank. And she must have told them for a reason."

"I suppose," Kathleen said.

"So let's say she made it all up," Susan continued.

"She didn't make up meeting Jerry in the city, Susan. They were together at the Four Seasons, remember."

"Jerry meets lots of people at the Four Seasons. You know it meant nothing."

"I don't agree with that. He met her there. And less than a month later, they run into each other at a resort in the Caribbean. It could be a coincidence, but I doubt it."

"Are you going to ask Jerry about it the next time you see him?"

"No. There's always someone listening. We don't talk about Allison at all. I'd feel much better if we could. I have so many questions." Her voice dropped to a whisper. "I think I just heard someone on the deck."

"Kathleen, Susan . . . it's Peggy. I have something for you."
She knocked on the doorjamb.

Kathleen glanced over at Susan, who shrugged. "Come on
in. The door's open."

Peggy walked into the room. A gigantic brilliant pink straw
tote bag dangled from one hand. "I didn't know what to do
with this. I was going to turn it in to the office, but then I
thought of your husband. He's really the closest thing Allison
had to a relative on the island. Perhaps he should have this."

"What is it?" Kathleen asked.

Susan was quicker. "Is that Allison's bag?" She reached
out for it.

Peggy pulled the tote out of Susan's reach. "Yes. She left
it on our deck the afternoon before she died. I saw it and
brought it in when the rain began and then forgot all about it."
Peggy paused. "When I realized she was dead, I just kept it.
Frank said I should turn it in to the office, but I told him that
the office didn't have any more right to it than I do. Anyway,
here it is. If you want it."

"We do!" Susan said.

"I was thinking it should go to Kathleen," Peggy pointed out.

Kathleen accepted the bag. "Thank you. It was very nice of
you. And—and thank you for talking to us."

"Oh, my dear, we should start a support group—women
who've been wronged by the men they love."

"I don't think—"

"I know. You've had a shock and right now you don't believe what I've told you. All I can say is that I have a nice
broad shoulder to cry on when you come to accept the truth.
Now I'd better get going. Frank is in the bar trying to drink all
the rum. I plan on helping him."

"Thank you," Kathleen said again, closing the door behind her.

Susan didn't even bother to wait until the door was closed

to grab the bag from her friend's hand and dump it in the middle of the bed. She scrounged around in the mess of paperbacks, sunscreens, scarves, combs, and small makeup bags, finding what she was looking for in just a moment. "The key!" She held her treasure up in the air. "The key to Allison's cottage. Now all we have to do is wait until dark."

"But it won't be dark for hours. What will we do until then?"

The question was answered for them the moment they stepped off the deck in front of Kathleen's cottage. The bridge-playing brigade enveloped them.

"Oh, Mrs. Henshaw." Ro Parker led her three companions to Susan and Kathleen. "I've been wondering where you were. We've been talking and we have a theory."

"And we have reservations for dinner, as well," the man by her side added. "We hoped your husband would be able to join us, Mrs. Henshaw."

"I—we—" Susan glanced over at Kathleen. "We aren't actually sure what we're doing for dinner," she said slowly. "Do you think we should wait for Jed?"

"If you don't think he would mind us going on without him, I think we should accept these people's kind offer," Kathleen said.

"Well, that's just fine. Let's go to the bar and order some rum punch and get to know each other better."

"I'm terribly sorry, but I don't remember your name," Susan confessed to the man by her side.

"You can't remember it. Probably never knew it. My name's Randy Burns."

"Burns—but I thought you were married to Ro."

"Nope. You're thinking of Burt. I'm married to Veronica—that foxy redhead in the green dress who's standing next to the man who is married to Ro."

"Do I hear someone talking about me?" The gray-haired man walking on the other side of Veronica peered around her and grinned at Susan. "Ah, Mrs. Henshaw. Good to see you again. Although, of course, the circumstances could be better."

"Call me Susan, please, and it's nice to see you again. And particularly nice of you all to think of us when you were making reservations for dinner."

"Hell, we've been thinking of you all day long. The girls are keeping themselves amused trying to figure out this murder thing. Cardplayers are good at puzzles, you know. We think we have an edge on the rest of the guests here."

Susan smiled. Lila's prediction that guests would get involved in trying to figure out who murdered Allison had been right on the mark. "I'm sure Kathleen and I will be interested in what you've all come up with," she said.

"Then let's find a place to sit, get us some drinks and something to munch on, and have a nice chat."

"I'll have a white wine spritzer," Susan said.

"You're not in Connecticut, for heaven's sake. Have a rum punch," Randy said. "This place makes the best rum punch in the Caribbean."

"And he should know. He's tried them all in his time," Burt said, sitting down between Susan and Kathleen.

"It is good," Susan admitted. "But—"

"But what? You find a place that has good rum punch, you drink rum punch," Randy said. "Bring a glass for everyone at the table," he called out to the bartender.

Apparently the order was specific enough. Six large glasses of rum punch appeared so quickly that Susan could only assume they had been poured and waiting.

"How about an assortment of those things on sticks?" Randy yelled out to the departing waiter.

"You'll have to excuse my husband, Susan. Since he retired

he's decided that manners don't matter," Veronica explained, leaning around Kathleen to make herself heard.

"Spent thirty-three years doing what other people wanted me to do," Randy explained. "Now I do what I want to do. Know I'm not gonna live forever, so I'm spending the time I've got left living for myself."

"Perhaps you're being just a little insensitive," Burt suggested. "Considering that there's been a death and all."

"Sorry." Randy took the cherry out of his drink with a shaking hand and managed to find his mouth. "Love these little buggers, even if they are full of sugar."

Susan, thinking that Randy apparently had more than enough alcohol already, was glad when the selection of "things on sticks" arrived as promptly as their drinks. "How long have you four known each other?" she asked, picking up a skewer loaded with fruit and chicken.

"Over thirty years. We met when Ro and Veronica shared a room in the maternity ward at Sibley Hospital in Washington, D.C. Ro'd just had Ronald, our oldest boy. Veronica was there with her second: Molly. We talked about those two kids getting married one day."

"And did they?" Susan asked.

"Fat chance. Little Molly—well, she's not so little now—she's been married three times, all of them losers. And Ronald, the apple of his mother's eye, is gay. He's been in a relationship with the same man for almost ten years. Nice guy, real nice guy. He's an endocrinologist. Strange how things work out, isn't it?"

Susan could only agree.

# TWENTY-ONE

CONSIDERING THE FACT THAT MURDER WAS THE TOPIC OF the hour, dinner was surprisingly festive. Susan thought that the large quantity of rum consumed undoubtedly contributed to the conviviality of the group. No one seemed to have any new information, but everyone had theories, which they defended energetically.

"I can see why they love playing bridge," Susan said. "They're the most competitive foursome I've ever met. I had thought the cards just might be an excuse to be social and drink, but I'll bet they all play to win."

Susan and Kathleen were strolling on the beach, killing time until the last guests went to bed.

"You know what was interesting?" Kathleen said. "Veronica's husband—what's his name?"

"Randy."

"He didn't drink."

"Of course he did! He even ordered most of the drinks."

"He ordered them, but he didn't drink them."

"Who did?" Susan asked.

"Veronica. She kept exchanging her empty glass for his full one. The first time I saw her do it, I thought he might not have noticed. But the second time she did it, he looked over at her and smiled."

"So she was drinking two rum punches for every one that the rest of us had," Susan said.

"Yes."

"Lord, I'm amazed she can still stand up."

Kathleen giggled. "Actually, she was sitting down when we left her. Perhaps they'll just call James and he will carry her to her cabin."

"It's strange that Randy would pretend to be drinking," Susan mused.

"Maybe he's a reformed alcoholic and doesn't want anyone to know."

"I suppose that's possible, although, in my experience, people who give up anything are unlikely to keep the news to themselves. The reformed alcoholics I know usually insist on talking about how their lives have changed in minute detail—usually while I'm enjoying a glass of wine."

"I know what you mean. Maybe Veronica is the alcoholic—prereform—and Randy is helping her to hide her addiction."

"Then he's the codependent every addict dreams of finding."

"Yeah, it's probably too weird to be true."

"But we really don't know much about these people," Susan said. "Almost anything could be true."

"I suppose. Did you learn anything tonight?"

"Not really. What about you?"

"Nope." Kathleen bent down to pick up a small white disk from the sand.

"What's that?"

"Sea urchin shell. Funny that they're so black and dangerous when they're alive, and the shell is so pale, fragile, and elegant."

"Hmm." Susan examined the shell in her friend's hand for a moment. "Think we should go back?"

"Probably. If everyone's not in bed yet, at least most of the people who are still up have probably had enough rum punch not to pay any attention to what we're doing."

"Good. I'll be glad to get this started. As anxious as I am to poke around Allison's things, I can't imagine how we're going to do it in the dark. And we can't risk turning on a light. The shutters on the windows offer a fair amount of privacy, but anyone outside would be able to see lights turned on in the cottage."

"We'll use flashlights."

"Where will we get flashlights?"

"They are in the nightstands on either side of the bed. At least they are in our cottage."

"You're kidding!"

"No. I guess the power goes out a lot here. Hadn't you noticed all the candles scattered around?"

"Sure, but I thought of them as romantic."

"They're also practical."

"I guess. So we'll stop in your cottage, pick up the flashlights, and if no one is around, go see what Allison brought here."

"Sounds good to me. Let's go."


Allison's cottage was immaculate. Two pairs of sandals lined up next to the door and folded beach towels lying on the couch were the only immediate signs of her occupation.

"Do you think someone's cleaned up her stuff?" Kathleen whispered.

"I don't know. The bedroom's upstairs. Let's go up."

The bedroom looked more occupied, with clothing strewn about, books lying open next to the bed, cosmetics and creams crowded together on the small dresser.

"Do you think we can risk turning on a light?" Kathleen asked.

Susan walked over to the doors to the balcony. "I think it's risky. Someone might see them. But the balcony faces the water. If we open these, the moonlight will shine in, and if we keep the flashlights aimed at the floor, I don't see how anyone outside will know we're here."

Kathleen had picked up a little tub of moisturizer and was examining the label. "This stuff sells for hundreds of dollars an ounce. I guess Allison was doing pretty well financially."

"Listen, it may have been years since I saw her, but I have no doubt that she had had every tuck, lift, peel, and injection ever invented. A few hundred dollars spent on cream would have been the least of it. She probably thought of it as protecting her investment."

"Was she always gorgeous?" Kathleen asked, opening the dresser drawer and beginning to rummage through an extensive collection of lacy underwear.

Susan walked over to her side and offered to help. "Not even pretty. Wow! Looks like she was ready for a romantic evening or two."

"Or a dozen," Kathleen said, picking up a tiny thong made entirely from black Chantilly lace and dropping it back onto the silky pile.

"Jerry has nothing to do with this—this stuff," Susan said.

"I—I don't know anything anymore," Kathleen said sadly.

"Kath—"

"I know. This is no time to give up. We're just beginning. We have to help Jerry. Etc. Etc." She slammed shut the top dresser drawer and opened the one below it.

Susan grabbed her friend's hand. "Shhhh!"

"I—"

"Shhh!" Susan repeated. "I thought I heard a sound downstairs!"

Kathleen clicked off her flashlight and froze.

"Could have been the wind. I'll go down and check it out."

"But—"

Susan had slipped down the stairs before Kathleen could finish. She was back in less than a minute.

"Can't see anything and the door's still closed. Must have been the wind or something outside."

"Or someone outside."

"Maybe someone who doesn't want to be seen any more than we do."

"Maybe someone looking for something," Kathleen said, returning to her search through Allison's drawers.

Susan went into the bathroom and looked through the prescription bottles scattered among the expensive cosmetics before returning to the bedroom.

"Learn anything?" Kathleen was going through a pile of bikinis on the dresser top.

"Nothing interesting. Allison had some sleeping problems, took lots of vitamins, and was on hormone replacement therapy."

"Nothing interesting," Kathleen agreed, sweeping the pile of swimsuits back into the drawer. "Too bad Allison didn't keep a diary telling us all about her life."

"I can't believe it."

Kathleen turned and discovered Susan standing by the bed, the drawer to the nightstand open, a leather-bound book in her hand. "What's that?"

"I think it's that diary you were yearning for." She directed the light onto the book and flipped through the pages. "And it looks like she's been writing in it daily ever since January first."

"Sensational!" Kathleen paused a moment. "I think I hear something outside again. Grab that diary and let's get out of here."

Susan nodded, tucked the book inside of her shirt, and the two women hurried down the stairs, across the first floor, and out the door, running right into James and his female companion.

"Oh!" Susan felt the diary slip southward. "Hi. We're—we—"

"We were just looking around," Kathleen said. "And now we're done. Good night." She grabbed Susan's arm and pulled her back toward their own cottages.

"I—yes, good night," Susan called out, clutching her midriff and holding on to the book. "Boy, do you have a lot of nerve!" she whispered to her friend. "I'd probably still be back there trying to explain what we were doing if you hadn't just brazened it out."

"They were glad we didn't hang around. They had no business being there, either."

"Oh." Susan turned and looked back at the row of two-story cottages. "Good point. I hadn't thought of that. Oh, hurry. Let's get inside."

"What?"

"Just go!"

"What was all that about?" Kathleen asked, as Susan carefully closed the door to her cottage behind them.

"Someone was standing on the balcony of the Parkers' cottage, looking at us through a pair of binoculars."

"Oh, no. Who was it?"

"I have no idea. Whoever it was seemed to be wearing one of those white terry cloth robes that hang in all the bathrooms here. It's a pretty good disguise. One person wearing one in the dark looks pretty much like the next person."

"That's true."

"Maybe they didn't recognize us."

"We did come straight back to your cottage," Kathleen reminded her. "Whoever's up there could make a pretty intelligent guess."

Susan frowned. "Oh, well, nothing we can do about that

now. Besides, maybe this will tell us who killed Allison." She pulled the notebook from beneath her shirt.

"Great."

"Hey, I was wondering where you two had vanished to." Jed walked out of the bathroom, a towel wrapped around his waist and a comb in his hand. "I asked around and no one had seen you since dinnertime."

"Did you get something to eat?" Susan asked, reverting to concerned wife.

"How's Jerry?" Kathleen asked, feeling the same thing. "Oh, my goodness, I was supposed to bring him dinner!"

"He's fine. We had dinner together. The food wasn't as good as it is here, but there was a lot of it. His biggest problem is boredom."

"Boredom?" Kathleen asked.

"Yes. The lawyer we hired has Jerry writing out everything he can remember about Allison. I thought Jerry would object, but he seemed delighted to have something to do."

"I wonder if we could get a copy of whatever he writes," Susan said.

"We could ask." Jed had pulled the robe off the wall hook and was slipping into it as he spoke. "Kath, the lawyer—his name is Jude Armstrong—wanted to talk to you as soon as possible. I suggested breakfast tomorrow. At seven. That's when the restaurant opens," he added somewhat sheepishly. "I know I shouldn't make appointments for you, but he wanted to see you before he visits Jerry and—"

"No, I'm glad you did. I'll ask for a wake-up call."

"That's right. You'll be up late tonight reading," Susan said, going over to her side of the bed and picking up a paperback with a bright cover and a clever title. "You wanted to borrow this, remember?" She gave Kathleen the book along with Allison's diary. "It's a real page-turner."

"But don't you want to read it first?" Kathleen asked.

"No. I'm going to go to bed. I'll get it back in the morning. Okay?"

"First thing in the morning," Kathleen agreed.

# TWENTY-TWO

SUSAN SLEPT BADLY THAT NIGHT, ROLLING AROUND SEARCH-
ing for a comfortable spot in bed, flipping her pillow so many
times that Jed, the mildest of husbands, finally protested and
threatened to find a comfortable lounge outside for her to
sleep on. Susan had gotten up, showered, and returned to bed
only to fall into a deep sleep.

When she woke up, the sun was shining through the louvers over the windows and Jed was gone. She could hear
the cheerful voices of people strolling by on their way to breakfast. She sat up. Breakfast! Kathleen! The diary! Susan slipped
from the bed and hurried to the bathroom. Ten minutes later,
she discovered Jed in the process of demolishing a large omelet and plantain fries.

"Want some coffee?" he asked, pulling back a chair for
his wife.

"Yes. And food. What's that?"

"Crab omelet. Fabulous. I highly recommend it."

"Then that's what I'll have—with fruit," she said to the
waitress who had appeared by their table.

"Can't beat the service here," Jed mused as their waitress
hurried off to the kitchen with his wife's order.

"One of the things people keep saying is that everyone on
the island—the natives—wants to work here and that they

*161*

work very hard to keep their jobs once they have them." Susan frowned.

"You look like you just had an idea," her husband said.

"I did." Susan didn't bother to explain. "Have you seen
Kathleen this morning?"

"Yes, she and Jerry's lawyer were just leaving as I arrived
for breakfast. They were going off to see Jerry. She said to tell
you that she'll be back as soon as possible and that she left the
beach bag in her cottage for you." He rummaged through the
pockets of his shorts and then handed her a key. "She said to
give you this."

"The key to her cottage."

Jed shrugged. "I guess so. But you are going to hang
around long enough to eat, aren't you?"

Susan was dying to see what was in the diary she had discovered last night, and she was pretty sure that Kathleen had
read it and left it in Allison's beach bag back at her cottage.
But they were on vacation, Jed had looked lonely sitting all
alone, and, besides, she was starving. "Of course," she answered, smiling at him.

"Then I'm going to have another cup of coffee and chat
with my wife."

Susan's smile vanished. "It hasn't been a great vacation,
has it?"

"Not quite what we planned. I keep wondering what's going to happen if we have to go home before Jerry is cleared."

Susan leaned across the table, trying to prevent their conversation from being overheard. "Jed! We couldn't leave him
here!"

"Kathleen is going to have to get home to her kids. And
I'm due back at work in less than a week. Susan, no one
knows how long it's going to take to get Jerry free."

"What does his lawyer think?"

"He's not optimistic. The authorities have one suspect. They're not busy looking for another. The truth is that unless you and Kathleen come up with someone else, Jerry's going to be tried for murder."

"Does he know that?"

"He's a smart guy, Susan."

"How is he doing really?"

"Not bad. The lawyer is good, and Jerry feels confident that he'll be well represented if this does go to trial. Strangely enough, he seems more worried about Kathleen than himself."

"Sounds like he has his priorities wrong. Kathleen's not going to be okay until he's okay."

"I've told him the same thing, but he keeps worrying about her. Damn." Jed put down his fork. "I can't tell you how much I wish he could talk with us without being overheard."

"Can't the embassy do something about that? Isn't Jerry entitled to some privacy?"

"I get the impression that they're doing the best they can. And Jerry's lawyer seems to think things might improve— and you might find the real killer."

"You don't believe that."

"You and Kathleen don't know anyone here. You don't have any contacts in the police department. Susan, we're in a foreign country, for heaven's sake. I know you're doing the best you can, but—"

"I know what you're saying, Jed, and I've been worried about that, too, but what I need is an ally who knows the—the lay of the land around here. And I think I've figured out who just might help us."

"Who?"

"That doesn't matter now," she answered, smiling at the woman who had brought her food. "But I've got a question, Jed."

"What?"

She waited until they were alone to ask it. "I don't know what you think about Allison. Did you like her?"

"Not particularly. And I can tell you something else." He leaned closer and lowered his voice. "Jerry didn't like her at all."

Susan looked up from her dish of mangoes. "Back when he was married to June?"

Jed nodded. "I remember when Allison introduced him to her sister. He came back to the office and said something about being surprised that such an awful girl could have such a wonderful sister."

"I never guessed."

"Well, he didn't mention it again until a few years after he and June were married. They didn't live in the same town. Allison didn't come to visit much. To tell you the truth, her name just didn't come up."

"Why didn't you like her?" Susan asked.

Jed frowned. "She flirted."

"With you?"

"With me. Probably with all men."

"Really? She always struck me as so . . . I don't know . . . so homely and dull. She wore such dowdy clothing."

"Just because a woman doesn't wear designer clothing doesn't mean she isn't interested in men. At least, not in my experience."

Susan opened her mouth to ask exactly what experience he was referring to, but realizing that changing the subject wouldn't be productive, she resisted. "Did she actually make a pass at you?"

"Not really. She just flirted."

"Did she make a pass at Jerry?"

"It's possible. I know that he was very uncomfortable being with her for a while."

"When June was alive?"

"After she died."

"How soon after she died?" Susan asked.

"Sue, you know I'm not as observant about this type of thing as you are. And I don't remember exactly. I do remember all four of us going to dinner at the Hancock Inn sometime after June had died."

"We all went there the day after her funeral."

"I'd forgotten that evening. What a horrible time. I really thought Jerry was going to crack up. A man shouldn't have to live with that much pain."

Susan nodded. "It was awful, wasn't it? I remember we went out because no one wanted to cook and I thought it would be a good idea if Jerry got away from the house. I was completely wrong, of course. I still remember Jerry sitting at the table, looking down at his cranberry-glazed Cornish game hen with tears pouring down his cheeks. I haven't ordered that meal at the inn since that dinner."

"That isn't the dinner I'm thinking about," Jed said. "This was later. Allison had come out from the city to pick up some of June's things."

"She did that a couple of times," Susan said. "But go on. Why did you think Jerry was uncomfortable with Allison?"

"He told me so. He was glad she was going to have some of June's things, but he wished she could do it without insisting on visiting him. He even tried to be away on business when she was in town."

"But she didn't stay in the house with him," Susan said. "He moved into that condo almost immediately."

"That's true. I don't remember where Allison stayed."

"I don't think she ever spent the night in Hancock after the week of June's funeral. But you're saying that Jerry didn't like seeing her."

"Hated it. At the time I thought that she reminded him of June and the accident and all, but later he said something that made me wonder if maybe Allison had been hoping to take June's place."

"She was in love with Jerry?"

"I got the impression that he thought so."

"Or maybe she just wanted what her sister had had," Susan mused, thinking of the book Allison was supposed to have written.

"I don't know," Jed said. "Do you want to go see Jerry?"

"Yes, definitely. When are you going?"

"This morning. But I'm playing gofer. Whatever Jerry and Jude want or need, I get or do. So I don't know if I'll even see him."

"And Kathleen's there now," Susan said. "Why don't you go see if they need anything now and I'll hang out here? I have a few things to do."

"Okay. You finish your breakfast and do whatever you're planning, and I'll head on into town. You know, we need a place to leave messages for each other," Jed said. "I spend a lot of time looking for either you or Kathleen. Why don't you just write where you're going on the bathroom mirror before you take off?" He suggested their usual method of communicating.

Susan shook her head. "No, the women who clean the cottages would read them."

"Why would that be a problem?"

"We really don't know who was involved in Allison's murder," Susan reminded him. "It doesn't make any sense that any of the staff were involved, but you never know."

"Okay. If you want to leave me a message, write it in the front cover of the book I'm reading—the Grisham on my side of the bed—and I'll write to you there, too. Okay?"

"Pretty smart. Are you going right away?"

"Yup." Jed stood up and paused. "Listen, Susan . . ."

"I will be careful," she assured him, offering her cheek for a good-bye kiss.

"I'm depending on that." He leaned down to kiss her before leaving.

Susan concentrated on her breakfast. It was delicious and she was hungry, so she didn't become aware of the difference between today and yesterday until she had finished her eggs and was spearing the last chunk of pineapple with her fork. Then she looked up and scanned the area. The restaurant was about one-third empty, and many of the diners were finishing their meals, as well.

And no one was paying any attention to her. No one was coming up to her to tell her about Allison. No one was asking her about the murder. It was hard to believe that less than twelve hours ago, most of the people eating here now had been eager to discuss the murder and the time they had spent with Allison. Susan put down her fork and frowned. What had changed?

She placed her napkin beside her plate and stood up. She felt in her pocket for the key Kathleen had given Jed and smiled. She was going to discover what Allison had written in her diary. Susan headed for the Gordons' cottage.

The key Susan pulled from her pocket was adorned with a wooden bird painted black. She put it into the small hole under the doorknob and turned. Nothing happened. She took it out, put it back in, and tried again. Nothing. Susan frowned, shook the doorknob, and was shocked when the door swung open, revealing the inside of the cottage. Susan hurried in and closed the door behind her, taking care to turn the dead bolt.

The room had not yet been cleaned. The bed was unmade, a damp towel was flung across the desk chair, and Allison's big straw bag had been placed in the middle of the dresser.

Susan hurried over to the bag and rummaged through it. No diary! She took a deep breath, looked around, and began to search the room. It was a small cottage, and ten minutes later Susan was sure of one thing: The diary wasn't here.

# TWENTY-THREE

SUSAN WAS SITTING ON THE EDGE OF THE UNMADE BED PLAY-ing with the unused key when Kathleen walked in the door.

"What does that open?" Kathleen asked.

"Who knows," Susan answered, tossing it on the nightstand. "Do you have it?" she asked immediately.

"Have what?"

"Allison's diary."

"Of course not. It's in the beach bag. I left it here for you. Didn't Jed tell you?"

"It's not here now," Susan explained.

"Are you sure?" Kathleen asked.

"Yes, positive."

"Someone must have come in here and taken it." Kathleen walked around the room, pulling open drawers and peering into them. "It doesn't look as though anything else is missing. Why would someone take that diary and nothing else? And how could anyone have known that we had it?"

"Kathleen, that doesn't matter now. What did it say? You did read it last night, didn't you?"

"Yes, but . . ." She paused.

"But what?"

"It didn't say anything. At least, it didn't say anything significant. It was a diary about food and clothing and exercise and dieting."

"You're kidding."

"No, apparently Allison's New Year's resolution was to lose ten pounds."

"So she's just like every other woman we know," Susan muttered.

"Well, yes—and no. Allison apparently did it."

"No, not like every other woman we know," Susan agreed. "But is that really all there was? No comments about other things in her life? How she ended up vacationing here? Stuff like that? Anything at all about Jerry, or Hancock, or June?"

"Nothing. Really." Kathleen walked over to the window and peeked through the louvers. "Now what do we do?"

Susan frowned. "There are two things I need to do today. First, I want to see Jerry. Do you think he'd like that?"

"According to Jed, his biggest problem is boredom." Kathleen looked back at Susan. "I'm sure Jerry'd love to see you, but you can't get any information from him. It's like Jed said, he's never alone. I—well, I wonder if you wouldn't be better off here talking to people and trying to find out if anyone saw anything the night Allison was killed."

"You know, everyone seems to want to talk to me about the time they spent with Allison, but, except for Ro, no one has told me anything significant about that night. Maybe I do need to stay here, but I'd hate it if Jerry thought I was ignoring him."

"Oh, Susan, you know Jerry would never think that! And he's so confident that he'll be released."

"Then I'd better get to work here and see what I can dig up. The next time you see him, you'll give him my best."

"Of course!" Kathleen glanced at her watch. "I told Jerry I'd order more meals for him. Guess I'd better get going. I'm going to bring him a late breakfast. I'll find you as soon as I get back. Okay?"

"Sure. I'll be around." Susan spoke her last words to Kathleen's back as her friend hurried off. Susan sighed and sat down on the bed, feeling completely alone.

She wasn't going to look further for Allison's diary. If Kathleen hadn't destroyed it altogether, she would have hidden it in a place where it wouldn't easily be found. Whatever Allison had written must have been incriminating. So incriminating that Kathleen didn't dare share it with Susan.

Susan was shocked and confused. She needed time to think and she needed to keep investigating. She couldn't imagine that it was possible to do both at the same time. Unless . . .

It was the best thought she'd had in days: time for a massage. It would relax her, and for once, a talkative masseuse would be a plus instead of an annoyance. She hurried off to the gift shop, determined to snag the first free appointment of the day.

"A cancellation. It's serendipity, Mrs. Henshaw. We just had a cancellation. Lourdes will be able to take you immediately."

"That's wonderful. I'll go on back to my cottage and get ready."

"Excellent. Lourdes just left to get some supplies. I'll send her over as soon as she returns."

"I'll be waiting," Susan assured her as she left the little gift shop.

She didn't have long to wait. Lourdes was at her door, folding massage table at her side, in minutes. Susan greeted her and let her in.

"Where you want me to set this up?"

"Same place as last time," Susan said, pointing. There was very little extra floor space in the cottage. "Can you think of any other place?"

"On deck outside is possible. I keep you covered with towel

while I work. The big cottages—their decks are more private. I set up my table out there and guests can have massages in fresh air."

"Oh, that's nice, isn't it? But I think in here would be just fine."

Lourdes flipped open the table and laid a couple of soft, thick towels on it, setting her lotions and oils up on the nearby dresser while Susan climbed on and settled into place. "Your vacation not going well," Lourdes said, running her hands over Susan's naked shoulders. "Your muscles tighter than before."

"Yes, well, it's been difficult."

"Murder always difficult. Makes problems for many people. Not just for murdered people."

Susan sure wasn't going to disagree with that. "I'm worried about my friends," she admitted.

"You should worry. Police on this island—pah, they no good. They lock up your friend. You worry. You worry plenty."

Susan's stomach turned over. But she had to concentrate. "The last time I had a massage, Allison—the woman who died—had failed to keep her appointment with you. But you did give her massages, didn't you?" she asked.

"Yes, every day since she arrive except for that day. She take care of her body, that woman. How she look, how she feel—it matter plenty to her."

"She was in great shape, wasn't she?" Susan said.

"Yes. She work at it. She say she work at her whole life. That may be true. Nothing come easy to some people."

"That is true," Susan agreed. "Did she tell you much about her life?"

"Yes. Some people like silence while I work. But not that woman. She was a talker."

"What did she say?"

"You think I tell you something to help free your friend." It was a statement, not a question.

"I hope you will," Susan admitted. "I don't know the other guests, or the staff, or the island police."

"But you know Ms. Allison McAllister, yes?"

"I knew her long ago," Susan admitted. "But it had been years since I saw her, so many years that I didn't even recognize her."

"She worked on herself, that one. She tell me she spent much of her life doing what other people tell her to do. Then she change and spend life taking care of herself."

"I wonder what happened that caused her to change."

"A death. A great love."

"What?" Susan jerked her head up.

Lourdes applied firm pressure to Susan's shoulders. "You not relaxing. We should not talk about this if it upset you. Massage do you no good if you not relaxed."

"The more I know about Allison, the more relaxed I will be," Susan assured her.

"Maybe that not true. Maybe you know more, you learn more, your friend look more and more guilty."

"I won't believe that. I've known Jerry for decades. I know he would not kill anyone."

"We women are sometimes very foolish when it comes to the men in our lives."

"Jerry is a friend. Not the man in my life," Susan said.

"I not talking about Jerry. I not talking about you. I talk about Ms. Allison McAllister. She foolish. She fall in love with this man Jerry who is now under arrest."

"She told you that?"

"Yes. She tell me that. And she tell me more."

"What? What did she tell you?"

"She tell me this man in love with her, too."

"I don't think that's true."

"Then why that man spend so much time with her?"

"What time? How much time? How do you know he spent any time at all with her? We arrived the day before she was killed."

"You and Mr. Henshaw arrived the day before she was killed. But Mr. and Mrs. Gordon. They arrive before you."

"That's true. But still . . . they got here in the middle of the day. And they went into town for dinner that first night."

"They go into town for dinner because Mr. Jerry Gordon did not want to see Ms. Allison McAllister. At least, that what she say."

"To who? Whom? Whom did she say that to?" Susan finally managed to ask a question in what she hoped was a grammatical manner.

"She say that to him."

Lourdes was working on Susan's left ankle, and for a moment, Susan couldn't believe what she had heard. "To him? Allison said that to him? When?"

"When she saw him in office. I was there. I help out in office sometimes in evening when my massage appointments finished and Lila want to take a break or need to check on work in kitchen."

"They came in together?" Susan asked.

"No, no. Your friend, Mr. Jerry Gordon, come in first. He ask me to get a cab for him and his wife. They want to see the town is what he says."

"So you called him a cab."

"I call the company that this place recommends, and they say that they can send a car in half an hour. Mr. Jerry Gordon say that just fine and he will go tell his wife. But then, before he can leave, Ms. Allison McAllister come in."

"Was she looking for him or did she just happen to come in at the same time?" Susan asked.

For the first time, Lourdes hesitated before answering. "I think she come in looking for him. She not seemed to be surprised that he there, and she start talking to him right away."

"What did she say?"

"She say he not be able to run away from her again."

"Again? You're sure she said again?"

"I sure. Then he say that he come to island to be with his wife and he going to be with wife no matter what. And she say ha."

"Ha! Like a sarcastic ha? Like she didn't believe him?"

"She say ha. I do not know what she mean, but she look angry and he look angry. And then he say that she should not be here. That she have things to do someplace else."

"What? He said what?"

"He say that Ms. Allison McAllister should not be here. That Ms. Allison McAllister has things to do somewhere else."

"And did she say anything to that?" Susan asked, hoping the answer was not another *ha*.

"She say that what he think and that he wrong. That she does have things to do and they have to be done here. And he say that she lied to him, that he was a fool, that he hoped she died. And he left. He angry," Lourdes added in case Susan had missed the point.

Susan grabbed the towel to gain as much privacy as possible under the circumstances and rolled over onto her back. "Have you told the police any of this?"

"The police on this island are idiots. All idiots. I tell them nothing," Lourdes answered proudly.

"Thank goodness for that," Susan said.

"But James, he nearby in employees' lounge. He hear, too. I do not know what he tell anyone."

Susan rolled back over onto her stomach. She wasn't relaxed. Her shoulders still ached. But she knew whom she had to see next.

# TWENTY-FOUR

Unfortunately James wasn't available. "Out teaching a guest to use a scuba tank," the young man said. He had taken James's place arranging towels on the chairs and lounges around the pool. "He be back soon, I hope. I'm running out of towels."

Susan just smiled and continued on toward the resort's office. If she couldn't see James right away, she'd have to make do with Jerry.

Lila looked up from her paperwork and put a professional smile on her face when Susan walked in the open doorway of the resort's small office. "Mrs. Henshaw. Can I help you?"

"I hope so. I want to see Jerry Gordon. Could you call me a taxi and then tell the driver where I'm going? I'm afraid I don't know exactly where Jerry's being held."

"I would be happy to, but if he doesn't know you're coming, you may not be allowed to see him. It's not open house down at the embassy, you know."

Susan, who never knew exactly how to react to people who were polite by profession, realized that she didn't like this woman very much. "I'll take my chances," she answered, smiling back.

"Then I'll order you a taxi. Do you want the driver to wait for you, or would you rather call another cab when you want to return? Waiting costs next to nothing, I might add. There are few planes arriving at this time of the day, and the driver would most likely be idle if you weren't using his services."

"Then I'd like him to wait," Susan decided. "I'll just go get my purse and I'll be back here in a moment."

"That will be fine."

Susan didn't see either Jed or Kathleen on the way to her cottage. She took a few minutes to write Jed a message in his book telling him where she was going and what time she was leaving. Kathleen, she decided, would most likely figure it out on her own. The taxi was waiting for her when she arrived back at the office. She climbed in the back of the 1964 Chevrolet Biscayne and gasped as the driver zoomed off, causing a blizzard of coral pebbles to fly into the air behind them.

Since Susan and Jed had arrived at Compass Bay in the dark, this was the first time she was seeing any part of the island other than the resort itself or its neighboring beaches. She was stunned by its beauty and its poverty. The taxi driver sped down the narrow roads, inadequately paved and in danger of crumbling into the sandy soil or being reclaimed by indigenous tropical plants. Children, accompanied by scrawny dogs, hung out in bare yards around broken-down houses. Big black birds scavenged in open garbage cans. Just when Susan began to wonder where the town was located, they arrived in it.

The town was charming. Comprised of a few streets of brightly colored storefronts and open-air restaurants, it was only slightly more crowded than the country they had been passing through. At the end of the main street, a few buildings had been built from gray stone on an outcropping of rock over the ocean. The cab stopped in front of the largest of these buildings, and the driver turned around and smiled at Susan.

"I wait, yes?"

"Yes, you wait. I'll be back soon."

"Take your time," he urged, helping her from the car. "Take your time." He leaned against the hood of his car, crossed his arms, and closed his eyes.

Susan turned and walked up the stone steps to wooden French doors standing open to catch the breezes coming off the water. No one seemed to be around, and she continued on into the building, her sandals slapping on the tile floor. Susan walked down the long center hallway lined with offices. She peered in open doorways, seeing desks littered with papers, but the employees were evidently somewhere else.

Continuing on through the hallway, she came to another pair of French doors, which opened onto a large porch where a party was in progress. About thirty people were sitting around, talking, laughing, and consuming Danish pastry along with mugs of coffee and dainty glass cups filled with pink punch. Susan stopped, unwilling to break into the group. Jerry was being held somewhere in the building. She'd just go back outside and see if she could figure out where.

"May I help you?" A tall woman with long flowing gray hair and darkly tanned skin detached herself from the group and came up to Susan.

"I'm looking for Jerry Gordon. I understand he's here somewhere." Susan glanced at the happy gathering before continuing. "I'm Susan Henshaw. I'm a friend of Jerry—"

"I know exactly who you are, Mrs. Henshaw. And I'm sure Mr. Gordon will be very happy to see you. He's being held on the ground floor. Well, it's actually a basement. I'd be happy to take you there."

"But your party—" Susan began.

"Is drawing to a close. One of our colleagues is getting married and moving back to the mainland. We're celebrating his good fortune and mourning his coming sadness."

"I don't understand."

"Everyone is happy to see him married, but we will miss

him and he will miss the island. This is a remarkable place to live, Mrs. Henshaw—not for everyone, no doubt—but those of us who fit in here have found something special, and most of us feel a keen sense of loss when forced to give it up." She smiled and then pointed down the hallway. "I'm neglecting my manners. I'm Frances Adams. I'm the highest-ranked United States government employee on the island."

"Then you're the woman who managed to have Jerry imprisoned here rather than in the local jail," Susan said.

"Yes. Don't give me too much credit. The police department here is unwilling to antagonize the wealthier people on the island, some of whom are the owners of the few places we have like Compass Bay. They were happy to have our help. If anything goes wrong during Mr. Gordon's incarceration, they will not be to blame."

Susan walked behind Frances Adams and considered her elegance and style. Susan had always admired women who didn't deny their age by dyeing their hair and then wearing it in a puffy, short, middle-aged style, but flaunted their streaks of gray and managed to turn them into something individual and even sexy. She doubted if she would have the nerve to adopt the style herself, but she admired those who did. "Well, I'm glad you helped Jerry. I understand the jail here is pretty awful."

"Worse than awful." Frances Adams turned a corner and started down a wide stone stairway, worn by many decades of use. "How is your investigation coming? Have you found any other viable suspects . . . if you don't mind my asking," she added when Susan didn't answer immediately.

"I don't mind you asking, but I was just wondering how you know I'm looking into Allison's murder."

"Mr. Gordon told me. He says you have solved murders in the States. I believe he is counting on you to get him out of this situation."

Susan began to chew off her lipstick. "I'm doing the best I can, but . . . The problem is that I know Jerry and I know Kathleen, his wife now, and I knew his first wife, June. June was Allison's sister and I thought I knew Allison. I mean the Allison I knew then isn't the Allison that I met here."

"Are you saying you believe someone borrowed her identity? That she isn't who she claimed to be?"

"Oh, no, nothing like that. It's just that she's so different from when I used to know her. There's probably nothing odd about it at all. People do change."

"Do you think so? In my experience very few people do change. Not really. Oh, they may look different and many of them claim to be different, but underneath it all they remain the same. It takes an unusual person to actually become someone other than who they started out to be. But you may know much more interesting people than I come across on this little island."

Susan doubted it. She tried to explain. "I know what you mean—sort of—but the Allison I knew years ago wouldn't have inspired enough feeling for someone to have killed her. She was . . . almost negligible. I know that doesn't sound very nice, but . . ."

"It doesn't, but it does make sense. Certainly a person who is murdered must be a person who inspired strong passions—in the killer if no one else."

Susan had never considered this before. They had arrived at the bottom of the stairway. Four uniformed men were sitting around a makeshift table, playing cards. Another man, cradling a large gun in his arms, leaned on the wall next to a metal door. "Is Jerry in there?" Susan asked, nodding toward the door.

"Yes. It's not as bad inside as it looks. Decades ago that space was used to store valuables traveling through the island—

rum, spices, precious metals, and the like. It's secure, but airy.

"Why don't I ask if Mr. Gordon can see you now?"

"I'd appreciate that," Susan answered.

Frances Adams smiled at the armed guard and approached slowly. They spoke for a few minutes. Frances pointed to Susan, the guard looked at her, and Susan looked back. The guard pointed at the cardplayers, who looked around and smiled. Susan smiled back at them and then at the guard. By the time they had all greeted each other, everyone was smiling except for the guard with the gun.

Frances Adams left the guard and walked back to Susan, who thought the smile on Frances's face now looked a bit forced. "You can see him, but the guard at the door is not happy with all Mr. Gordon's visitors. He said that usually prisoners can only be seen by their lawyer and their family. I told him you were almost family, but it didn't help. May I suggest you keep this visit as short as possible?"

"I will," Susan assured her as the guard turned and, with much clanking of old-fashioned skeleton keys, unlocked the door and stood aside for her to enter.

"I'm needed upstairs," Frances Adams said. "When you leave, just follow that corridor." She pointed toward a long stone hallway. "It will lead you back to the front of the building. Please call me if you have any questions . . . or problems," she added, looking over toward the armed guard.

"I will," Susan said, and quickly entered the doorway. The guard followed close on her heels.

Much to Susan's surprise, the room was spacious and light. Stone walls had been stuccoed and painted a soft turquoise. The wall opposite the door boasted three large windows with magnificent views of the sea and some small islands in the distance. The bars on the windows didn't interfere with the beauty of the scene. Although sparsely furnished with a narrow bed, a small table, and two chairs, the room was still attractive and almost cheerful. Jerry was sitting on one of the chairs, which had been drawn up in front of the window on the right, but he rose to greet her with a huge smile on his face.

"Susan, I can't tell you how happy I am to see you."

Susan reached out to hug him and was stunned when the guard grabbed her hands. "Ow!"

"We're not allowed to touch," Jerry said sadly. "She doesn't know the rules," he explained to the guard. "She won't do it again."

"No, I won't," Susan assured him, trying to control her nervousness and her temper. Her wrist was stinging as a result of the man's rough handling.

"You only have a few minutes," he growled, and leaned back against the door, replicating his former position outside the room.

"Sit down. I can't tell you how much I've wanted to see you," Jerry said.

"I've wanted to see you, too. I—"

"Susan, I've been thinking. About my life and my past, and I think that Kathleen and June are very much alike."

"Really . . . I—"

"Yes. In fact, I'm sure of it. The more I think about it the surer I am."

"Well—"

"Of course, you could say the only thing they had in common is that they were both married to me, and that's true, isn't it?"

"Yes, but—"

"But I believe their situation made them alike in many, many ways."

Susan realized she wasn't going to be allowed to speak a full sentence unless she interrupted. "Kathleen isn't—"

"She's much more like June than it may appear at first glance," Jerry said firmly and loudly. "You must realize that she and June are in the same situation, and the end result could be the same."

"You mean Kathleen might die in an accident?" Susan was completely perplexed.

"No talk about death. Visit is at an end," the guard said, putting his gun between Jerry and Susan to emphasize his point.

"But—" Susan cried out.

"This is fine," Jerry said quickly. "You think about what I said, Susan. Think and you'll realize I could be right."

# TWENTY-FIVE

Susan's taxi driver was waiting, leaning against the trunk of his car, eyes closed. Susan started toward him and then stopped. She was upset, and the thought of returning to Compass Bay was completely unappealing. Leaving her driver to continue his nap, she turned and walked toward the center of town.

Jerry and Kathleen, she remembered, had come to town for dinner their first night on the island. She wasn't really hungry, but she was thirsty and nervous; stopping for a drink seemed like an excellent idea. The first restaurant she came to was a run-down bar—a surprisingly active bar considering the time of day—and she continued on to the next. THE COCONUT HUT: DINE IN PARADISE read the brilliantly painted sign above the door. Susan decided she could use a little paradise and went in.

The air-conditioning felt wonderful although she had walked less than a quarter mile, and when the hostess appeared, Susan was happy to be escorted to a small table in the back of the room.

"I don't need a menu. I'll just have a large lemonade and . . . and a glass of ice water," she ordered. The hostess hurried off, and Susan picked up her purse. She probably had a pen, and she wanted to write down what Jerry had said while it was fresh in her mind. Frances Adams had said Jerry was depending on Susan for his release. He must have known she would, if possible, have come to see him. He must have planned what he would say. So why did his words make absolutely no sense?

June and Kathleen had only two things in common: They had both been Jerry's wife, and they both were the mothers of two children by him. Period. They didn't come from the same background. June had been brought up in the suburbs, attended an excellent women's college, and married Jerry soon after graduation. Kathleen grew up in New York City, attended Hunter College, and fulfilled a childhood dream when she joined the police force. Being a suburban housewife had been a natural avocation for June; for Kathleen it was an ongoing struggle. June was domestic by nature and by training. Kathleen took good care of her family and her home because she cared about them, but she had had to learn to do it and it hadn't been easy. Accustomed to meals on the run or take-out in New York City, Kathleen had been unfamiliar with many of the phrases common in cookbooks. It was only recently that Kathleen had managed to pull off large dinner parties with as much ease as June had the first month of her marriage.

Susan picked up the pen she had found in her purse and moved the paper place mat closer, continuing to think about Kathleen and June without writing a word. Of course, there were things about wives that only a husband would know, but Susan couldn't imagine that Jerry had been referring to such private, personal things. They were both good mothers, but their style was different. Although Kathleen seemed more casual than June, she was just as concerned and involved. Like June, she served her time as class mother, but while June brought elaborately decorated cupcakes to class parties, Kathleen found a bakery that made delicious health food bars and passed them out to Emily's and Alex's classmates.

June had never seemed to need anything outside of her home and family. Kathleen had been eager to start her own security company as soon as her youngest was in nursery school. Kathleen loved her life, but sometimes Susan worried that it was too confining. Kathleen needed excitement. And June didn't. June was . . . well, June was dull.

Susan was surprised. She had never thought of June that way. June had seemed perfectly happy to do what was expected, but nothing more, nothing surprising or fun. Susan hadn't been looking for anything else when they had been friends. Busy with two young children, Susan was content to make it through the day without a crisis call from the school nurse or a torrent of sibling rivalry upsetting the balance of family life. But, if June had been alive when Chad and Chrissy were older and less demanding, would she and Susan have remained friends? As she had told Kathleen yesterday, Susan doubted it. Oh, they would have seen each other—their husbands' relationship would have guaranteed that—but close friends? The type of friends she and Kathleen had become? Susan knew it wouldn't have happened.

The waitress delivered a tall glass filled with ice cubes and bright yellow liquid. She had forgotten the water, but this looked so refreshing that Susan didn't complain. She grabbed her drink and downed more than half in a few quick gulps. And gasped.

"There's alcohol in there," she protested, setting down the glass with a bang.

"Rum, triple sec, and Absolut Citron. Just like the sign says," the waitress replied, nodding to the drinks menu posted on the wall. "Call me if you want another," she added before slinking off toward the bar.

Susan blinked a few times and looked down at the glass. It

was cold, it was refreshing, it was delicious. She picked it up again, finished it off, and looked in her purse for money. Appreciative of the mistake the waitress had made, she left a generous tip before heading to the bar to pay her bill.

"I had a lemonade," she explained to the bartender.

"Looked like you needed it when you came in," the bartender replied. He was young, tanned, and blond, and wouldn't have looked out of place playing on Chad's soccer team at Cornell.

"I guess I did," Susan said, paying the reasonable bill.

"Say, don't you have some connection to that man they say murdered his ex-wife that they're holding over at the embassy offices?"

"How do you know that?"

"It's a small island and murder's big news. So, who are you? A relative?"

"I'm a friend. He didn't murder anybody. And the woman who died was the sister of his dead wife, not his ex-wife."

"Really? You know, he and that woman were in here the day she died."

"No, I think he and his wife were here the night before Allison died."

"I make a pretty good living being nice to the customers, lady, but I gotta tell you, you're wrong. He was here with the dead woman. Belinda—that's the woman who waited on you—works days. She had to be at her son's school—some sort of play or something—so I was alone. I waited on them myself. There was a picture of the dead woman in the newspaper. I'm sure it was her here with him. If you know what I mean."

Susan, who was familiar with the poor grammar habits of even the most well educated young people, nodded. "Did you overhear what they were saying? I'm not accusing you of eavesdropping or anything, but it could be important."

"I eavesdrop all the time. That's part of the reason I took this job. I'm a writer. Well," he added modestly, "I want to be a writer. And, let's face it, at twenty-two years old I don't have a hell of a lot of life experience to write about. Came down here to get some. And if I can grab a piece of someone else's life experience, it's just fine with me."

Susan's spirits lifted—someone who could report on Jerry and Allison together. What a find! "So what did you hear?"

"Yeah, well, not a lot. There was a Lakers game on the radio and I sort of spent most of my time listening to that," he explained sheepishly.

"Then did you notice anything about them? Did they appear happy? Sad? Angry with each other?" She added the last question reluctantly.

"All of the above," he answered. "I watched them carefully. A man with a woman he wants to impress is likely to be a good tipper. Didn't want to miss any signals."

"So how did they seem happy and sad at the same time?"

"Not at the same time. It was sort of sequentially."

"Do you remember the sequence? No, wait, first—did you notice if they came in together?"

"They didn't. She came in first. Sat right down where you were sitting this afternoon and ordered the same thing you did. One large lemonade."

Susan wondered if Allison had known about her choice's amazing alcohol content. "Did she seem happy or sad or anything like that?"

"She seemed just like lots of ladies that come in here—impatient. You know, she looked at her watch a lot, shook her foot, tapped on the table."

"Like a woman waiting for a man who's late."

"Yup. You got it."

"Did he keep her waiting for long?" Susan asked.

"Sure did. About half an hour. I thought she was gonna get up and leave when he walked in the door."

"And did she seem glad to see him?"

"Seemed surprised that he'd finally shown up, if you ask me. I was surprised he did, tell you the truth. He didn't look real happy to see her. He sat down and ordered a double Scotch. Not a real popular drink around here. Most people on the island, especially the tourists, stick to drinks with lots of rum and lots of sugar."

"You must have delivered his drink."

"Yes, and a second large lemonade for her," he answered helpfully.

"And they talked? Yelled at each other? Laughed? What?"

"They just stared at each other and drank mostly. Every once in a while one of them would say something to the other, but mostly they just drank. It was a little weird. They made a point of meeting and then might as well have been alone."

Susan wasn't sure what to make of that. If Kathleen's information was to be believed, Jerry and Allison had seen each other recently in New York City, so any awkwardness here wouldn't stem from the time that had passed since they last met. On the other hand, they might have been worried about running into someone they knew. "Did you seat Allison?"

"No, she came in while I was busy with something else. I didn't even see her. She probably seated herself."

Susan turned and looked at the table. Allison had chosen to meet Jerry in a public place. She hadn't been worried about being seen. Her choice of seat could have indicated that she actually wanted someone to witness their meeting. Susan realized that anyone believing Jerry was the murderer could use this against him. If Allison had suspected Jerry might cause her harm, she certainly wouldn't have wanted to be alone with him. She frowned. She had come here to relax, and think, and get a drink. What she was getting was confused.

"You know," the bartender broke into her thoughts. "Now that you've mentioned it, I've been thinking and it's like a little weird that they met here right before he killed her, isn't it?"

"I suppose."

" 'Cause he could have done it after they left here, right? Why wait until that night back at Compass Bay? Why not just off her here?"

"Maybe he didn't want to be seen."

"Hey, drag someone behind one of the buildings here and no one would be likely to see you. You know, that's interesting," he added, apparently intrigued by his own thoughts. "He could've killed her here and he didn't. Why, I wonder."

"I can't imagine."

"Yeah, but you're not a writer. I have a writer's imagination. I can think of lots of reasons. You know what?" he asked, his face brightening. "I think I've just realized something. I think I've had an—an ep—an eppy-something. What is it people call it?"

"Do you mean an epiphany?" Susan asked.

"You got it! An epiphany! That's what I just had. I'm not going to hang around here and wait to get old to have something to write about. I'm gonna write mystery novels. I'm gonna write about people killing people and getting away with it . . . until the last chapter."

"Sounds like a mystery novel to me," Susan agreed, starting toward the door.

The bartender may have found a new career, but she was more puzzled than ever.

# TWENTY-SIX

SUSAN HAD A LOT TO THINK ABOUT ON THE RIDE BACK TO
Compass Bay. She made two decisions. First, she would tell
Kathleen what her conversation with the bartender had revealed. She wanted to know if Jerry had said anything about
his meeting with Allison to his wife. And, second, she would
not mention Jerry's insistence on the similarity between his
two wives to Kathleen. It could only hurt her.

But she couldn't find Kathleen. Jed, enjoying a late lunch
poolside, reported not seeing her all morning, but offered to
buy them both lunch when she appeared. That way, he explained, yawning, Susan could tell them both about her visit
with Jerry. Susan just smiled and walked off. Kathleen wasn't
in her cottage or on the beach. Susan thought for a moment
that she had discovered her stretched out on a lounge by the
bar, but that sunbather turned out to be male.

Susan exchanged greetings with the other guests, but
didn't ask about her friend, not wanting to increase the attention their group was already receiving. She was ready to give
up and rejoin her husband, when she noticed something unusual lying next to one of the kayaks turned upside down beside the dock.

Once Susan realized what she was seeing, she abandoned
her reluctance to draw more attention to their group. She forgot everything in her overwhelming urgency to get help. She

screamed, and within minutes help had arrived—if everyone in the resort, staff and guests, could be called help.

Kathleen was unconscious, sprawled on the beach, half-hidden behind a lightweight plastic kayak. Susan, trying to control her own panic, couldn't see anything obviously wrong—no blood, no bullet holes, no scarves wrapped tightly around her neck—but she was relieved when the female half of the honeymooners identified herself as a doctor and took over the examination.

"Does this woman have diabetes or any sort of condition that might cause her to pass out?" the young woman asked.

"No, nothing like that," Susan assured her.

"No, I see now." The doctor gently cradled Kathleen's head in her bejeweled hand. "She has quite a large egg here. She must have slipped and fallen and hit her head on the stone wall."

Kathleen began to regain consciousness. Susan was slightly amazed to hear her friend say "What happened to me?" just like actors returning to consciousness in movies and on TV. "You fell and hit your head," Susan said, speaking up before anyone else could.

Kathleen looked up at her friend. "My head does hurt. I—can someone help me back to my cottage? This sand isn't very comfortable."

"You shouldn't stand up right away," the doctor insisted, firmly pushing Kathleen's shoulders back into the sand.

"Go get the board! Right away!" Susan recognized Lila's voice. And so, apparently, did her staff. People dashed off, and in moments, James had organized three other men and, with their help, placed Kathleen on a glossy surfboard, and carried her back to her cottage.

Lila and the doctor went in, the carriers came out, and Susan, as well as most of the other guests, waited on the beach for some word. Soon Lila reappeared. "Mrs. Gordon is going to be just fine," she announced.

"I want to see her," Susan spoke up.

"You're Susan Henshaw?" The doctor appeared by Lila's side. "She wants to see you. But she really should be kept quiet. If she shows any signs of concussion . . ."

"I'll give you a yell," Susan answered. "My son played on every school team possible when he was young. I know about concussions."

"Excellent. Then I'll leave her in your hands."

The lights were off in the Gordons' cottage. Kathleen lay on the bed, a damp washcloth folded in half and draped across her forehead. Susan tiptoed across the room, enjoying the cool breeze generated by the ceiling fan. "Kathleen?" Susan whispered.

Kathleen opened her eyes and smiled. "Susan, thank God! Someone hit me!"

Susan dashed to her friend's side. "Are you sure? How do you know? Do you know who did it?"

"I'm sure. I didn't fall, for heaven's sake. I was sitting on one of the kayaks on the beach. It was turned upside down, and someone smacked me on the head with something very hard. I swear I saw stars."

"Do you have any idea who did it? Did you recognize any distinct scent that might offer a clue? Or see anyone out of the corner of your eye? Or anything?"

"No. Nothing. I may have heard someone coming up behind me, but I didn't turn around and look. I wanted to be left alone."

"How long were you unconscious?" Susan asked.

Kathleen languidly lifted her left arm and peered at her watch. "Not terribly long. Maybe half an hour."

"Where were you all morning? Jed said he couldn't find you."

"I took a walk on the beach." Kathleen sighed and closed her eyes again. "I didn't want to see anyone. I'm so worried about Jerry, and I just can't think of anything to do to help him. Except . . ."

"Except what?"

"I don't know. It's probably a stupid idea. I'll tell you about it . . . later."

"Are you feeling nauseous?" Susan asked. "Shall I call the doctor back?"

"No, I'm fine."

"Really?"

"Really. You know, this might help Jerry."

"How?"

"If he's guilty, why would someone want to hurt me? Doesn't it make sense that the murderer hit me over the head? So isn't that proof that Jerry's innocent?"

"I suppose you could say that," Susan agreed reluctantly. If Kathleen, after her experience as a police officer, could believe that, she might actually be suffering from a concussion.

"I think we should call the local police and tell them what happened to me just now," Kathleen insisted, starting to sit up.

"Okay. But you have to lie down. And I need to talk to you before we call anyone. I saw Jerry!"

"How is he?" Kathleen asked as though she hadn't seen her husband herself an hour or so before Susan's visit.

Susan smiled. "He's just fine. He—he sent his love." Well, she told herself, he would have if he hadn't been so busy babbling about the supposed similarities between his two wives. "But I stopped in a bar downtown before coming back here."

"Susan, that doesn't sound like you! Did Jerry say something that upset you?"

"No," Susan lied. "I was thirsty. I ordered lemonade. I had no idea that it would be full of rum and vodka."

Kathleen grinned. "Not a bad surprise."

"Well, I wasn't driving. Anyway, the bartender told me something that surprised me, too."

"That Jerry and Allison met in his bar the afternoon of the day she was killed."

"You know! Kathleen, how do you know that?"

"He told me. Remember I was looking for him that day? Well, I was furious that he had vanished like that without telling me, and that night we had a big argument. I asked him what was going on, and he—" She stopped and looked toward the front door. "Look outside and make sure we can't be overheard before I go on, will you?"

"Of course." Susan leapt up and looked out the door. It was a gorgeous afternoon, and the guests and staff could have been models posing for photographs advertising the joys of Compass Bay. They were swimming, sunning, kayaking, playing cards in the bar. No one was skulking around the Gordons' cottage eavesdropping on Susan and Kathleen. "We're fine," she assured her friend, coming back inside and moving near the bed. "Now go on. You and Jerry had an argument and . . ."

"And he told me that Allison had been following him around ever since we got here. If he sat by the pool, she pulled up a chair close by. If he went for a walk on the beach, she appeared there. He said he had gone into town to get away from her, and she was sitting in the bar he went into as though she was waiting for him to arrive."

"Really? But how would Allison have even known he was going to be in town?"

"I wondered that myself. But I was in the office the other day when the honeymooners—I suppose we should call them the doctor and her husband rather than the honeymooners now—well, they asked Lila to call them a cab to take them to town, and it occurred to me that Allison could have been following Jerry around and overheard him do the same thing. Then she left before he did and just waited for him to run into her there."

"I suppose that's possible. It's an awfully small place. It would be easy for that to happen." Susan thought for a moment. "I think we should call the police and tell them about the person who assaulted you."

"Oh, I do, too. Maybe they'll free Jerry before dinner."

"Kath . . ."

"Susan, I know it's not realistic, but I can hope, can't I?"

"Sure. You stay here. I'll go over to the office and call them."

"Great." Kathleen closed her eyes, and Susan headed off on her errand.

Lila was in the office and she looked up, concerned, when Susan walked in. "Is Mrs. Gordon feeling worse? Shall I call for a doctor?"

"No, Kathleen's fine. She wants to talk to the police. I wonder if you would call them for her."

"Of course. May I ask what's the matter?"

"I think Kathleen should be the person to talk about this," Susan said.

"Of course. There should be an officer at her cottage in a very few minutes. Perhaps the lawyer who is handling Mr. Gordon's case should be called, too." Lila's hand hovered in the air above the phone.

"No, I think just the police. Thanks. I'll go back and tell Kath that they're on the way."

"Good. Mrs. Henshaw . . ."

"Yes?"

"Our island police may not wear fancy uniforms or have a lot of sophisticated equipment, but they're not idiots."

"I—I don't know what you're saying," Susan admitted.

"Just that they are not as credulous as you would like to believe."

"I don't believe that they are anything like that," Susan said firmly, turning and heading back to Kathleen's cottage.

As Lila had promised, two uniformed police officers were on the deck of the cottage almost before Susan had finished telling her friend what Lila had said.

As well as being prompt, they were polite, professional, and completely unwilling to believe Kathleen's story.

"I think you fell and hit your head," the youngest officer stated. "Head injuries can be strange. You may have imagined the big man coming up and hitting you."

"I didn't say anything about a big man! I said someone! How do you think I got this bump on my head if someone didn't hit me?"

"You fell. You hit your head. It happens," the older man said in an offhanded manner.

"I'm telling you that I was assaulted. You should file a report. You should be asking me questions. You should start to look for whomever it was who did this to me! You are holding my husband without any real reason at all, and there is someone loose here who has criminally assaulted me! That person and the murderer could be—very possibly are—the same person! And you're doing nothing!"

"Mrs. Gordon, we are not doing nothing. We will file a report, which will require much paperwork. We will investigate your allegation that this strange man—or woman—knocked you out. If there is a crime here, we will do our very best to find the person who committed it. But there is no connection that I or my partner can see between this and the brutal murder of Miss Allison McAllister. Except for the involvement of your family in both crimes."

"I—what? But that's ridiculous!"

"Not so ridiculous. Let me tell you a story."

Kathleen ground her teeth so tightly that Susan could hear them skid, but she merely nodded and the police officer began.

"Years ago when my father joined the police force, there was another murder on the island. A young woman kill another young woman. She think if this other young woman dead, then the woman's fiancé will fall in love with her and marry her. But he did not love her, and in time, he found another woman to love. So, as you might guess, the woman who murdered his first fiancé murdered the second. That's when we caught her, of course."

"So what? You just proved what I was saying to you! If you think Jerry killed Allison, do you think he assaulted me, too? While you have him locked up? Are you nuts?" she asked, sitting up in bed and scowling at the men.

"This is a small island, Mrs. Gordon, but we have our bad people, too. A person who is locked up, a person of means as your husband appears to be—" He stopped and looked around the luxury cottage before going on. "A person like that could hire a bad person to do these things for him."

"My husband would not hire someone to hurt me!" Kathleen said, standing up and yelling right in the oldest officer's face. "Get out of my cottage. Now!"

"We must file report. We'll be back for you to sign it," the younger man said.

"I won't sign anything," Kathleen said, turning her back on the men. "Now please leave my cottage."

# TWENTY-SEVEN

"YOU SHOULD LIE BACK DOWN," SUSAN SAID, TRYING TO guide Kathleen toward the bed. "Please, Kath. You can't help Jerry unless you take care of yourself."

Kathleen sat on the bed. "I don't seem to be capable of helping Jerry period."

"I'm going to call Frances Adams. Maybe she can help us."

"Who?"

"Frances Adams. The American embassy representative on the island."

"Oh, yes. I met her. That might be a good idea," Kathleen said quietly.

"Are you all right? Are you feeling nauseous? Faint?"

"I'm just terribly tired. You know, I think I will lie down for a while. Maybe take a nap."

"I shouldn't leave you alone."

"You should. I'm okay, Susan. Just unhappy and tired. You go do what you have to do. Maybe you can help Jerry. I sure don't seem to be able to."

"I'll call Ms. Adams."

"And I'll take a nap."

"You shouldn't be alone."

"I'll be fine. One thing about these louvered windows—someone will hear if I call out."

"I guess so. You know one thing that bothers me about this place?"

"What?"

"The lack of phones. I hate the fact that Lila or someone in the office overhears all our conversations."

"We should have brought international cell phones. You can rent them. Jerry actually suggested it, but I didn't want him checking in with work and vetoed the idea. What an idiot I was."

"You had no idea all this was going to happen."

"You can say that again." Kathleen closed her eyes.

"Do you want me to wake you up for dinner?"

"When are you going to eat?"

"Around seven?"

"I'll meet you in the restaurant. Save me a seat."

"Sure. See you then."

"Uh-huh."

Susan smiled. Kathleen was already drifting off to sleep, so she quietly shut the door and started toward the office, stopping to stick her head in the gift shop. James was lounging against the wall, smiling seductively at the attractive young woman who was sitting behind the cash register pretending to work. Susan thanked him for his help in organizing and moving Kathleen, then explained that her friend was resting. "She promised me she would yell out if she needed something. Since you're close by, I wonder if you would just keep an ear out—just in case."

"Of course. Lila expects us to do all we can to help the guests. I'm here until six tonight. If she calls, I'll run."

"Thank you so much," Susan said, thinking that she was going to have a lot to remember when it came time to pass out tips.

Lila was in her office with the door closed. A woman Susan

didn't recognize was manning the desk. "I need to make a phone call," Susan said.

"Of course, Mrs. Henshaw. Do you need a phone book?"

"I want to speak to Frances Adams. She works for the United States embassy office."

"I can get that number for you. We have it right here in this little book." She flipped through the pages of a small, worn notebook and found the number immediately. "I can dial for you. Phones on this island are not what you're used to in the United States."

"Thank you. I'd appreciate that." Susan didn't say any more as the door to Lila's office opened and she came out, followed by the two officers who had been so horrible to Kathleen. In an example of dreadful timing, their appearance coincided with the call going through.

"Ms. Adams," the young woman announced in a tone no one could ignore and handed Susan the receiver.

"Thank you." There was nothing she could do but take the call. "Hello, Ms. Adams. This is Susan Henshaw. . . . Of course, Frances. I—" She paused and looked at her audience. "I'd like to speak to you about something. . . . Wherever it would be convenient. . . . Let me write down the address." The woman who had dialed the embassy for Susan pushed a pencil and paper toward her. "Thank you." Susan wrote quickly. "I'll be there in less than half an hour. Bye." She handed the receiver back. "I must go get my purse and talk to Jed. Could you call me a cab and tell them this is where I need to go? Thanks."

Susan turned and walked away without even acknowledging the police officers' presence. Back at her cottage she found Jed napping after his large lunch. Susan woke him enough to tell him what she was doing and then wrote a note in case he woke up later and couldn't remember a thing she had said. Finally she grabbed her purse and took off.

Susan's cab once again splattered coral chips into the sky as it took off toward town. As they approached the more populated area of the island, her driver made a sharp turn and entered what looked to be jungle. The trees narrowly parted for the dirt road, and the buildings disappeared.

Susan leaned forward so the driver could hear what she said over the noise of his engine. "This isn't the right way!" she yelled. "I'm going to see Frances Adams. She works at the United States embassy offices."

"Yes. Ms. Adams. That's where I take you," he yelled back, swerving to avoid a scrawny black chicken busily pecking at something in the middle of their path.

"This isn't the way to the embassy, is it? We don't seem to be going downtown," Susan called back when she could sit up again.

"Not embassy. Not downtown. Ms. Adams. You wait. You'll see."

For the first time the possibility of kidnapping occurred to Susan. Who had told this driver where to take her? She was alone in a foreign country. No one knew where she was. She could vanish, and no one would ever be the wiser. Jed would look for her. Kathleen would look for her. She wouldn't have succeeded in helping Jerry, and he might rot in a foreign prison. She was busily creating a plot for a B movie, when, pulling the steering wheel sharply to the right, the taxi driver flew between two large stone columns and entered paradise.

It was, quite simply, the most beautiful place Susan had ever seen. Deep green lawns were bracketed by wide beds where tropical flowers rioted. The white pebble drive led up to a pale peach stucco house fronted by a wide mahogany veranda. White stone steps led down to the ground, and Susan could imagine Cole Porter, wearing a white tuxedo jacket, martini in hand, descending to greet his guests.

Instead Frances Adams, in well-worn jeans, a white linen

camp shirt, and pink plastic flip-flops on her feet, appeared at the top of the stairs, waved, and called out a greeting.

The cabdriver slowly approached the house, got out, and opened the door for his passenger. Susan fumbled around in her purse.

"I pick you up. You pay me then."

"That's fine, but how will I call you?"

"Ms. Adams knows how," he explained, and climbed back in his cab and drove off.

"I like that driver," Frances Adams said. "He doesn't make a mess of the drive the way many of the other drivers do."

"This is incredible," Susan said, looking around. From the vantage point of the house, the garden seemed almost to embrace them. "And absolutely gorgeous."

"It had what gardeners call good bones when I arrived; the main beds were laid out and most of the walls built. The house was in disrepair, but still very beautiful. I've lived here for sixteen years and put most of my free time and much of my money into this place. Gardening is a passion.

"But we're not here to talk about me. Come inside. We'll have some tea and talk."

Susan followed her hostess up the broad stairs, through open French doors, and into a spacious hall that ran straight to the rear of the house. The doors at the far end of the hallway were also open, and Susan spied a small swimming pool in the middle of another even more beautiful garden.

"The living room is that way." Frances Adams pointed to the right. Susan saw an elegant room with formal furniture and a huge crystal chandelier hanging from the ceiling. "But I usually only use it for official functions. Let me show you my bolt-hole, my library."

They turned to the left, crossing the highly polished hallway and through more French doors into a large room, lined on three sides with floor-to-ceiling bookshelves. Two large, worn deep couches covered in claret linen faced the wide windows on the fourth side of the room. Behind one couch, a scarred table supported a computer, printer, and a mess of papers and books. Frances Adams nodded at the computer. "My downfall. I am addicted to books—all books, but my particular passion is old gardening books. It was bad enough when letters and catalogues from stores and dealers around the world arrived by mail. But the Internet, alas, has made it all too easy for me to indulge.

"Please, have a seat. Would you like some tea?"

"Not really," Susan admitted.

"Then how about a drink? I have some rum that is made in the hills on an unnamed island. It's not completely legal to make and is never exported. We drink it in very small glasses. It's quite a treat and something few tourists get to sample."

"How could I pass that up?" Susan said, wandering around the room and examining the books, as her hostess walked over to a small table set between the windows and poured two tiny drinks from a cut-crystal decanter.

"Here is yours," she said, offering one to Susan.

Susan tore herself away from the bookshelves and sat down on the closest couch. She picked up her glass of dark hazel liquid and took a sip, suddenly nervous.

"Wow! That's amazing," she exclaimed, blinking.

"It is, isn't it? Now, what did you come here to see me about?"

"I'm—this is going to sound silly," Susan started.

"It's about the murder, I assume? And your friend, Mr. Gordon?"

"Yes. You see, Kathleen, Kathleen Gordon, his wife—you've met her."

"Many times. A lovely young woman. Go on."

"She was assaulted today."

"Good heavens. Where?"

"At Compass Bay. She was sitting on the beach when some-one came up from behind and hit her on the head with some-thing. It knocked her out. She was unconscious for a while before I found her."

"You found her?"

"Yes. You see, I was looking for her, and I saw something lying next to one of the kayaks—they're kept on the beach during the day—and it turned out to be Kathleen."

"Who had been unconscious for a while, but no one else found her before you."

"Exactly, and when we called the police, they refused to do anything. Assault is a crime. And Kathleen and I think that it's possible that the person who killed Allison hit her, so if only the police would look—" She stopped talking. The expres-sion on Frances Adams's face puzzled her: Frances Adams looked skeptical. And she looked very, very sad.

"Your friends are lucky to have someone like you who cares so deeply about them."

"I don't just care about them. I know them. Jerry is not a killer."

"You have much more experience with this type of thing than I do. And I can't say I'm sorry about that. But my under-standing is that you have found murderers among your friends and neighbors."

"Yes. I—" Susan glanced back at the computer. "The *Han-cock Herald* is on-line. You looked me up!"

"Yes. You have quite a bit of experience. So perhaps you will understand my next question. Do you believe we are all capable of murder?"

"Perhaps . . . under the right circumstances . . . mothers protecting their children . . . You think Jerry killed Allison!"

"I have, in fact, absolutely no opinion about that. Well, that's not true. I believe he's a very nice man and I hope he didn't kill her. But, no, I can't be sure he's innocent. And the police are convinced he's guilty. Your story about Kathleen's assault must sound suspicious to them."

"But—"

"Think about it. Compass Bay is a small resort. I understand the cottages are two-thirds full right now. So say there are close to thirty guests there. And full staff is twenty-seven . . ."

No wonder everything flowed so smoothly, Susan thought, distracted by the statistics.

". . . so you're telling me that almost sixty people were close by Mrs. Gordon lying on the beach and they did not spy her body. You, on the other hand, just happened to be there and find her."

"You think I'm lying to you!"

"No, I don't. But I think Mrs. Gordon loves her husband very much, and she is trying to direct the attention of the police away from him and came up with this fake assault to do so."

"I can't believe—" Susan started.

"I am perfectly aware of the fact that you don't believe that. But, I'm afraid that's what the police believe and the facts certainly can be read that way. Mrs. Henshaw . . . Susan . . . you had better work very hard and very quickly to find the real murderer. Because right now, everything points toward Jerry Gordon as the guilty party."

# TWENTY-EIGHT

Susan was still upset when she arrived at Compass Bay. She didn't bother to smile at Lila, working behind the front desk. She didn't stop at the gift shop to see if Kathleen had called out. She didn't even stop to see Kathleen. She stormed into her own cottage. Jed would make her feel better in this crisis as he had done in every crisis during the thirty years of their marriage.

If only he would wake up.

Miserable and impatient, Susan shook her husband awake. It wasn't an easy task. He muttered and pulled away from her without opening his eyes.

"Jed! Wake up! You've been sleeping all afternoon. I need you."

"Sus—" His right eye opened.

"Jed. We have a real problem. No one believes Kathleen was assaulted."

"Kathleen . . . assaulted. Is she okay?" Both eyes were now open, but Susan stopped shaking him. When she found Kathleen on the ground, she had screamed. Everyone had come running. Everyone except for Jed.

"Have you been sleeping all afternoon?" Susan asked.

"I . . . all afternoon? What time is it?"

"It's almost six o'clock. You were going to take a nap right after lunch."

"I guess I did." He sat up and shook his head. "I haven't felt like this since I got drunk my freshman year of college." He looked at his wife. "Did you say six o'clock?"

Susan glanced over at the clock on the nightstand. "Six-oh-three."

"And Kathleen. You said she was hurt."

"She was. Jed, you haven't heard anything all afternoon?"

"I've been completely unconscious. Almost like I was drugged or something."

"I'd bet anything that that's just what happened to you. You were drugged. At lunchtime. By someone who didn't want you to find Kathleen."

Jed looked at his wife. "I don't get it. I'm still a little woozy. Tell me what's going on. From the beginning."

"I went to see Jerry."

"Is everything okay?"

"Sort of. He kept telling me that Kathleen and June were very much alike. It's not true, of course. I've thought about that so many times since I saw him. Kathleen is almost nothing like June."

"Of course she isn't. Go on."

Susan smiled, glad her husband agreed with her. "Anyway, while I was in town, I went into a bar. I know, it's not like me, but I was thirsty and that's not the point. The point is that the bartender had seen Allison and Jerry there together the afternoon before she was killed. They weren't exactly getting along."

"Let's just hope he doesn't tell this to all his customers."

"True. Anyway, I came right back here to find Kathleen. I didn't tell her what Jerry said about June, but I did want to see if she knew Jerry and Allison had been together. But I couldn't find her anywhere. I was looking down on the beach when I saw her arm sticking out from beneath a kayak. She was unconscious. I screamed. Everyone in the place came. Well, everyone except you. I must have been upset. I should have realized you weren't there. Did you know that the bride is a doctor?" she asked, changing the subject.

"No, go on. What had happened to Kathleen?"

"Someone hit her over the head. She thinks she was unconscious for quite a while." Susan looked at her husband, waiting for his response.

"And no one else saw her in all that time?" he asked.

"That's the problem," Susan said. "No one did. I didn't think of that. And neither did Kath. We called the police because we thought that the murderer must have been the one who hit her. Well, I still think that's possible."

"But the police don't agree?"

"Of course not. Apparently everyone thinks Kathleen was just pretending to be hurt—despite the large lump on the back of her head—and no one is going to investigate anything. I went to see Frances Adams."

"Again? The woman must be getting tired of us!"

"Maybe. But, although I didn't like what she was saying, she did manage to get me to see what everyone else is thinking.

"Anyway, that's the story of my day. It's been horrible. Every time I think I've found something that might help Jerry, it has turned out to be just the opposite."

"Where's Kathleen now?"

"In her cottage. She's sleeping, too. You know, I should check on her."

"Good idea. You do that and I'll use the bathroom and join you two. It sounds as though we could all use a drink before dinner."

Susan hurried next door to the Gordons' cottage, realizing, guiltily, that she should have checked on her friend's condition before waking up Jed. Not bothering to knock, she opened the door and peeked in.

She need not have worried about disturbing Kathleen. A quick look around the room was all it took to be sure that her friend wasn't there.

This time, she didn't scream, although the room was in a shocking state. The bedding was on the floor, dresser drawers emptied onto the bare mattress, and looking through the open door into the bathroom, Susan could see makeup, shampoo, and the like spilled onto the countertop and tile floor.

"Good God!" Jed appeared in the doorway behind her.

"Kathleen's missing," Susan said.

"You're sure she's not just hiding under all this mess?"

"No. She may be hurt. Doesn't it look to you as though there was a struggle?"

"It looks to me as though someone was searching for something." He walked in and picked up a paperback from the floor and replaced it on the nightstand. "You know, this could all have happened after Kathleen left the cottage. She could be sitting on the beach reading a mystery novel or drinking some rum punch."

"Or unconscious under a kayak," Susan said. "Okay. Let's look around. If we find her, fine. But we can't search the beaches in both directions. If she doesn't turn up right away, I say we call the police. Or Lila. Or maybe we should call Lila first and then call the police."

Jed looked at his watch. "I'll look around all the cottages west of here. You take the gift shop, bar, restaurant, pool area, and beach. Keep an eye on the time." He looked at his watch. "We meet back here in fifteen minutes. There's a murderer loose. Don't take any chances."

"You, too!" Susan turned and got to work.

They met back at the Gordons' cottage as planned, Susan arriving a few minutes late.

"Where have you been?" He sounded worried.

"Saying hello in what I hope was a perky manner to half the guests in the resort. It's predinner drinks time, you know. I didn't want them to think something else odd had happened. You didn't find her?"

"No, but James was down by the water putting away the kayaks. He says he's been walking between the cottage and the beach for the past hour or so and hasn't seen anything unusual."

"Did you tell him about this mess and all?"

"Just asked him if he'd seen Kathleen. He said no and—"

"That he'd been walking back and forth, etc."

"Yes. Exactly."

"So we call the police," Susan said.

"And we tell Lila," Jed added, following his wife toward the office.

Actually, Lila called the police. Susan couldn't tell whether or not Lila believed her, but it was obvious that a possible intruder at Compass Bay wasn't something she could ignore. Once again the police arrived almost immediately. Once again there were two men. This time, however, Susan was pleased to note that they listened with great seriousness to Susan and Jed and assured them that they would immediately organize an all-island search. While Susan gave one Kathleen's description, the other got on the phone with headquarters.

"I think they're doing all they can," Lila said when the three of them were together again. "Perhaps it's time for dinner . . ."

"Definitely," Jed agreed.

"But, Jed, we forgot to tell them that you were dr—"

"Let's go, hon. Our reservation was for seven. We don't want to be late." He grabbed her arm with more force than necessary, and Susan got the idea at once.

"Yes, you're right! Thanks for your help," she added to Lila as her husband guided her away.

"Why did you do that? The police should know if you were drugged!"

"They should and they will in good time. But, Susan, if I was drugged, it happened here."

"You think one of the staff did it? Which one?" Susan peered around at the numerous servers on the crowded patio restaurant.

"I've been thinking about that. Assuming that my food was tampered with, it may have been someone in the kitchen or the waiter or maybe the bartender. I had a beer with my meal. Draft, not bottled. Or . . ."

"Or?"

"Or it could have been someone who stopped at my table to chat. Let's sit down and I'll try to think who I spoke to during lunch."

"You have reservations for three, I believe, Mr. Henshaw," the hostess said, approaching them with a slip of paper in her hand.

"Yes, Mrs. Gordon won't be joining us this evening," he answered. "I wondered if you could find a table with some privacy for Mrs. Henshaw and me. It's been a long day, and my wife has a slight headache."

Now, Susan had never had a "slight headache" in her life. She either felt fine or as though a brick had knocked her over the head, but she tried to look appropriately wan and droopy as the hostess led them to a small table on the patio around the pool.

"I'll tell a waiter to serve you here," she said before walking away and leaving them alone.

"This is pretty good. If we speak softly, no one should overhear."

Susan scooted her chair slightly to the right so she could look up at the restaurant without turning further. "So who stopped at your table?"

"Lord, Susan, you know I'm not good at names."

"Then just describe them to me."

"Well, all the bridge players were there. They were play-ing at a table right next to mine, and whoever was dummy usually took the opportunity to order another drink and stop over and chat. That foursome really packs away the alcohol."

"Well, three of them do anyway," Susan said. Their waiter came for their drink order and to announce the dinner spe-cials. "So tell me who else appeared at your table," she asked when they were alone again.

"Well . . ." The sun was sinking into the sea in the west, and Jed's face reflected the vivid hues of the sky. He frowned.

"What about the honeymooners? They didn't stop to talk to you, did they?"

"As far as I know, they followed their usual pattern and didn't leave their cottage until well after the rest of us had eaten both breakfast and lunch."

"So they're out."

"Yes."

"What about Joann and Martin?"

"Yes. How she nags him. Now if someone had to die, why couldn't it have been her? My guess is that Martin would be a very happy widower, although he would never put it like that."

"So they stopped at your table?"

"Yes, but not to see me. Ro was dummy and sitting with me, and Joann wanted to talk to her about a kayaking trip. She sat down and chatted for a while, managed to let everyone within hearing know that she was tired of kayaking with her husband—apparently he can't keep up with her—and then they both headed over to the pool. Joann needed to work on her tan."

"How about Peggy and Frank?"

"I don't think I know who they are."

"Good-looking couple. He has bright red hair. Around our age. They're from Connecticut. They're very athletic. Always swimming laps in the pool or taking off on long kayaking trips. They're here on their second honeymoon and like to tell everyone about it."

"Oh, I know them. They stopped by and talked for a while. In fact, she gave me a message for you. She wanted to be sure you knew about some sort of scuba-diving class that James is holding tomorrow afternoon."

"Really . . . I've always wanted to try that. Remember when we were in Bermuda with the kids and Chad learned? He's always said that was one of the best trips we ever took."

"I think that may have had more to do with the bikini-clad instructor than the submerged flora and fauna."

"Oh, well, I'll probably be busy tomorrow anyway."

"This trip sure isn't turning out to be the relaxing vacation we planned," Jed said.

"No, but it may be getting better. Lila is on her way here. With two police officers—oh, no."

"What?"

"Those officers were here this morning. They think Kathleen only pretended to be assaulted. I wonder what they're going to say this time. Now that she might have been abducted and her cottage searched."

It turned out that the officers were in a rut. This time, however, it was Susan they didn't believe. And this time they

threatened her with arrest if she—or any of her companions—
continued to waste the island police department's valuable
time.

# TWENTY-NINE

SUSAN WAS SO ANGRY SHE COULDN'T SLEEP. SHE WAS ALSO nearly paralyzed with worry. Jerry was in jail. Kathleen had been assaulted and then disappeared. And Jed, her husband, the person she loved more than anyone else in the world, had been drugged. The police refused to help out, and apparently, the embassy couldn't. Jed, claiming to still feel the effects of whatever had caused him to sleep all afternoon, had dropped off as soon as he lay down. Susan hadn't even bothered to take off her robe, and finally tiring of trying to read, she put down her book and wandered out on the deck.

It was still early and Compass Bay was hopping. Susan leaned against the deck rail and watched the vacationers. The bridge players were still at it, sitting at a round table, illuminated by the lights of the bar nearby. She wondered if the convenience of the light outweighed the convenience of so much alcohol close by. The honeymooners were sitting together on the breakwater, their arms locked around each other. This really was a resort for couples. Susan spied two women she didn't recognize chatting together by the pool, legs dangling in the water. They probably were here with the two unknown men sitting at the bar. New guests had arrived. Their vacations wouldn't be tainted by Allison's murder.

She spied Joann and Martin heading down the path toward

their cottage. They would soon pass by her. She hurried back inside, not wanting to talk to them.

Getting ready for bed, she realized that, in the morning, someone was going to have to tell Jerry about Kathleen's disappearance. She went to sleep hoping that somebody didn't have to be her.

Jed's long nap combined with a good night's sleep had him up at dawn.

"Sue. Hon. I'm going to go see Jerry. I'll tell him about Kathleen and . . . and I guess I'll take it from there."

Susan, drowsy with sleep, muttered agreement, punched her pillow, and rolled over to find a cool spot on the mattress.

She woke up an hour later and stared at the ceiling. She was alone. Her friends were in terrible trouble. Not knowing what to do, she decided to head over to the restaurant. Food didn't sound terribly appealing, but a cup of coffee might be a big help.

She found a seat by the wall and, her back to the still empty restaurant, stared out at the sea. A young woman approached almost immediately, and Susan looked up, expecting a menu. She was handed a folded sheet of notepaper. "Your husband called. He said to give you this. I'll find your waiter." Susan grabbed the paper and opened it anxiously.

"I'm with Jerry. I told him about Kathleen, and while he looked a little worried, he didn't seem unduly upset. I'm going to see his lawyer. Maybe we can do something here. You stay there and relax."

Susan frowned. Just like a man. Jerry "didn't seem unduly upset." What did that mean? And how could she stay here and "relax"? Relax? Surely Jed knew she couldn't relax while all this was going on!

On the other hand, Jed knew his message would be read by others, possibly the murderer. What, really, could he say?

Susan boiled the note down to facts: Jed was going to stay in town. She should stay here. "Coffee. A full pot, please," she ordered from a nearby waiter, busy setting the tables.

He dashed off and returned immediately, pot in hand. Susan sipped from the cup and felt her spirits rise. Jed must be planning to do something in town. He didn't need her help. Now she had to decide where her efforts could best be used here.

She considered the various possibilities. The thing to do, she decided, was spend as much time as possible with the people who had known Allison here before she was murdered. There must be a connection between at least one other guest and Allison—and that person must have killed her.

"Would you like to order breakfast now?"

"Ah . . . yes. I'll have the crab and avocado omelet and some fresh fruit."

"Of course, Mrs. Henshaw. Shouldn't take any time at all."

Susan smiled and looked back at the water. She'd see who showed up next for breakfast. If logic and orderly investigation couldn't solve this murder, she would just have to depend on serendipity.

As luck would have it, the next guest to arrive was looking for her.

"Susan Henshaw! You're just the person to take my husband's place this morning."

"Doing what?" Susan asked, turning and looking up at Ro Parker.

"We're taking the kayaks out to see the eastern beaches. They're almost entirely deserted and well worth the trip. And, I don't know about you, but I could stand to burn some calories." Ro pulled up a chair, sat down, and lowered her voice. "We heard about your friend vanishing. I just want you to know that I, at least, don't believe her vanishing act means she—or her nice husband—really did kill Allison. I just wanted you to know." She put her hand on Susan's arm and gave it what she probably thought was a friendly squeeze.

Susan knew anger would get her nowhere. "Thanks." She leaned closer to Ro. "What are people saying about Kathleen?"

"Oh, dear. Well, I know she's your friend, but I must say her stunt yesterday didn't win her many friends here."

"What do you mean?"

"Well, pulling a vanishing act makes her look very guilty."

"But she was abducted. Her room was searched!"

"I know it looks like that. And I suppose it's just possible. But, if you want to know what people think . . ."

"I do."

"They think she's taken off to try to deflect suspicion from her husband."

"But her cottage—"

"She trashed it before she left. I don't believe it, but you said you wanted to know what people were saying."

"I suppose I shouldn't be surprised. No one here really got to know Kathleen or Jerry before all this happened. There's no reason to believe in their innocence."

"And everyone knew Allison. She was quite gregarious and so charming. She fit right in with all the various little groups here.

"Oh, there's my husband. Do tell me you'll come out with us. He'll be so relieved not to have to go."

"What time? And how long will we be gone?"

"We're leaving around ten and we'll be back before one— for a late lunch. Now tell me you'll come."

Susan made up her mind quickly. "I will."

"Fabulous. We're meeting on the beach. James is going to fit us all out with life vests and such."

"I'll be there." The timing sounded just about perfect. That would give her a few hours to think about what Ro had just said. Susan would never have described Allison as gregarious.

When she had visited her sister in Hancock, she had refused to socialize without Jerry or June by her side. In fact, Susan herself had tried a little matchmaking and been discouraged. Convinced Allison was just shy, she had given up. But this new Allison, thin and gorgeous, had also, apparently, had a personality transplant. She had jumped into the social waters of Compass Bay with enthusiasm.

It was time for Susan to do the same.

At least she had an opening line.

By the time Susan met the bridge foursome on the beach, she had spoken to the other three couples who had spent time with Allison.

Abandoning any pretense that she was doing anything other than investigating a murder, she used the same approach each time. "I'm trying to find out what happened to Kathleen. When was the last time you saw her?" she started by asking Joann and Martin.

Martin looked up from his bowl of oatmeal with a startled expression on his face. "Sorry? We thought everyone knew what had happened to her. She left the resort, didn't she? Ran out on her husband."

"Martin! We know nothing of the kind!" Joann spoke sharply. Susan noticed she was eating the macadamia nut pancakes with coconut syrup with a side order of pork bangers. In terms of calories and cholesterol, their two breakfasts were complete opposites. "I'm sorry, Mrs. Henshaw . . . Susan. My husband sometimes lacks tact. Of course, we are all shocked and concerned about the disappearance of your friend. I myself believe she was driven insane by the shock of learning that her husband is a murderer and she has done herself some dreadful harm. We're on an island. Such an easy place to disappear."

Susan reminded herself that she was investigating and that

defending her friends wasn't going to get her anywhere or help her learn anything new. "I can't image Kathleen doing anything like that. She's upset that her husband was wrongly accused of murder, but Kathleen was a police officer in New York City before her marriage. I don't think there's a whole lot that shocks her or could send her over the edge."

"A police officer," Martin said. "Amazing. She's so sensational looking. Who would have guessed."

Joann looked at her husband with such anger that Susan thought for a moment that she was going to strike him. "Good-looking women, Martin—if you call that anorexic scrawniness good-looking—are used as decoys. She probably spent her time on the police force dressed up as a hooker trying to attract johns."

"Really?" Martin had a smile on his face. "Well, I wouldn't know anything about that—at least, nothing I would admit to," he said to Susan, raising his eyebrows over twinkling eyes.

Susan sincerely hoped Martin had time to enjoy his vices, whatever they were, since he seemed to be having a perfectly miserable vacation.

"Finish your cereal, Martin. You don't want to become constipated again."

Susan tried not to gasp at Joann's hideous manners. "Did either of you see Kathleen yesterday?" she asked, getting back to her point.

"I saw her early in the morning," Joann answered promptly. "She was getting into a taxi. I assumed she was going to town to shop or something rather than running away."

"She wasn't running away at that time, dear," Martin said mildly. "I saw her later than you did."

"When was that?" Joann asked as though such a thing wasn't possible.

"When you were looking around the gift shop. Remember you asked me to return to our cottage and pick up that scarf you were hoping to match? I saw Mrs. Gordon go into her cottage. That must have been almost two hours later. If she was going to jump in the ocean, as you implied, dear, she hadn't decided to do it then. She waved and smiled at me. She seemed quite perky."

Susan realized that Kathleen must have just returned from seeing her husband.

"Playacting. She probably did a lot of that when she was on the force."

Susan decided she wasn't going to learn anything more by staying here. "Thanks. I don't think Kathleen killed herself. But I am worried about her and I appreciate your help."

"Anything we can do," Martin assured her.

"I hope this breakfast isn't going to take you all day," Joann snapped, picking up her fork and impaling a sausage.

"I think not, dear. That's one of the advantages of limiting one's caloric intake."

Susan hurried off. No need to hear Joann's response if she could avoid it.

Frank and Peggy were almost finished with their meal when she found them. They were sitting on the patio, looking out to sea and not speaking.

"Do you mind if I interrupt?" Susan asked, walking up behind them.

Frank looked up. "Nothing to interrupt. We're just having one of those wonderful intimate meals in which Compass Bay specializes."

"So much for our second honeymoon," Peggy said.

Susan just smiled awkwardly and asked her question. "You know my friend Kathleen is missing?"

"We do. We were just talking about that," Frank began.

"Yes, the poor girl. It's so different than our situation. We were able to heal and grow, develop personally even though

Frank had done something so reprehensible. She apparently didn't get the chance."

"My wife believes Mrs. Gordon was murdered."

"My husband believes she has killed herself in her grief over discovering her husband was unfaithful. I believe therapists refer to that as projecting. He thinks, no doubt, that I should have thrown myself into the sea upon discovering his unfaithfulness. I believe women are stronger than that and I believe I have proved it."

"It doesn't have anything to do with women being strong, or not being strong," Susan said. "I'm worried that you're right. I don't think Kathleen was murdered, but I do believe some harm may have come to her. When was the last time you saw her? Do you remember?"

"Yesterday. Around lunchtime," Peggy said positively.

"My wife is right about this one thing. We were walking by her cottage and she stuck her head out of the door. Said hello and stuck it back in again."

"What do you mean, right about this one thing?" Peggy turned on him. "It just so happens that I'm frequently right about a lot of things. And it wouldn't hurt you to admit it once in a while."

Susan left without even bothering to thank the couple. She didn't want to interrupt.

# THIRTY

THE HONEYMOONERS HAD NOT YET LEFT THEIR COTTAGE
when Susan walked down to the beach to join Ro, Veronica,
and Randy, all three properly outfitted in bright-orange life
vests. Burt was there to "say bon voyage"—his words. He
said just that and then took off, heading for the bar. Ro stared
at his back, a frown on her face, and then turned back to Susan. "I understand you've spent the morning asking some of
the guests when they last saw your friend."

"Yes."

"Well, we've been talking about that and we came up with
something you might find very interesting," Veronica said,
looking up from the task of tying the strings of her sun hat to
her vest.

"What?"

"We saw her at different times, and she was acting rather
strangely." Ro picked up the story. "You see, Burt noticed her
first. He always notices gorgeous women, but I'm a very un-
derstanding wife. As long as he just looks, I always tell him."

"When did he see her?" Susan asked, trying to get back to
the point.

"Right after you left her in her cottage. She walked out—
toward the office—and stopped when she saw that there were
people in the gift shop. He said that he got the impression that
she didn't want anyone to see her."

"And she went back into her cottage."

"Yes. Burt thought she was looking a little shaky. He thought about asking her if she needed help, but she went inside, and he decided to leave her alone."

"And I saw her next. At least that's what we figured out when we were all talking," Veronica jumped in. "I went back to our cottage to get some sunscreen. Sometimes we can't find a place to play that is in the shade, especially in the morning—the sun just bounces off the water—and the door to her cottage was open. She was sitting on the bed, rubbing her head. I called out and asked her if she needed a doctor, and she said no, she was absolutely fine."

"Which makes what happened next so interesting," Ro added.

"What happened next?"

"First, I should tell you that when I was coming back with my sunscreen the door was closed," Veronica said. "I assumed your friend was lying down—"

"But she wasn't even in the cottage!" Ro interrupted. "Randy and I went for a short walk just a few minutes later, and we saw her walking on the road."

"Outside Compass Bay?"

"Yes, isn't that strange?"

"And there's something even stranger," Veronica said. "We think she saw us and hurried back into the resort."

"I'm not so sure that she saw us," Ro added. "I don't think we can be so sure about that."

"And why would she have hurried into Compass Bay the back way if she hadn't been seen?"

"What back way?" Susan demanded.

"Oh, there's a staff entrance. About a hundred feet down from the regular entrance—no arch or palm trees or anything like that—just a door in the wooden fence that runs between the cottages and the road."

"I never even realized there was a fence behind the cottages," Susan said.

"That's because everything is oriented to the sea. There aren't even any windows on that side of the cottages," Ro pointed out.

"There's a path back there. It's how the staff moves between cottages. Didn't you ever realize that you don't see them walking around much?"

"I never even thought about it, but you're right. The staff is remarkably unobtrusive, isn't it?"

"That's the way we're told to play it, ladies," James said, joining them and their conversation. "And gentleman," he added, seeing Randy.

"You mean there's a part of Compass Bay that isn't public?" Susan asked.

"Of course there is!" Ro spoke before James could answer. "There's the path behind the cottages, and a fairly large laundry room back there, too. And the staff lounge, too. Right, James?"

"You're a longtime guest, Mrs. Parker. You probably know your way around here better than most of the staff.

"I see you've all chosen your kayaks so, as soon as I find Mrs. Henshaw a life vest that fits, we'll start on our way, if everyone is ready to go.

"Now, I think this jacket will be perfect for you, Mrs. Henshaw. May even be the one you used the last time you were out."

"It may be. It feels fine," she added. "James, I was wondering." She looked over at her companions. "I have a question or two."

"You know Lila doesn't like us talking about the guests, and I can't afford to get in trouble. Maybe . . ."

"What if we talked later? When we can be alone? I just want to ask a few questions about Kathleen."

"Later. When we are alone. I want to help you and your friends if I can."

"That would be great!"

Following James's directions, the paddlers set out.

"Hey, are we gonna get caught in a thunderstorm?" Randy called out, pointing toward the horizon where dark clouds were forming.

"No. The storm comes tonight. We'll be home long before any rainfall."

"Funny how we've stopped watching TV or reading the paper or checking out the weather forecast since we've been here, isn't it?" Veronica said, paddling up to Susan.

"You know, that's true. I guess part of being on vacation is leaving the world behind."

"Which you haven't been able to do, unfortunately," Veronica added.

"No."

Veronica looked at Ro, Randy, and James. Stronger paddlers, they were about five hundred feet away. "Ro is one of my oldest and best friends, but I don't always agree with her."

"Of course not."

"I think she's wrong about your friend."

"Kathleen?"

"Yes. Ro thinks she staged this whole abduction scenario to cast doubt on her husband's guilt."

"And you don't?"

"I don't want to upset you. So I didn't say anything before— not even to Ro—but I think she may be suffering from dementia from her concussion and she may have just wandered off."

"Why do you think that?"

"She looked so distraught when I saw her in her cottage and . . ."

"And?" Susan prompted.

"And I think I may have seen her leave Compass Bay by the

employees' entrance. I'm not sure. It was getting dark and I just saw something out of the corner of my eye. But I went back to my cottage for a second, and I know I saw someone moving between the Gordons' cottage and the gift shop. It could have been Mrs. Gordon. The person was tall with long hair."

Susan pursed her lips. There seemed to be an excessive number of guests at Compass Bay who fit that description. "You could be right. She could be confused and wander off . . ."

"I was thinking of amnesia."

"Oh. But she knew who she was after she was attacked—" Susan shut her mouth.

"Attacked? I thought she fell and hit her head on the beach wall."

"That's possible, but it's also possible that she was hit with something. I mean, Kathleen is in good shape and she doesn't drink excessively or take drugs. Why would she suddenly fall and hit her head on a perfectly smooth sand beach?"

"I never suggested that she had been drinking," Veronica said. "Why would you think of that?"

"Why else would she fall down like that?" Susan asked, bewildered by Veronica's hostile response.

"People are always judging. I had thought that with all the problems your friends were having, you might be different. But I guess I was mistaken!" Plunging her paddle in the water with a strength Susan would never have suspected, Veronica skimmed across the surf to rejoin her group.

Susan remembered Veronica and her husband's strange drink exchange too late to change to a subject that they both might find acceptable. Oh, well. She was now about a quarter of a mile behind her companions. To her left, the breeze off the water bent palm trees toward the silvery sand of deserted beaches. To her right, the water reflected the darkening sky. A pair of pelicans flew overhead. Looking down into the water, Susan saw her own reflection blending with the colorful fish below. It was beautiful. It was quiet. It was a perfect spot to think through everything that had happened in the past few days. Susan began by considering the possible suspects. Allison had made a point of being friendly with everyone who was staying at Compass Bay (except for the honeymooners), so why couldn't one of them be the killer? Peggy and Frank were from Connecticut. Perhaps they had known Allison. Perhaps Frank's affair had been with Allison. Peggy claimed to have forgiven, but Susan got the impression that her feelings weren't exactly under control. What if they had arrived here for their second honeymoon only to discover the woman who destroyed their marriage already in residence? Would Peggy have killed her husband's lover for revenge? Would Frank have killed his ex-lover for any reason at all?

Susan wasn't sure that made sense, and she suddenly realized that she wasn't going to find out—at least, not now. Now she had more serious problems. Her kayak, no longer floating on the water, was on the way to becoming a submarine.

"Hey! James! Ro! Veronica! Randy! Hey!" She held her paddle across her chest with one hand and waved the other. "Hey! Help!"

The quartet turned at her call and waved back, big smiles on their faces. For a few seconds, Susan wondered if they were glad she was about to sink into the water, if her kayak's demise was intentional. Then she realized the wind was blowing away from her. They couldn't hear her. She grabbed both ends of her paddle and raised it in the air above her head. In Maine, this was known among kayakers as a distress signal. Either the same was true in the Caribbean or it was such an unusual thing to do that it couldn't be ignored, but as she watched, James spun his kayak around and began to paddle toward her.

Susan smiled, relieved, although she knew he wasn't going to be fast enough. Gently, as though rocking a baby to sleep, her boat sank below the surface. Supported by her life vest, she clutched the paddle and waited for rescue. Looking down, she spied a green parrot fish doing figure eights around her knees. A nearby pencil-thin barracuda, thankfully, didn't show the same interest.

"Mrs. Henshaw! Are you all right?"

"I'm just fine. Can't say the same for my kayak," she added.

"That's not important. Now we have a problem. How can we get you onto my kayak?"

"It won't support us both," Susan protested.

"I can swim by your side."

"I have a better idea," Susan said. "Why don't I just hang on to the back and you can kind of tow me in?"

"That would work, but . . . are you sure that's what you want to do?"

"I'm sure. The water is wonderfully warm. If you're strong enough to paddle back carrying the extra weight . . ."

"No problem. Let's make everyone understand what we're doing and we'll start out."

Ro and Veronica appeared with Randy, paddling vigorously, trailing behind. James explained their plan.

"What a horrible thing. You could have drowned!" Ro exclaimed.

Susan, busy trying to figure out how to hang on to the ropes tied to the rear of James's boat without getting rope burn, just smiled.

"And now Mrs. Henshaw gets a free ride back to Compass Bay. The rest of you will have to paddle for yourself."

No one said anything more. As the tide was coming in, they easily made it back to shore. As soon as Susan's feet hit the sandy sea bottom, she dropped the rope and swam. If anyone had asked, she would have described the last half an hour as innocuous.

Apparently Lila didn't feel that way at all. She was waiting on the beach, towels in hand, ready to help Susan (who didn't need it) out of the water and up onto the sand.

"Mrs. Henshaw! Are you all right? Should I call a doctor?"

"I'm fine. Absolutely fine," Susan assured her honestly. "Your kayak is sitting on the bottom of the ocean, but I'm fine."

"I'm certainly glad to hear that. But why don't I find Lourdes and she can give you a massage on the house."

"Well, I . . ." Susan hated to refuse, but she really had other things to do. "I need to meet Jed," she lied. "I'll just go back to my cottage and shower."

"If you're sure . . ." Apparently satisfied, Lila directed her attention elsewhere. "James, you'll be in my office as soon as the kayaks are secured."

"Yes, ma'am." Before he turned back to his task, Susan was surprised to see the expression on his face. He looked afraid.

# THIRTY-ONE

Jed was nowhere to be found, and Susan decided that the shower she had used as an excuse to get away by herself was an excellent idea after all. She had learned a lot this morning, but nothing intrigued her as much as Lila's reaction to the kayaking accident. The woman had been what Susan's children would have called "off the wall." Why would a simple accident upset Lila more than a murder or Jerry's arrest or Kathleen's assault? Susan was pouring cream rinse into her palm when the answer struck her. It hadn't been an accident. Someone had tried to kill her. Lila wasn't seeing what happened as an individual accident, but as the latest event in a line of horrible events. Events that could damage the reputation of Compass Bay.

Her kayak must have been sabotaged! But by whom? Susan scrubbed the salt from her skin and thought. The person who did it must have known that Susan was going to end up with that kayak. And who would have known that? James . . . No, in fact, James had been up at the kiosk when Ro, Randy, and Veronica picked out their boats. It had to be one of those three people. Or all three? Susan played around with that thought before discarding it. Regarding them as a foursome was fine, but they were four individuals. And she needed to consider each individually. And she shouldn't, she realized, exclude Burt. Burt may not have gone on the trip, but he certainly was around when the other three were selecting their vessels. He could have made a hole in the remaining kayak while the others were busy putting on their vests and dousing themselves, yet again, with another layer of sunscreen.

But how could she find out? Those who were willing to answer her questions when she asked about Kathleen wouldn't necessarily answer questions about their friends. On the other hand, anyone overlooking the beach could have seen what was happening. Susan tried to remember if she had noticed anyone nearby.

It was hopeless, she finally decided, flipping off the shower and grabbing a thick towel to wrap around her hair. She was tying her robe's sash when she heard someone at the door. "Jed? Is that you?"

"No, Mrs. Henshaw. It's me. Lourdes."

Susan hurried across the room and opened the door. "Hi."

"Miss Lila send me here. She think maybe you need massage after your ordeal this morning."

"How nice, but I told her that I was fine."

But Lourdes was already inside the cottage. "If you not mind, Mrs. Henshaw, I would like to talk to you. If you do not mind."

"Of course not. Is something wrong?"

"Yes. Something is very, very wrong. We are all very, very upset."

"What is it?"

"We worry about James. We all worry about James."

"Why? He's just fine. You should have seen the way he paddled his kayak back to land—"

"James is very strong. But that will not keep Lila from firing him."

"Why would she do that? He seems to be the person who keeps this place running smoothly."

"Yes. That's right. James is very, very important at Compass Bay. But Lila is very, very angry at him. Things like today not supposed to happen. Guests are not supposed to be in accidents."

Susan didn't know how to respond to that. Apparently it was okay if guests were murdered, assaulted, or kidnapped, but a hole in a kayak was unacceptable. Susan knew she had never been in any danger. The water was warm; she wasn't terribly far from shore; help was nearby. What was Lila so upset about?

"James is a wonderful man. Mány, many people who work here owe much to him. And he has large family that he supports. It is very important that he stay at Compass Bay."

"Is Lila going to fire him?" Susan asked, appalled.

"Ms. Lila is very, very mad," Lourdes said again.

"What does he want me to do?"

"Oh, no! You not understand. I ask you for help. Many of us on staff, we ask you for help. James not ask. James not know I am here."

"You and . . . the other members of the staff—what do you think I can do to help?"

"If you could, please, go talk to Lila. Tell her that James saved your life. That he did nothing wrong today. That you feel terrible if he be blamed for your unfortunate accident."

"Look, all of that is true. Well, he probably didn't save my life. I wasn't in any real danger," Susan said. "But why do you think anything I can say will help?"

"Lila care most about opinions of guests. That is what Lila care about."

Susan sighed. She might as well try to help James. She certainly wasn't helping anyone else. "I'll go talk to her immediately."

"But not tell her that I come see you," Lourdes urged.

"Of course not." Susan was fairly sure Lila's image of her

was so low that nothing could damage it—although she was also fairly sure Lila wouldn't appreciate her butting into Compass Bay's business.

"You go now. Before something stupid happen to James."

"Yes. But will you do me a favor? Would you find out if anyone has seen my husband recently?"

"Yes. You do James favor. I do you favor." Smiling broadly, Lourdes left the cottage.

"Well, no time like the present," Susan informed her reflection in the wall mirror.

Lila was at the front desk flipping through some reservation forms. She looked up with a smile, which disappeared when she recognized Susan, only to be replaced immediately.

"Mrs. Henshaw. What can I do for you? I hope you've recovered from your ordeal. Perhaps you've reconsidered my offer and would like a massage?"

"I'm absolutely fine," Susan said. "I wanted to tell you how wonderful James was when I discovered my kayak sinking. He didn't waste a minute getting to me and bringing me back to land. He wanted me to get up in his kayak, but I thought it would be better if he just towed me behind. He was wonderful," she repeated.

"Ah, well, many of our guests grow quite fond of James during their stay."

"He must be quite a valuable employee," Susan said.

"All our employees are valuable to us," Lila said. Obviously she was losing interest in their conversation; she picked up the papers she had been sorting through when Susan entered the room. "Oh, Mrs. Henshaw, I almost forgot. There's a message here for you. The call must have come in while you were out this morning."

It was from Jed. "Still with Jerry. Everything okay. He says we don't have to worry about Kathleen anymore. Repeat. Anymore."

Susan frowned. "Thanks."

"Everything okay?" Lila asked.

Susan suspected that the other woman had read the note before passing it on, so she merely nodded. She turned and then remembered the reason she was here. "You will give James my thanks for everything he did today, won't you?"

"Of course. But you can tell him yourself, you know. Or leave him a note at the employees' lounge."

"Where is the employees' lounge?"

"Right across the street. The little stucco building beside the parking lot."

"Maybe I'll do that," Susan said, folding the piece of paper and sticking it in her pocket.

"Watch the traffic. There aren't a lot of cars on the island, but there are even fewer safe, competent drivers."

"Thanks for the warning." Susan turned and left the office, walking across the large patio, under the bougainvillea-covered arch that formed the entry to Compass Bay. Taxis had picked her up and dropped her off here, but she hadn't paid any real attention to the unpainted stucco building sitting in the middle of a dirt field on the other side of the street. Cautiously looking both ways down the deserted street, she headed toward the run-down building. A few of Compass Bay's brightly colored chairs, broken-down and in disarray, sat around the building. French doors were open and Susan could see even more utilitarian furniture inside. She walked in.

The building was deserted. Rusting metal chairs stood about equally disreputable metal tables displaying the remains of a meal. A large mouse—Susan refused to think *rat*—scurried across the filthy floor. The place was a mess except for the large bulletin board hung on an unpainted wall. Messages, printed in heavy black marker on thick white paper, had been hung neatly. Curious, Susan wandered over close enough to read them.

The first was a listing of each cottage and its occupants. Under the names (first and last of each member of the party) was the check-in and checkout date, the guest's hometown and state, and services that had been reserved. Susan noticed that the honeymooners were scheduled for sequential massages every other afternoon, as well as room service breakfast to be delivered daily—and promptly—at eleven A.M. Beside this order someone had written *"KNOCK FIRST!!!!!!"*

Moving even closer and squinting, she realized that each guest's name had been annotated, and, some, judging from the variety of handwriting, by more than one person.

Next to the Henshaws' cottage number and their names was written "neat & nice" then a couple of stars, and finally "detective wannabe." Slightly insulted, Susan continued her perusal.

The Gordons were depicted by three amateurish sketches of skulls and crossbones and a lot of exclamation points. Susan frowned.

Joann and Martin weren't well loved by the staff, she noted. "Pickie!" someone with minimal spelling skills had written. "Kayak 1–3 MWF" read another. "Slobs!" said yet another note.

Susan was intrigued by the note next to Veronica and Randy's cottage: "Large pitcher of rum punch—no ice— room service at four P.M. each day—do not be late!" "Nothing else matters, man!" someone else had added. "One drink for my lady and one more for the road," an apparent Sinatra fan had scrawled. It had been edited by another, turning it into "5 drinks for that lady and none for the road." The final editing said, "That's no lady, that's his wife—STAY AWAY!"

Equally interesting was the complete lack of comment next to Ro and Burt's cottage. Names. Dates. Nothing else.

But Rose Anderson also had nothing written by her name. Was that because there was nothing to say about the shy, timid woman, or had someone erased any notations—as Susan suspected had been done next to the Parkers' names?

"Mrs. Henshaw. I understand you've been looking for me."

Susan turned and discovered James leaning against the doorjamb, arms folded across his chest.

"Yes," she answered. "I wanted to thank you for all you did today. And I have some questions."

# THIRTY-TWO

J ED WAS SITTING IN THE BAR, A LARGE, UNTOUCHED GIN AND tonic on the table before him. "If you're not careful, the staff will be leaving notes in the staff lounge about your drinking habits," his wife said, sitting down beside him.

"What?"

"It's not important. Jed, I know where Kathleen is!"

"So do I. At home in Hancock. How do you know?"

"How do you know?" she asked at the same time.

"You first," Jed urged.

"James told me. Apparently he's related to the owner of the taxi company and knows the driver who took her to the airport."

"Not surprising. That young man seems to know everyone on the island—and be related to at least half of them."

"How do you know about Kathleen?"

"Frances Adams told me. Kathleen called her—"

"From Connecticut?"

"Yes, let me explain. Do you want a drink of your own?" he asked, as Susan picked up his glass and sipped.

"Yes, but that's not important! Go on! Tell me everything!"

"There's not a whole lot to tell. Kathleen called the embassy office this afternoon while I was with Jerry. She spoke to Frances Adams, who came down immediately and told us about the call."

"Why did she take off?"

"Kathleen said she left Compass Bay and flew home to see if she could discover anything that would help Jerry."

"And what did she find out?"

"Nothing. She told Frances Adams that the trip was a waste of time. And, of course, now she has another problem."

"What?"

"The island police are not at all happy about her leaving. They're threatening to arrest her if she returns to the island."

"Can they do that?"

"Apparently so. At least, they can hold her, which is really the same thing. Frances suggested that she remain in Connecticut until this is all resolved."

"Boy, is she an optimist! I can't imagine how that will happen."

Jed instantly looked concerned. "So you didn't come up with anything today?"

"I've asked what seems like a hundred questions, and visited parts of the resort I didn't even know existed, but I can't tell you that I've learned anything that will help Jerry." She frowned and picked up his drink again, raising one eyebrow at him.

"Go ahead and finish it," Jed offered.

"I wonder what Kathleen thought she would learn about Allison in Hancock," Susan mused.

"She wasn't investigating Allison," Jed said, waving to a passing waiter. "She was interested in June's death. We'll have a pitcher of rum punch and two glasses," he ordered.

"And a large glass of water, a notebook and a pencil, and . . . and whatever you have available to eat," Susan added. "I'm starving.

"You know, that might be important," she continued. "Kathleen must think there's something suspicious about June's death. Does she think it was murder?"

"I don't know. But I don't remember there being any suggestion of that at the time."

"No, I don't, either. And I'm sure we'd remember," Susan added.

Jed leaned across the table and lowered his voice. "Sue, if that auto accident wasn't an accident, doesn't that suggest that Jerry is a murderer?"

Susan considered that. "I wonder if that's what Kathleen is thinking."

"I have no idea. I sure wish I'd had an opportunity to talk to her."

"Can't we call?"

"No. She said she was heading into the city to check on some things and she would call as soon as she had something to tell us."

"But—"

"Frances Adams said the less communication the better, Sue. She is concerned that the police department might decide that the embassy office is interfering with the investigation and take it out on Jerry."

"Is that all Kathleen said?"

"She had seen Jerry's parents. At least, she mentioned talking to his mother. They're worried, but the kids are fine. Kathleen wanted Jerry to know that, of course."

"Did she explain why she trashed their cottage before leaving?"

"Not a word about that. Oh, here are our drinks."

"Cook just pulled these from the oven. Be careful, they hot," their waitress said, putting a big tray of fried plantain and soft-shell crabs and two dipping sauces on the table between them. The young woman stooped closer to Susan's head and continued. "We thank you for good words about James," she whispered so quickly and quietly that Susan was sure she alone heard.

"What was all that about?" Jed asked.

"Probably another of James's relatives . . . or girlfriends. They were worried that he might get in trouble after my kayak sank today."

"Your kayak sank?"

"Yes. There was a hole in it."

"How in God's name did that happen?"

"Shhh! Jed, not so loud! I don't know how it happened. It just did. James towed me in."

"James put a hole in your kayak?"

"No! He saved me. Well, not exactly saved me," she explained. "I had on a life vest and we weren't that far out. I could probably have gotten back by myself."

"We? Good heavens! You were with the bridge players, right?"

"Three of them. How did you know?"

"They stopped by when I sat down and asked how you were doing. I told them I hadn't seen you all day long, and they said something about you having a story to tell me over dinner. I was hoping they meant that you had figured out who killed Allison."

"And instead I'd had a kayaking accident. Sorry."

"Are you sure it was an accident? It's strange that the hole was in your kayak and not someone else's."

"I know. I thought about that. Look, where's the pencil and paper that the waitress brought?" she asked, looking around.

"Right here under the napkins." Jed pushed a pad with COMPASS BAY printed across the top of each sheet of paper and a pencil across the table to his wife.

"I'm going to list the possible suspects—the people who might have killed Allison, and drugged you, and assaulted Kathleen, and maybe even damaged my kayak. Then we can write down motives and . . . and . . ."

"That's the problem, isn't it?" Jed asked gently. "Motive.

The only person who is connected to Allison, Kathleen, you, and to me is Jerry and he's been locked up since the day after Allison died."

"Peggy and Frank are from Connecticut."

"Did they know Allison?"

"Not before coming here. At least, that's what they claim." Susan looked up from the untouched pad of paper and looked around. "You know what's weird?"

"Everything?"

"Yes, but look around. How did one person get away with all these things? Murder. Assaulting Kathleen. Ripping up her cottage."

"She might have done that herself, Sue."

"Oh, yeah, that's right. But someone put a hole in my kayak. How does one person do all that in this small place without being seen?"

"Now that's a good question," Jed agreed, staring out at the row of cottages lining the beach.

"And the other odd thing is how chummy Allison was with everyone before we arrived."

"Well, a single woman alone. Maybe she was just lonely."

"Maybe, but there's something odd about that. I know I'm missing something. It's as though Allison thought that everyone's opinion of her mattered a great deal." The honeymooners walked by, smiled at Jed and Susan, and continued on.

"Good-looking couple, and funny how they look so similar from behind," Jed said.

"Jed, they're not important. Concentrate! We were talking about how Allison wanted everyone to like her."

"You know, that's sort of sad. I mean, it might have mattered if she had lived, but . . ."

Susan started so violently that she knocked her drink over into the appetizers.

"Susan, are you okay? What are you looking at? Was it something I said?"

"It's something you said, and something I said, and something I saw . . . and I think I know who killed Allison."

"That's wonderful!" Jed said, sounding relieved.

"No," she answered. "It's not! It's really, really awful."

"Susan . . ."

"And the problem is that we need evidence. No one is going to believe us without evidence. Unless we have evidence, Jerry won't be released." She stood up.

"Where are you going?"

"Downtown. To a bar. To get a drink."

Jed looked down at the mess on the table. "We could just order something else here."

"No. I do know one thing: I'm never going to find out what I need to know by asking questions here at Compass Bay."

# THIRTY-THREE

"HOW DID YOU EVER FIGURE IT OUT?"

Even in the leisurely Caribbean, everything could change in twenty-four hours. Yesterday Susan had been asking all the questions. Today she had all the answers.

Well, almost all the answers. Kathleen's plane was landing in less than an hour, and Susan was hoping she would be able to fill in a gap or two in the story. Until then, Susan and Jed were spending the day lying in the sun on either side of Jerry Gordon, replenishing his glass of rum punch as needed and explaining to curious guests what had happened.

"I know I was lucky to be held under the embassy offices, and the view was spectacular, but I sure did miss the sun—and the alcohol—while I was there," Jerry said, stretching out and putting his hands behind his head.

"So tell us, how did you ever figure it all out?" Ro Parker repeated her question. "Did you look for clues? What did you find? How could you possibly have guessed what really happened?"

"Better tell her. She's been driving me nuts since word that you had discovered the murderer's identity spread around Compass Bay last night," Burt urged.

"Oh, you!" his wife responded. "You're just cranky because you can't seem to attract the waiter's attention this morning."

"It's true that the standard of service has fallen off dramatically in the last twelve hours," Veronica chimed in.

"Guess you can tell who really ran this place," Randy spoke up. "And I have to admit I'll really miss James. Seems to me he personified the high standard of service that kept us coming back to Compass Bay year after year."

"Has anyone heard if they've found him yet?" Rose Anderson appeared on the edge of the group and asked timidly.

"First, before you start to complain about the service, before we worry about the murderer's whereabouts, please tell us how you figured out who killed Allison McAllister," Ro asked again.

"It was a combination of things," Susan began. "You see, I couldn't connect Allison to anyone else at Compass Bay. Anyone except you and Jed and me," she continued, turning to Jerry.

"I kept thinking about that myself," he admitted.

"Well," Susan continued, "since I couldn't connect Allison to anyone except us, I couldn't figure out who might want to kill her. I also couldn't figure out who to ask about her. All the information I had about Allison was from the guests she spoke to before we arrived. And, like all of us, she just talked about the parts of her life that she wanted to talk about. Then it occurred to me that I was actually getting a fair amount of information. Allison had talked to you all more than . . . well, more than anyone ordinarily would. She came here alone and I assumed that she was lonely. But then it struck me that she was saying very specific things about herself and her life, all of which connected her to the Gordons. She was obsessed with them. She even wrote a semiautobiographical novel that made her sound like a victim of her sister. According to Rose, she got a big advance for it. I guess sibling rivalry is a hot topic these days."

"June was always kind and generous to Allison—despite the tension that existed in their relationship," Jerry spoke up.

"Allison also made sure everyone knew about my own experience investigating murders," Susan continued. "And that struck me as odd. I have two great kids. My husband has a great job. I live in a wonderful town. There's a lot you could tell people about me. Why did everyone here know about my sleuthing? Frankly, I was beginning to be embarrassed about it, and then it occurred to me that Allison must have told everyone for a reason."

"What was that?" Rose spoke up.

"She wanted me to investigate—or rather—be involved in a murder investigation at Compass Bay." Susan looked around and suddenly felt like a teacher trying to explain the theory of relativity to a group of second-graders: Everyone's face was blank. "Allison came here planning the murder of Kathleen Gordon," she explained.

"What?"

"Why?"

"How do you know?"

"I know it because she, in fact, did some other fiction writing. She wrote a diary that purported to record the last month and a half of her life. A month and a half during which she continued her passionate love affair with Jerry and during which Jerry promised to get rid of his wife and marry Allison. At least that's what it said."

"You know, whatever happened, you can patch up your marriage," Peggy said, leaning forward and patting Jerry's arm.

"It was complete fiction," Jerry answered. "I love Kathleen. I couldn't stand Allison. Period."

"Men sometimes—" Peggy added.

"Peggy, shut up!" Frank roared. "Not all men have affairs. Not all men are married to you!"

There was a moment of silence while they all took this in. Then Susan continued her explanation.

"The diary was supposed to be discovered after Kathleen was murdered. I suppose Allison herself might have suggested that the cottages be searched. But Kathleen and I found it when we were searching Allison's cottage. Kathleen read it and then claimed it had been stolen from her cottage. Kathleen doesn't lie very well. I knew she had gotten rid of it somehow—probably just dumped it in the ocean."

"You never asked her about it?" Joann spoke up.

"Sure I did, on the phone just a few hours ago. But I already knew Kathleen and Jerry were innocent. I just didn't realize immediately that Allison must have been trying to prove the exact opposite. You see, nothing made sense because the wrong person died."

"Why? Why did the wrong person die?" Randy asked.

"Because one tall, long-haired blond looks pretty much like the next in the dark. Allison had made herself over, and she had made herself into a copy of Kathleen. She was out on the gazebo in the dark; James came up behind her, strung a fishing line around her neck, and pulled it tight. He's strong. She would have been dead within minutes. And, probably, James realized that he had killed the wrong person."

"She came to the island to find someone to kill Kathleen," Ro said.

"Yes."

"Why would James, or anyone, do that?"

"Money. James liked working here, but he was living on the expectation of good tips. And tips are not a dependable source of income. In fact, there was no guarantee that he would even continue working here from day to day. When my kayak sank—and I think that was probably an innocent accident—there was a serious concern among the staff that he'd be sacked. Lila was furious with him. She couldn't blame

Allison's murder on the staff, or Kath's concussion . . . or the knockout drops put in Jed's lunch—"

"Why was that anyway?" her husband asked.

"You were sitting in the restaurant, waiting for me to show up. James probably thought you might see him with Kathleen. He couldn't risk that."

"But why hit Kathleen?" Burt asked.

"I think he probably wanted to scare her away. But what no one knew is that Kathleen was a cop. She doesn't scare easily."

"That's true," Jerry said proudly.

"Anyway, Lila doesn't expect accidents to happen here— ever. Those kayaks should have been checked for damage before they were put out on the beach. And that's James's job. This is a good place to work. Everyone kept repeating that. Everyone on the island who isn't driving a taxi wants to work here. There's probably no one on the staff who isn't aware of being replaceable. One slip up and you're out."

"Sounds like Lila," Burt Parker said approvingly. "She runs a tight ship."

"And she's hired many of James's friends, relatives, and girlfriends. A lot of people depend on his continued employment. When he saw the opportunity to make some money to free him from this situation, he took it.

"Of course, the fact that Allison picked James to help her out was part of the problem I had investigating. Everyone here, with the exception of Lila, was protecting him. He could come and go without ever worrying that anyone would say anything to incriminate him. No matter what he did here he'd get away with it. Taking girlfriends on the beach at night was against the rules, but James knew no one would report him. There was probably no one else in the resort who could— quite literally—get away with murder.

"In fact, I had to leave Compass Bay to discover that he and Allison had been meeting."

"Where did you go?"

"There's a restaurant in town—the Coconut Hut—"

"More a dive than a restaurant," Veronica said.

"Yes, I suppose."

"But their lemonade is sensational," Veronica went on, looking around as though hoping one would appear before her right now.

"And their bartender is a very observant young man, thank heavens," Susan said, trying to return the conversation to the topic at hand. "He was working the day Allison was killed, and he saw her meeting with Jerry."

"That meeting was completely accidental!" Jerry protested.

"And wouldn't have happened if James had shown up," Susan added. "The bartender said Allison waited impatiently for someone to appear. She was probably amazed when Jerry walked in instead of James."

"I was trying to get away from Allison, and I couldn't believe it when I walked in that door and there she was. I really thought I was going to go mad," Jerry said. "I even considered making up some sort of excuse and taking Kathleen back to Hancock. Instead, I got back to Compass Bay as soon as I could and told Kath I wanted to eat dinner in town. I just wanted to get away from Allison and to keep Kathleen away from her. I thought things would be better when you and Jed arrived," he added, looking at Susan.

"Did you ever think that Kathleen might be in any danger?" Jed asked, sitting up.

"I never thought that Allison might be planning to kill her, but, yes, I did get the feeling that she was trying to damage our marriage. I mean, I couldn't believe it when I saw her walking down the dock toward us the first afternoon we were here. She was wearing a tiny bikini; her hair was shimmering blond and hanging down her back; she looked like Kathleen. Not beautiful like Kath, of course, but like an . . . an imitation of her."

"Which is why you couldn't take your eyes off her, right?" Susan asked.

"Why I—but you weren't even on the island yet. How did you know that?" Jerry smiled. "Kathleen must have told you that."

"She did. She thought you were . . . well, infatuated with Allison."

"God, no! I couldn't stand the woman. And I was shocked. I didn't trust Allison. The fact that she had turned herself into a replica of Kath made me very uncomfortable. I thought she was up to something, but I never even considered something like planning a murder."

"You and she had been meeting in the city, right?" Susan asked.

"We met once in early January. She called me up at work and asked if I'd take her to lunch. I couldn't think of any reason to refuse, so we met at the Four Seasons."

"Didn't she look the same there as she did this week?" Peggy asked.

Jerry paused a moment to consider her question. "No, I don't think so. Her hair wasn't as blond and it was tied back somehow. She was wearing glasses, I think. And it was snowing outside. She had on some sort of black wool suit. She looked like every other woman in the city. We talked about general things. Nothing significant."

"Except that you told her we were all coming here for a vacation," Susan pointed out.

"Yes, I'm afraid I must have. I know I was thinking about it. The weather was awful. We had a new client at work who was making everyone miserable. Susan, when you came up with this idea for a trip and found Compass Bay, it was almost all I could think about for a few days. I probably told Allison about it before we'd finished our first course."

"Had you kept in touch with her after June died?" Jed asked.

"No. She helped me clean out the house, but I didn't see her for a long while after that. She sent Christmas cards and birthday cards, but, well, I'm not awfully good about that type of thing."

Susan smiled. In her experience, not many men were.

"Why were Allison and James meeting in town?" Frank asked.

"I don't know for sure. But my guess would be that James wanted to end their deal. He seems to be a nice young man, not a killer. So he suggested they meet away from here and in a public place."

"But Jerry met her instead," Susan said.

"Do you think Allison would have let him back out of their agreement?" Jed asked.

"Probably not. And she really had a lot of power over him. If she had gone to Lila and told her what James agreed to, he would have lost his job for sure. And everything he was trying to protect when he agreed to kill Kathleen would have vanished anyway."

"So maybe he did know that Allison was lying out in the gazebo. Maybe he knew who he was killing," Ro suggested.

"That is possible," Susan said slowly. "But we won't know unless James is found."

"Unless?" Jerry asked. "Don't you think he'll be found?"

"He has lots of friends, lots of relatives. My guess is that he was smuggled off this island by some of them and he won't be back. But the Caribbean is made up of many islands and has many more resorts. He'll take a new identity, find a new job, and in a few months he may be taking other American tourists out to see other coral reefs."

"That's entirely possible," Jerry agreed.

"Allison must have really hated you," Rose spoke up. "To want to kill your wife and then have the murder blamed on you."

Jerry looked over at her. "You know, she really must have. And I never had any idea. None at all."

# THIRTY-FOUR

"WELL, I'M SURPRISED TO FIND YOU THREE ALONE. I thought you'd be the center of attention after solving the murder."

Susan, Jed, and Jerry opened their eyes and realized Kathleen was back.

Jerry jumped up to give his wife a warm greeting. "Kath, I can't tell you how good it is to see you," he said, embracing her.

She smiled up at him. "It's good to be back. New York is freezing."

"Did you see the kids?" he asked.

"No, your dad took them to the movies while I was there. I wanted to look around the house, but I didn't want to upset them by popping in and then leaving immediately. As far as they know, I've been here the entire time.

"Your mother was sweet. Even solved a small mystery for me," she added, smiling. "Why didn't you tell me you can't swim?"

"What? Jerry swims. I've seen him in the water at the club hundreds of times," Susan protested.

"That's what I said to her," Kathleen admitted. "But his mother explained that Jerry never learned to swim. Some sort of inner ear problem when he was a kid. We've all seen him in the pool at the Field Club—standing in the water helping out the kids. That's not swimming."

"Caught," he admitted. "I've always been embarrassed about it. Everyone we know swims."

"So that's why you wouldn't go out in the kayak with Kathleen!" Susan said.

"True. That's an awfully big ocean to someone who doesn't really feel comfortable in the water. Sorry to disappoint you," he added, pulling Kathleen closer to him. "I should have told you before we got here."

"Jerry, I'm not disappointed. I don't care if you swim or not. I just didn't understand your reluctance to do things. If only you had explained." She sat down on the lounge her husband had just vacated. "So why are you three all alone?"

"If you had been here an hour ago, you would have found us surrounded," Jed said. "Everyone wanted to know what Susan had discovered and how she did it."

"So where are they now?"

Susan chuckled. "Lila decided it was time for the Miss Marple hour to come to a close. She announced a complimentary cocktail party for guests. I was abandoned in minutes. They're all down on the beach gorging on crab canapés and rum punch like there's no tomorrow."

"For one of them, that just might be true," Kathleen said.

"Who?" Jed asked, immediately concerned.

"Randy, Veronica's husband. They're an odd couple: She's drinking big-time, and he's abstaining but trying to hide it. Susan and I decided she was probably an alcoholic and he was the world's greatest enabler."

"And you found out something else?" Susan asked.

"He's seriously ill and his medication means that he can't drink. I traveled back from the States with a doctor, a very indiscreet doctor, who is treating Randy down here with medications that haven't yet been approved for use in the States."

"That's sad," Jerry said.

"Everyone here has their own story," Susan said. "I've been thinking so much about Jerry and June and Allison that I guess I haven't really gotten to know anyone else."

"You know what I've been wondering? I've been wondering how Allison knew what Kathleen looked like," Jed said.

"My fault," Jerry admitted. "Like the proud husband and father that I am, I showed Allison photos of my family when we met for lunch in the city. I made everything pretty easy for her, when you think about it."

"You're not at fault here," Susan said. "You have absolutely nothing to feel guilty about."

"She's right. You can't blame yourself for any of this," Jed added.

"Unless you suspected that Allison had something to do with the accident that killed June and the kids?" Kathleen asked gently.

Jerry looked over at her and frowned. "I had been thinking about that recently. When we met in the city, Allison said something weird. She said that sometimes some people deserved to die. It came at me out of left field, and I began to wonder how much she hated June and the kids."

"That's why you had their photos out," Kathleen guessed.

"Yes, I was looking for a photo of all four of them."

"Did you find one?" Susan asked.

"Lots, but they didn't tell me anything. I kept wondering, though—"

"So did I," Kathleen interrupted. "So yesterday I had some old friends from the department in the city bring up some files. June and the girls were killed in an accident. Your insurance company did everything possible to get out of paying out on those policies. They impounded the car, hoping to find something wrong with it that might limit their liability, but they couldn't come up with anything. Nothing mechanical and no one had sabotaged the vehicle. It was a terrible tragic accident and that's all it was."

Jerry broke the silence that followed her explanation. "You know what? I think crab canapés and rum punch sound like just the thing to cheer us up."

"And a nice way to begin our very short, but very romantic Caribbean vacation," Kathleen agreed, getting up and taking his hand.

"You two head on down to the beach," Jed said. "We'll join you shortly. Just don't drink up all the rum," he called out as they strolled away. "Thank God you figured out who killed Allison," he said, turning to his wife. "Now we can all relax."

"Hmm." Susan reached out and pushed a lock of hair off his forehead. "You know what question we haven't answered yet?" she asked, smiling at her husband.

"No, what?" He smiled back.

"What is it about the Caribbean that makes everyone feel so sexy?"

## COMPASS BAY RUM PUNCH

*3 tablespoons fresh lemon juice*
*3 tablespoons fresh orange juice*
*3 tablespoons unsweetened canned pineapple juice*
*2 teaspoons Mount Gay rum*
*2 teaspoons amaretto*
*1 tablespoon Myers's or other brand dark rum*
*a splash of grenadine for color*
*1 maraschino cherry*

Combine all ingredients and pour over ice. Drop maraschino cherry in glass and enjoy. Makes one drink.

Ballantine Books

proudly presents

*The Susan Henshaw Mysteries*

and

*The Josie Pigeon Mysteries*

by **VALERIE WOLZIEN**

Published by Fawcett
Available wherever books are sold

## *The Josie Pigeon Novels*

SHORE TO DIE
*The First Josie Pigeon Mystery*

PERMIT FOR MURDER

DECK THE HALLS WITH MURDER

THIS OLD MURDER

MURDER IN THE FORECAST

A FASHIONABLE MURDER

Published by Fawcett
Available wherever books are sold